BELOW THE LINE

BELOW THE LINE

JOHN MCFETRIDGE | SCOTT ALBERT

Signature
EDITIONS

© 2003, John McFetridge & Scott Albert

All rights reserved. No part of this book may be reproduced, for any reason, by any means, without the permission of the publisher.

Cover design by Terry Gallagher/Doowah Design.
Photos of John McFetridge and Scott Albert by Barbara Gilbert.
Printed and bound in Canada by Printcrafters.

We acknowledge the support of the Canada Council for the Arts and the Manitoba Arts Council for our publishing program.

National Library of Canada Cataloguing in Publication

McFetridge, John, 1959-
    Below the line / John McFetridge and Scott Albert.

ISBN 0-921833-88-1

    I. Albert, Scott, 1975- II. Title.

PS8575.F48B45 2003   C813'.6   C2003-903080-6
PR9199.4.M428B45 2003

Signature Editions, P.O. Box 206, RPO Corydon
Winnipeg, Manitoba, R3M 3S7

For Laurie, always.
—John

EXT. INDUSTRIAL AREA — NIGHT

A few cars are in the parking lot of an industrial strip mall. The store fronts are all dark, save for the end unit.

A car pulls up in front of the end unit.

FX of a camera shutter opening and closing as a middle-aged white man gets out of the car and walks to the door. As he pulls on the door handle we see a small handwritten sign, "AAAAA Massage."

INT. PARKED CAR — NIGHT (CONTINUOUS)

In the passenger seat, EDDIE, a cop in his early thirties, sits with a camera in one hand. He is balancing the zoom lens with the other.

Beside him, in the driver's seat, MIKEY, a little older, a little more tired, and a lot less interested, drinks coffee.

          MIKEY
Why do you bother taking pictures of him? We don't care who that slob is.

          EDDIE
You never know what we might need someday. Who knows what he might see?

          MIKEY
Right, some poor working stiff getting a quick blow job on his way home from work.

Eddie continues to look through the camera.

          EDDIE
We watch everything.

Notice of Filming

March 16, 2002

Attention: Neighbouring Residents of R.C. Harris Filtration Plant, Toronto

Please note that Little Italy Productions Inc. will be filming scenes from the two-hour movie for Showtime Network, Life and Death in Little Italy, at the R.C. Harris Filtration Plant on Thursday, April 25, 2001.

We are making arrangements to park the majority of our production vehicles at the parking of the filtration plant as well as at the parking lot of the Palm Beach Court apartment buildings. As well, we are making arrangements for the parking of our technical vehicles on the following streets:

- East side of Neville Park Avenue, south of Queen Street East.
- South side of Queen Street East between Victoria Park Ave., and Courcelette Avenue.

Please note that a member of our crew will be in the area on Thursday, April 25th at 5:00 a.m. to begin placing traffic cones at the above noted sections of the streets.

To those residents who normally park their vehicles overnight in the areas noted above, we respectfully request that if possible, your vehicle be parked down the street, or on an adjacent street, on the evening of Wednesday, April 24th.

All our production vehicles will be vacating the streets by 11:00 p.m. on the 25th.

Please note that, because the lawn bordering Lake Ontario will become a work environment, the lawn will be closed for the duration of our day there. Please do not allow any dogs to run unleashed near our work environment. Also please note to take caution when accessing the beach from the steps on Neville Park Avenue. Although we will be making safe all cables as they cross the street, we ask that you be careful of potential tripping hazards as well as the various pieces of equipment near the filtration plant.

Thank you for your support of Canadian filmmaking and Ontario location filming. We are looking forward to a successful filming schedule in Toronto. Meanwhile, please feel free to call me should you have any questions, concerns or comments.

Sincerely,
Morton Gibson
Location Manager

THE LOCATION MANAGER

Morton Gibson, the location manager, drove the van up Yonge Street and said, "The great thing about Toronto is that it can look like so many American cities."

Edward Nijar, the American director huddled in his bomber jacket, said, "So *that's* the great thing about it."

The key grip laughed.

Morton ignored him and said, "Even European cities. We shot *Peacekeepers* here. It was supposed to be Croatia." He was repeating himself to Nijar, saying the same things he'd said during the location scout the week before. Now on the tech survey a week before principal photography, Morton was saying it for the benefit of Judy Nemeth the line producer, Franz Woceski the DOP, the First AD, the designer and a couple of keys who were with them in the van.

"I worked on *Good Will Hunting* here," Judy said. "We did a little second unit in Boston but not much. This city is wonderful."

"It's been New York for *American Psycho,* Washington for *Murder at 1600,* Chicago for *John Q.* All over for *The X-Men.*" Morton turned off Yonge Street and parked in front of an old church that had been renovated into condos. As they got out of the van, Nijar and Woceski immediately walked away from the group towards the condo's front doors.

"The practicals will be all right," Woceski said in his Polish accent.

"A little bland," Nijar said, not even looking up at the lights over the large wooden doors.

Morton started to follow and Judy touched his arm lightly. "Let's try not to spend too much time here, okay? This is pretty straightforward and we should really nail down the exteriors."

"I thought we'd settled on everything."

"Edward's changed his mind about one of the alleys." She started to explain, trying to make nice to the Toronto location manager, excusing the impulsive New York director, but Morton was already nodding and heading inside.

"No problem. We've got lots more to choose from." He stopped and looked back at Judy. "Any other surprises?"

"No, everything else is locked down tight. This'll be a smooth shoot." They shared a smile. It was the first time Morton had worked with Judy, but they had developed an instant rapport, neither of them bothering with that faux cynicism so common of movie crews. They liked their jobs, so what?

Morton pushed his way past the crew members milling about the front door and knocked. A woman in her early thirties opened the door and smiled in recognition.

"Hello," she said. "Right on time."

"Time is money," Morton said. A smile creased the otherwise perfectly smooth white skin on her very pretty face and for a brief moment Morton thought it might not be sincere. He realized he shouldn't have mentioned money, the five-thousand-dollar location rental not being the main reason she claimed to be offering her home as a movie set. "All these people are on the clock, Ms. Sanderson," he said by way of explanation.

"Vanessa, please." The smile didn't change. She pushed a few strands of blonde hair back behind her ear. The tiny diamond stud in her lobe glinted. "How many are you? Would you like coffee?"

"No thanks, that's fine. We're all caffeined up. Oh, this is our director, Edward Nijar." Morton practically had to grab Edward to prevent him from wandering down the street.

When Nijar turned to Vanessa, his expression changed from disappointment and concern over the building to a slight smile. Still cool, he took her manicured hand in his own and said, "Hello."

She looked him in the eye and Morton stood beside them, not moving at all until Judy nudged him.

"So, um, Vanessa, like I said on the phone, we'd like to see a little more of your place today, if that's okay?"

Still looking at Nijar she said, "Yes, that's fine. Come on in."

The whole group trooped in and stood in the front entrance. A beautiful oak staircase wound its way up to a second floor landing and a large chandelier hung from the ceiling.

Vanessa said, "Let me know when you're done," and walked into a sitting room off the kitchen. All the guys watched her go, even Woceski, although he was the first one back to business, walking up the stairs.

On the second floor they opened all the doors on the landing, looking at the spare bedrooms, a kind of small library and the large bathroom.

Nijar hadn't seen the whole place when he picked the location. All they really needed was the front entrance and the staircase—a couple of cops come to talk to a gangster at his home—but the script was still being revised and they might put something in a bedroom.

Morton hung back. Judy lingered beside him, wondering what was up, and Morton winked as Nijar opened the master bedroom door. Then it was a Keystone Cop routine. Nijar took a step into the room, stopped in his tracks and was bumped from behind by Woceski, the First AD, the designer and the key grip. Then Nijar continued into the room and the rest followed, spreading out like an accordion.

Judy looked sideways at Morton and he motioned for her to go on in. She looked suspicious and walked into the master bedroom.

The rest of the people on the survey, all men, were standing at the foot of the massive bed, the biggest bed any one of them had ever seen, looking at the huge oil painting hanging on the wall above the wrought iron headboard.

The key grip said, "Well now, you don't see that every day."

On the canvas was a larger-than-life Vanessa Sanderson, naked and tied spread-eagled to the very bed it hung above.

"Toronto the Good, eh?"

Nijar was nodding. "Right."

The key grip said, "This is nothing. You should see what's going on in Brampton."

Judy stood in the doorway and looked at Morton, who was still out in the hall. He was fighting to hold back his laughter. Not like the first time he'd seen the painting, when he was doing the very first scout of the location. Vanessa had allowed him to wander around the condo with his camera by himself and when he'd gotten back to the front door she'd met him with a sly smile and asked, "Did you see everything?"

"Yes, I think I saw everything," he'd answered.

Vanessa Sanderson was the one laughing then. She'd said, "Do you think the film company will like it?"

"Some of them will, for sure." And Morton had gotten out as quickly as he could. He hadn't thought at that time that they would need to see any more of the place than the front door. He'd only looked around the whole condo because that's what location scouts do. Every building they enter is a possible location, if not for the movie they're working on at the time, then maybe for one in the future. He had thought that Vanessa might have moved the painting when he'd told her he'd be bringing a gang of people through the place, but really, it didn't surprise him that much that it was still there.

The rest of the survey was uneventful. Nijar didn't like anything else, and when they were leaving Vanessa came out of the sitting room to say goodbye. She looked directly at Nijar. She always seemed at ease, but she was clearly used to dealing with whoever was in charge.

"Did you see everything?"

Morton was disappointed that she used the same line. It was too rehearsed now.

Nijar held out his hand. "Yes, thank you. You have a beautiful home."

No blushing. She accepted it easily, as if he were saying it was cold outside. "Thank you. I was wondering, what kind of a scene would take place here?"

"Some policemen come to talk to a gangster."

Vanessa laughed. "This is a gangster's home?"

"We'll have to do a little redecorating."

"Make it a little more tacky," Herb, the designer, said.

"Who plays the gangster?"

"We haven't finalized the casting. Harvey Keitel maybe. Joe Mantegna, Joe Pantoliano, Anthony LaPaglia. Someone like that."

She was impressed. "Well, if there's anything I can do..."

Nijar shook her hand. "It was very nice to meet you."

No one said anything as they piled back into the van. Morton drove and Nijar sat in the passenger seat. Judy sat right behind Morton.

They had driven almost two blocks in silence before the key grip said, "What does that chick do for a living?"

Herb said, "I think she gets divorced." Most of the guys laughed.

Judy said to Morton, "Next up is the Cormier Mansion."

"Yeah. It's just up the street," he said as they continued on Yonge into Rosedale proper.

They drove through a stonework gate, which was standing wide open, and continued through the artificial mounds of landscaped nature, circling a baroque fountain, which was dry, and ended at the house. Four stories, an eight-car garage, giant stained glass windows and fifty empty rooms. The place was built in the sixties and had changed hands a dozen times since then. You could chart the ups and downs of the TSE by the number of times this property went on the market. The current owners were in bankruptcy hearings so often that they were desperate for the five-grand-a-day rental.

As they got out of the van, Judy again took Morton aside and he said, before she had a chance, "Don't spend too much time here, I know."

"Well, it's just that this location is completely locked down and quite flexible."

"We still can't burn it down. You might be going back to California in six weeks, but I still have to manage locations here."

Judy looked genuinely hurt. "I know that. I didn't mean we could be cavalier about it."

"Cavalier?"

"It's a word. It's the right word."

"No one uses that word."

"I just did."

"Hey, you two, quit flirting and open the damned door."

Morton turned and looked at the people standing by the enormous front door. He was shocked that someone would think he was flirting. He shot a glance at Judy. He wondered if she thought he was flirting. If she did, she didn't seem to mind, smiling at him from under that goofy wool hat.

"Where would we be without grips?" she said.

They walked through the empty mansion, with Judy trying to get everyone up to the third floor as quickly as possible. She didn't want to come out and say they didn't have the money to dress more than the one room they were using, and a little bit for the front of the place so it didn't look deserted in the exterior shot, but that was the reality.

In the empty rec room on the third floor Nijar and Woceski stood by the windows at the back. Woceski said something about covering them, but Nijar said, no, he wanted one of the gangsters to stand by the window and look out. "Surveying his estate, as it were," he said.

There was a bar in one corner of the room, with a big built-in mirror still behind it, but the rest of the walls were empty. Herb talked about the kind of paintings the gangsters would have, garish, too obvious, that sort of thing.

Judy stood beside Morton at the door. She whispered, "Just once I wish they wouldn't be so cliché."

Morton shrugged. "It's a necessary shorthand. Archetype stuff. Makes it easier, so we don't have to spend so much time on that development. That way, there's time for the rest of the story."

"Have you read this script?"

"Of course."

"I don't mean, have you skimmed it for locations? I mean, have you read it?"

"Yeah, I read it."

"So, do you think these gangsters are clichés?"

"I told you, not clichés, archetypes."

She looked at him sideways, not sure if he was being sarcastic or not. "Okay, do you think they are archetypes?"

"Sure. I mean, there's no real need to establish them as wildly original gangsters. They make money from prostitution, drugs, extortion, money laundering, the usual. We know that. We know them. Same thing with the cops. These guys are not particularly well educated or well travelled."

"You don't think it kind of takes away from the suspense that we already know all about these guys?"

"Well, the story isn't really a thriller, you know. It's not about catching the bad guy."

"It's not?"

"No."

"So what's it about?"

"It's about the fear of losing your privacy, of being watched all the time." Morton looked at Judy, and unlike all the other people he'd known from working on movies, she actually seemed interested in what he thought the movie was about. "It's a huge fear for people these days—Big Brother knows what you're doing, e-mail, credit cards. It's all a way to track your movements."

"You got all that from this script?"

"Sure. Taps right into the current *Zeitgeist*, touches the nerve. First scene of the movie is through a zoom lens. It's people watching other people, spying on them. That states the theme right there."

Judy nodded thoughtfully. "That makes sense. Touches that nerve."

She really seemed interested and didn't brush him off the way everyone else always did whenever he talked about anything other than the budget, the locations and the star gossip, so he went on. "That's the way movies work, you know, visually, emotionally, touching the nerve. There's a story about a studio executive who turned down *Jaws* because he said not enough people lived on the coast. He said, 'Who, in Nebraska, is going to be afraid of a shark?'"

Judy nodded. "Wow, was he wrong."

"Not really. He just didn't know that the nerve they hit wasn't fear of sharks, it was fear of drowning. People in Nebraska drown in swimming pools and bathtubs. Everyone's afraid of drowning."

"So you think this picture's going to hit that nerve of people's fear of losing their privacy?"

"Well, I don't know, I haven't seen the latest revision. I was told locations didn't change, so I didn't bother to read it."

She hit him with her daytimer.

Herb came over to them. "Can we really get a 200-pound mahogany pool table up those stairs?"

"No need," Morton said. "There's a service elevator right through there." He pointed to a door beside the bar.

"Okay," Judy announced to the room, "that's it for this location," and they were off to the next.

The R.C. Harris Filtration Plant was a beautiful art deco building constructed in the 1930s, a make-work project which provided employment for many of the tradesmen who'd lost their jobs in the Depression. The building had marble floors and stained glass windows and inlaid tile and a large expanse of lawn overlooking Lake Ontario. It was almost always used as a prison exterior.

"So what are we this time?" Albert, the manager, asked Morton as the rest of the group wandered around the front doors and Nijar and Woceski decided where the twelve-foot-high barbed wire fence would be put up.

"New Jersey Correctional Facility for Women."

"Women's prison. Will they want it pink?"

Morton smiled. It was a constant irritant for Albert that his gorgeous building was always a prison. It showed such a lack of imagination that it affected his opinion of the films themselves. Although even Albert admitted it was classier in *Murder in the First* than in *Half Baked*.

"Thanks, Albert," Morton said and wandered off to join the group.

"Okay, smart guy," Judy said, pulling Morton away from the rest and stopping in front of a bench overlooking the huge lake, "name another movie that states its theme right off the top."

"Well, most good ones do."

"Like?"

"Okay, well, um, any John Sayles movie."

"You like his movies?"

"The only real independent."

"Okay, but what about stating the theme?"

"Any one of them. Practically the first line in *Lone Star* is, 'you live someplace, you ought to know something about it,' and the whole movie is about knowing your roots and how big a factor they are in your life and being able to get past them."

Judy looked thoughtful. "Okay, what about *Good Will Hunting*?"

"Well, it's a bit of a mess, isn't it?" He looked at Judy a little apologetically. She didn't seem to mind. She was just interested. "I understand it went through a lot of drafts, that it was a spy thriller and stuff. But, you know, it's a rich boy's fantasy; the only way to get happy is to get 'out of here.' There's a difference between working class and ghetto."

"There is?"

Morton smiled. "Class is the unspoken evil of America. You can talk about racism, sexism, whatever, but the movies will never talk about classism. In the movies, all unions are corrupt and hold people back, and all wealth is good."

Now Judy laughed. "What are you, a communist?"

"Things haven't changed much since HUAC, have they?"

"Okay, now I'm not sure. Do you like movies or not?"

"I like car chases, big explosions and skinny naked chicks."

Before Judy could hit him again, the rest of the gang joined them. They were finished surveying that location and on to the next, The Hotel Novotel, which with its big awning looked so "New York."

It was after eight when they got back to the production office on Carlaw and people began drifting away slowly. Morton went downstairs and ran into the Transport Captain, Roger Doyle, on his way up.

"Hey, MoGib, how's it going?"

"Long day. You?"

"Hiring drivers. Everybody wants to drive Ainsley Riordan."

"She was in *Playboy*, you know."

"I've heard."

Morton liked Roger. As far as Transport went, he was great. Never complained about the cramped parking locations assigned, never had trouble with the maps. He always seemed friendly and on top of things. One of the Craft Service girls said she'd never met anyone who'd ever heard Roger raise his voice. There was a rumour he had once been a high-ranking guy in the Hell's Angels. Another rumour was that he had been in the armed forces, a peacekeeper in Bosnia doing land mine removal. Whatever, he got things done and didn't complain. That made him a saint on set.

"Think she might be high maintenance?"

"High maintenance? A Hollywood actress?"

Morton laughed. "Yeah, but really, it's all these tough guys playing gangsters that are more trouble."

Roger continued up the stairs. "You got that right."

"You just be careful with Ainsley."

"I can't imagine I'll say more than two words to her."

Morton went down to the tiny windowless office Locations had been assigned and started piling up the big red file folders to be returned to the OFDC Locations Library. On the wall above Morton's desk were pictures of the locked locations. He looked them over and sighed loudly. How many times had he used the Harris Filtration Plant? The Cormier Mansion? The parking lot off Shuter Street? New York, Chicago, Pittsburgh.

"Hope that doesn't mean you're too tired."

He looked up sharply and there was Judy standing in the doorway holding a bagel in one hand.

"What have you got in mind?" Hopeful.

"Edward wants to look at alleys at night."

Morton smiled a little and tried not to look too disappointed. "Of course. He's away from home, he's got no family here and no life except this movie. Why should it be any different for the rest of us?"

"Is it different for you?"

Morton started to speak but stopped and then laughed. "No, I guess not."

Judy handed him the bagel. "I'm going to tag along and so is Franz, but that's it."

"We going now?"

"Half an hour. Edward's still trying to convince Don Cheadle to play Trey."

"What's the holdup?"

"I think he read the script."

Morton couldn't tell how sarcastic she was being and he liked that.

The first alley they saw was "too wide open." It had been almost 9:30 when they'd finally left the office and neither Nijar nor Woceski seemed to be in any kind of a hurry as they walked up and down alley after alley talking about where the car would be stopped and where the shooting would take place. The scene would be an "execution-style" shooting. That meant a guy would get shot in the head. Morton figured that pretty much anytime a guy shoots another guy he's trying to "execute" him. Not much style in it.

Judy and Morton stood by the van at one end of the alley. She said, "So, Morton, what got you into film?"

"The short hours and easy money."

"Okay, why Locations?"

"The glamour. I could be in charge of Don Cheadle's garbage can."

"Can you be serious?"

Before he could answer, Morton's cellphone beeped and he flipped it open. "Locations… Un-huh… yeah, I know… right… okay, thanks." He closed his cellphone.

"What is it?"

"What?"

"What was that all about?" Judy asked, more insistent than she wanted to be, but struck by the fact that Morton answered his personal cellphone, at 10:00 at night, with "Locations."

"One of our scouts, Garry."

"He's working late."

"We lost the Emerald Isle."

"That sleazy motel?"

"That's the one."

"Damn. We loved that place. Two stories, balconies, hallways, parking lot. Sleazy. It had that great sign on the front desk, 'No Exotic Dancers.' Set Dec never would have come up with that."

Morton nodded, but didn't look too bothered by the news. "Still, we've really shot the shit out of that place. It's been in more movies shot in Canada than Shannon Tweed. Be good to find something new."

"I have a feeling that if there was something new to find, you'd have found it," Judy said.

"I don't know where you got this idea that I know what I'm doing," Morton said. "Come on. There must be a million motels around here."

Judy didn't look too optimistic. "I don't know. Most of those mom and pop operations went out of business a long time ago. It's all Days Inns and Motel 6s now."

"We'll find something." He noticed Nijar and Franz walking back through the alley towards them and said, "Let's not tell anyone just yet, all right?"

"Oooh," Judy said, a big phoney shiver running through her body. "Our first big secret."

"Doesn't this shitty city have any decent alleys? You know, a place that looks like a decent hit could go down in it."

"I think I know the look," Morton said. He glanced at Judy as they walked back to the van, and the glare she gave him stopped him from adding something about having seen a few dozen B-gangster movies, and they all had the same scene in the same alley.

Nijar popped a CD into the deck. Something he thought was cool and hip and was considering for the "soundtrack." Guitars droned, drums droned and a male singer droned.

"I love this band," Nijar said. As always, he sat in the passenger seat of the van. After a few minutes of pounding out the slow steady drone of the band on the dashboard Nijar let his hands rattle off a much faster beat and he turned sharply towards Morton. "We need an alley that's neighbourhood. These guys are all about *da neighbahood*. It's got to have that feel."

Morton nodded and looked straight ahead as he drove. He said, "And the neighbourhood isn't downtown. It's connected to the city, but emotionally, it's miles away."

"Yeah, right, that's it."

Morton looked in the rear-view and saw Judy staring at him, a slight smile on her red lips, her eyes twinkling, daring him to be sarcastic.

"So, there should be an overpass in the shot, the visual that shows the neighbourhood is connected, but that it can also be passed over."

"Yes! Now you're getting it," Nijar said with the most energy he'd had since his arrival in Toronto. He slapped Morton on the shoulder and said, "You stick with me, you'll learn."

Morton turned the van around and said, "Okay, I've got a couple of ideas." He didn't add, "Why didn't you just say it should look like every cliché shot of Brooklyn?"

A few minutes later they pulled up behind a three-story hotel on Lakeshore that backed up against the Gardiner Expressway near Parkside. A few years earlier the whole area had looked fifties, with the drive-in burger joint, the castle gas station and the motel-style hotel, but all that was gone now and everything had been renovated. Nijar didn't look too happy until Morton drove around back and he saw the expressway from underneath and the blank wall of the back of the hotel separated by an alley.

"It's got potential," Nijar said, opening the door of the van. "We'll have to cover this wall with graffiti. We can bring in some guys from New York for that." Then he and Franz were out of the van.

Morton stayed in the driver's seat and Judy stayed in the seat behind him.

She said, "Has he got any idea how much it'll cost to fly in a couple of guys from New York, put them up in a hotel, pay for their damages to said hotel, and fly them back, all for a day of spray painting?"

"I know it's hard to imagine, but we might have a few guys right here in Toronto who could deface a wall."

Judy laughed. "Right, of course. I forgot. Directors get to me."

"It's what they do. I was thinking about the money, too. I didn't want to show him these alleys because they'll all require unit moves for what will end up being a close-up of a guy getting shot in the trunk of a car."

"You don't think we'll have a standard establishing shot?"

Morton turned half around in the seat and looked at Judy. "You're starting to sound downright cynical."

"You started it." She kicked the back of his seat.

"Oh yeah, I'm telling Mom and then you'll have to sit in the very back seat."

Judy laughed.

Morton said, "There used to be a bunch of motels right over there but the whole place went high-rise condo. Too bad. It had that real Jersey shore bleak look he wants."

"Could you turn off that crap?" Judy said, motioning to the CD player. Morton turned it off right away and the silence was wonderful. "So you like movies, right?"

"Right."

"Is location manager your dream job?"

"At the moment. I don't know. I used to think I might like to produce."

"Really?"

"Yeah, but I don't really know anything about it."

"Oh, come on, there's nothing to it. You don't know anything about art, everything's too expensive and it takes too long and you yell at people."

"You're going to be a producer, aren't you?"

"That's the rumour."

"That's one of them."

"I know, I know, young ambitious woman, moved up the ranks pretty fast, must have fucked my way up, right?"

"I can't imagine anyone would sleep their way onto this production."

"What do you think I'm doing here?"

He shrugged. "Probably paying your dues. This was probably a production in trouble—first-time director, a lot of testosterone in the cast, foreign location—so somebody asked you to help out and you said okay, if you got something back."

"Wow, you think I drive a pretty hard bargain."

"Do you?"

"You're a pretty astute guy, Morton Gibson."

"Yeah, for someone from below the line."

"It's true what they say about the Canadian inferiority complex, then, is it?"

"It could just be me. The grips seem to know everything in the world."

"Let's not even get started on the camera girls."

Morton turned further in his seat, surprised by her use of the out-of-fashion sexist putdown of the whining of the almost exclusively male club of the camera department. "Right."

"But let's just say there's a grain of truth to what you say."

"Uh-huh."

"And let's just say I could get some financing, and some decent casting, and maybe even a good director. Maybe."

"Hypothetically, of course."

"Of course. And let's just say that hypothetically, I'm someone who is very organized and efficient and worked my way up through the production ranks. I know the set and how to run a good one."

"So far so good."

"But let's just say I'm not so good at spotting the screenplay that might hit an underlying nerve."

"No script? That shouldn't get in the way of your being a producer and making lots of movies."

"Let's say, for the sake of argument, I'd like to make good movies."

"Oh well, that's different."

Judy had leaned forward between the front seats of the van, her head resting on the passenger seat, and looked at Morton. He looked back. The only sound was cars speeding by on the Gardiner Expresswy ten feet above them. They'd moved past their initial instant rapport of a couple of people who liked working on movies and didn't care who knew it to the more intimate area of hopes and dreams where even the most uncynical fear revealing too much. This was personal.

But like a cheap B-movie with very convenient timing, the van door burst open and Nijar jumped in. "Okay, good one. Slap on a little paint, throw around some dirt and it could work. What else have you got?"

Judy disappeared back into the darkness of the van's middle seat as Franz sat down next to her.

"We've got one that might even be a little more urban."

Rubbing his hands together against the cold, Nijar said, "Urban, that's what we need. Urban, baby." He hit play on the CD and turned the volume up louder.

Main Street, south of Danforth and north of Gerrard, rises to an overpass above about a dozen railway tracks. On the west side is an old neighbourhood of brick homes and duplexes on a street that dead-ends at the overpass. From the right angles, the ones used in the Rob Lowe movie, *First Degree*, and with some imagination, it could look like a little piece of Brooklyn. A very little piece.

Nijar loved it.

Franz hated it, of course, but it was settled. Gangland execution-style murder would happen here, in the shadow of the Main Street overpass.

When they got back to the production office it was after eleven, but Nijar still took Morton aside and asked, as casually as he could, for Vanessa Sanderson's phone number. Morton didn't even say anything about the time, he just handed over the number. Franz headed back to the hotel and Judy went into her office to make some phone calls. It was just after eight in LA.

Morton went down to his office and got some more film for his camera. He was coming back up the stairs when he ran into Judy on her way down.

"You heading home?"

He looked sheepish. "Actually, I was going to check out a couple more motels."

"Now?"

"Might as well see them at night."

"Mind if I come along?"

"People will talk."

"People will talk anyway. Might as well give them something to talk about."

"Isn't that a Bonnie Raitt song?"

They drove out to Kingston Road first. Morton explained that even though it was in the heart of suburbia now, it used to be Highway 2 heading east out of town to Kingston and Montreal before the expressways were built. The old motels scattered between the fast food places and shopping centres were holdovers from another era and they looked it.

"Most of these motels are rented by the city now as shelters."

"Shelters? I don't get it."

"Homeless families. The downtown shelters are like barracks, with rows of single beds, and they're either male or female. Some pretty rough characters sometimes, not the best place for kids, so the city rents out these motels."

They were in the parking lot of the Have-a-Nap Motel and watched a minivan pull up and a middle-aged man in a business suit get out of the driver's side. A girl, who despite the make-up, miniskirt, boots and halter top couldn't have been more than sixteen, got out of the passenger side and they went into a room together.

"But living with the hookers and johns is perfectly fine," Judy said.

"I thought, as an American, you'd be more upset about the use of tax dollars to shelter the homeless families."

"Look, you Canadians always think—" she stopped suddenly and looked at Morton. He was smiling at her. "I can't believe you. It's midnight, we're sitting in the parking lot of a sleazy motel looking at baby hookers and dirty old men, trying desperately to fill a location for a movie neither of us would pay a dime to see and you're…you're…what are you doing, you're making jokes?"

"Sorry."

"Don't be sorry. But tell me, do you think there's a story in this?"

"Scouting locations? No."

"Homeless families. Would it hit that nerve, that fear in everyone that they are just a couple of bad breaks away from being homeless?"

"No, people don't think they're a couple of bad breaks away from being homeless. They think they're hard-working, law-abiding citizens and the homeless are lazy people who screwed up."

"Yeah, but the statistics show that the reality is, most homeless people are hard-working—"

"But there's no underlying fear. You ever hear anyone seriously say they're worried about ending up on the street?" Morton was serious. "It's a lot more realistic fear than UFOs, or ghosts or Big Brother conspiracies, but it would have to be one hell of a script."

Judy frowned. "Yeah, I guess."

They decided the motels looked okay and they'd show Nijar some pictures, but he'd complain the b.g. was too suburban and he didn't want to shoot the scene that tight. It was too late to drive out to Oshawa or Hamilton where there might be something in an industrial, steel plant kind of neighbourhood, but that might be where they'd end up. Morton said it would be a huge waste of money—with a unit move out of the zone—the travel per diems would kill them, and the lost time would be incredible. And all for thirty seconds of screen time.

Morton said, "Why don't you have another look at the script? Maybe it doesn't even have to be a motel."

"What do you mean?"

"Well, the reason it's a motel now is because the cop, what's-his-name, has left his wife and he's in transition. Motels, people coming and going, renting a space for a few hours or a day, that kind of thing. He's at the motel and that's where he has the meeting with Trey, and that's when the bad guy sees him, but something else could symbolize that his character is in flux. You know, he could be at a truck rental place, getting ready to move his stuff out."

Judy spoke slowly. "Right, yeah, that's true, I never thought about *why* it was a motel. I was thinking we could look at hotels, something like that. I just figured it was a motel because on a cop's salary he couldn't afford a hotel."

Morton smiled. "Well, I'm just making this stuff up as I go. But if it is supposed to symbolize his life in transition it could also be an empty apartment he's looking at, thinking about moving in. There are a lot of possibilities."

"Yeah, well, we'll have to talk to Spellman."

"Who's Spellman?"

"The writer."

"Is he coming to Toronto?"

"Shit, no."

It was almost 1:30 a.m. when they got back to the hotel but before Judy got out of the van she turned sideways and faced Morton. She obviously had something on her mind, something she'd been thinking about and wanted to say. Finally, just before it got too awkward, she said, "You know, Morton, you're a very interesting guy. You know a lot about the technical aspects of movie making and you also know a lot about the stories and how they work."

"I'm sorry," he said, genuinely, "I'll keep my opinions to myself."

"No, no, it's not that." She paused. "Although around Edward it would probably be a good idea." They both laughed. "But no. What I mean is, I was serious about producing. I think I can do it, but I may only get one shot at it. I have a few scripts I'm looking over, but, well, I was wondering, would you be able to take a look at them?"

"Me? I don't know, I—"

"I can probably get you some money, you know, reader's report fees, but I'd really like you to think about this as a...as more than just a reader's report."

"I don't know. The thing is, I'm usually so full of shit I wouldn't be of any use to you."

"Well, think about it." And she jumped out of the van.

Morton was stopped at a red light on deserted Bay Street when it started to sink in. Judy Nemeth, the American line producer on this feature had asked for his input on script selection for something she was going to produce. She was connected, she was owed, and most importantly, *she* actually knew her stuff. She was one of the few people he'd ever met on a movie set that actually liked movies.

A car horn blared and Morton realized the light had changed. He stepped on the gas and tore down Bay Street to Adelaide and headed east. At 1:30 in the morning the traffic was pretty light. He thought about Judy the producer and could really see the potential. Since she had arrived in town the relaxed atmosphere of the pre-production crew had tightened up just enough. No one felt pressured but everybody got a bit more efficient. She seemed to know what had been done in every department, what needed to get done and if there was any chance they'd be ready to shoot anywhere near the scheduled start date.

So she's good, big deal, Morton told himself. Plenty of efficient young Americans cut their teeth on Canadian sets these days. It doesn't affect the hierarchy at all—we're drawers of water and hewers of wood, Morton thought. We're labour. We're below the line. He drove a little faster onto the Eastern Avenue overpass, past the Don Valley Parkway exit, past Broadview and towards his own little house almost in the Beaches. She might come back and shoot the thing in Toronto—as long as the exchange rate stayed close to where it was now—but she'd turn into every other person who's ever said, "Give me a break on this one and I'll remember you." Yeah, right. Remember me for the next time you need a location manager.

Still, she seemed so sincere.

No, Morton was too old to get caught up in those movie dreams anymore. Years ago he would have bought it hook, line and sinker. Man, how many producers got how much extra effort out of how many crews by promising big paydays on "the next one" that never materialized? Why should we expect above-the-line positions, Morton wondered, when the reasons the Yanks come here is for cheap below-the-line labour and government kickbacks. It's like the auto industry: so many assembly lines in Canada, so many plants, so much automaking labour, but it's not like we have our own car industry. There's no Canadian car company, no one designing cars here. Why should the movie business be any different?

Morton pulled up in front of his little one-story "railway house" in the middle of a long row of identical houses. A hundred years ago Irish labourers had lived in them while they built the railway. Cheap labour. He sat in the van.

He would make a great team with Judy Nemeth. She did have the connections to get the financing (in the US, of course. It's a very old joke in Canada that Canadian producers "have everything together except the financing"), she did run a good set, and he knew Canadian crews and locations. And more than anything, he knew movies. He loved movies.

He got out of the van, shaking his head. It was quiet on this little side street that was really more of an alley. Stop being a moron, Morton. She's just saying those things to get more work out of you.

Except it was almost 2:00 a.m. and he was still working. How much more could she expect? Morton unlocked the door, went inside and directly to his bed. He sat there looking at the posters on the wall. *Cuckoo's Nest*, *The Commitments*, *Three Kings*. And lots more.

The movies have a mystique, a cachet, a glamour that no other form of storytelling can come near. No one would ever say, "I don't go to movies," the way they say, "I don't watch TV," even though everyone knows they do. Even though TV may have left the movies far behind when it comes to character development and storytelling. The movies have no genre separation, there are no literature or sci fi or mystery sections at the multiplex. Just making a movie is a big deal. Any kid who's managed to splice together ninety minutes' worth of 16mm is a "filmmaker" and taken seriously, let into the club. There's no slush pile for indie films. Some festival somewhere will show it. Someone, somewhere will find that tiny homage to Godard.

Morton collapsed on his bed. How many times had he been through this? How many drunken nights had he spent deep in passionate debate about movies? Movies, for God's sake. Special effects space cowboys and teen sex comedies. But there was something there. Something at the core. Something that touched the nerve.

The movies may have been the first ever working-class art form, made popular by the droves of factory workers trapped in dank urban caves who were desperate for a glimpse of the wide open Wild West that no stage play or pulp novel could deliver, but they were also big business.

Years ago, when Morton was a serious young photography student trying to decide between exhibits in art galleries or photojournalism in far-off war zones, he'd stumbled into a job scouting locations. It was fun, it was exciting, and it paid well. It led to more work and even promotions, until finally, he was a location manager.

And, for a while, he had big dreams.

Morton studied movies and business. He had big plans. Production manager, line producer, producer. Making good movies, real stories. Finding a great short story in a literary magazine that really cut to the heart, telling the real story of peacekeepers or the defining moment of some bus driver's life. He didn't want to be a writer or a director, he wanted to discover new directors, develop screenwriters. Just like Judy Nemeth.

Except she was really doing it. Morton had smashed his head against that brick wall for years and given up. He spent a few more years convincing himself he was happy at his level; he was a very good location manager and never felt out of his element or in too deep. He never wanted to get back on that treadmill where the next big break was always slightly beyond his grasp, where he never felt he was living his life, where he was in a constant waiting period, where just up ahead everything would be different. No, he was content.

He also lived by himself in a one-bedroom house.

Morton slept uneasily, waking up every hour. He tried not to remember that line from Bruce Springsteen, something about a dream being a lie if it doesn't come true. No, his life was dictated by movie moments.

Driving back to the office a little after rush hour the next morning, Morton made up his mind. He didn't need the aggravation. He didn't want to upset his life. He was too old to start over with those kinds of dreams. He really was happy as a member of the crew. Working on movies was fun, a series of small victories, people working as a team. It had the perfect mix of artistic expression and technological intricacies. He didn't want his life to be one of those *Rocky* clichés where the character throws away his secure life for one last shot at his dreams only to fall hard and have a breakdown. No, it wasn't worth the risk for his shot at the big time just so he could say he took his shot. Working on movies was fun, but life wasn't a movie.

Judy was already in the office at 9:30. "You're right. It doesn't need to be a motel. He's left his wife, but they may get back together. Nothing's permanent at this point. So the location only needs to symbolize that. I really like the idea of the empty apartment he's looking at."

"The metaphor's a little clumsy." Morton said. "I haven't even had a cup of coffee."

"I'm on my third. It'll work and it has the added bonus of being cheap."

"Have you asked Nijar about it?"

"Asked? No. I'll just tell him. It'll give him something to blame on me. You know, studio interference, all that crap."

Morton laughed. "You don't really look like a fat guy smoking a cheap cigar."

She shrugged. "A suit's a suit, someone to blame. So look—" But before she could say anything, she was interrupted by Garry, the location scout.

"Come on, people. It's time for the inspirational speech from the producer. This'll be the best creative writing in this whole production."

Morton said, "Garry."

Judy said, "It's okay," and they walked into the office bullpen.

Most of the crew was there, dozens of people. Renée Jato and Edward J. Nijar were at the front of the room.

True enough, it was some inspirational creative writing. Renée started right in with what a great crew they'd assembled and what a terrific project it was and how excited everyone was. Nijar looked distracted. He probably thought he looked cool.

Morton had heard it all before. Most of them had. He looked around the room. The usual suspects. Some things had changed in 10 years. Now the grips had laptops and Palm Pilots with the schedule on them and there were some straight guys in the pretties—not Steven, of course. Morton saw him, well dressed and smiling slyly. A young 40-something. Single. Too bad. Maybe he'd meet someone on this show. Morton glanced at Garry, who was standing there rolling his eyes, and for a moment thought the chemistry might work. Then he shook his head. No way.

Renée went on about how hard it was going to be, what kinds of sacrifices they'd all make, but that's the only way great movies get made.

Nick, the production manager, was rocking back and forth on his toes. He was experienced, thorough, and knew the city well. If this show didn't run really smoothly... Well, Morton couldn't imagine that with Nick and Judy Nemeth it wouldn't. Unless he was wrong about Judy.

And there was Roger Doyle. Talk about calm. No matter what, that guy never lost his composure. Always had a great crew. As long as Roger didn't have to talk to any of the movies stars, it would be fine.

What marriages will fall apart on this show? Morton wondered. Who'll get laid? Fall in love? Movie crews can be the greatest mix of people. Where else do you get truck drivers and make-up artists and electricians and accountants and photographers all working together? Gay guys and tough-talking movie stars and teamsters. For six or eight weeks everybody knows everything about everyone else. No secrets on set. It's like summer camp, or high school. Morton cringed. High school, shit.

Judy was standing right behind him, listening to everything Renée said.

And then Renée handed it over to Nijar. "We came to Toronto," he said, "because, quite simply, you are the best crews in the world. Professional and creative. We ask for your input. We *want* your input. Maybe this isn't the biggest movie *you've* ever worked on—but it sure is for me." He paused for the soft laughter at his humble, self-deprecating remark. "And I'll really be needing your experience. We've got a great cast and I promise you all, we'll be back next year with an even bigger show, and you are all wanted on the voyage."

The applause wasn't bad. Morton had heard better, but he'd heard a lot worse. As he looked around the crowd he was once again struck by the insincerity of it all. Yet another arrogant, obnoxious Hollywood director who was coming for the cheap labour, and all the star-struck locals who'd do anything to accommodate.

All right, Morton figured. At last, finally, this is it. This is my movie moment. This is where I speak from the heart and tell it like it is. This is where I tell Judy Nemeth I can see through her manipulation and I'm not going to start dreaming again. I'm not going to set myself up for another sure crash and burn. I'm happy with what I am. I'm content. I don't need to take my shot. I'm not gonna fly now. I have a good life.

"So," Judy said as they were walking away from the bullpen, "what do you think? I have a few scripts in my office. Think you might be able to look them over? See what we can do? We'd make a great team."

And Morton said, "Sure, I'd love to."

One of the scripts wasn't half bad, a really heartfelt story about some nurses on strike. Luckily there are plenty of empty hospital wings in Toronto, so locations wouldn't be a problem. The script was set in Cleveland, but as Morton pointed out, that's one of the best things about Toronto—it can look like so many American cities.

Italy Productions Inc.

345 Carlaw Avenue, Suite 317, Toronto, Ontario M4M 2T1
Tel: 416.463-1266 Fax: 416.463-1950
Set Cell: 416.526-3516

CASH PAY DUTY OFFICERS

Date:_____

Location:_____

Signature below verifies receipt of cash as indicated from Italy Productions Inc., as payment for off-duty police services.

Name:_____

Badge #:_____

Division:_____

Municipality:_____

Category:_____
(i.e. Sergeant, Motorcycle, ETF, etc.)

Social Insurance Number:_____

Hours of Work:_____ To:_____

Total Hours:_____ at:_____ Per Hour

Total Payment:_____

Signature for cash received:_____

THE LOCATIONS PA

At least the parkas from *Samurai: The Series* were warm. He shoved his hands deeper into the pockets. This damned *Life and Death in Little Italy* hadn't even given out hats yet. Nothing.

He walked along the deserted street dropping an orange cone every few feet. The middle of the night, freezing cold. Locations work. Tomorrow this place would be jumping, a full unit, 25 trucks, Winnies, full crew. He'd be sleeping.

By the time he got back to his cube van it was completely cold inside. The heater would take forever to warm it up.

"Four fucking years of film school."

THE PAID DUTY OFFICER

Working for the movies was nothing like it is in the movies. Randy stood with one hand on his radio and one hand on his gun as the grey Crown Vic rolled up to the sidewalk. He didn't go to movies very often, but he didn't have to—the chick that got out, he'd seen her in *Playboy*. Name like Angie Reardon, something.

"Missed me that issue," the other cop, Chris, said and kicked at the sidewalk.

Randy laughed. "It's a good one." He watched as a guy exited the Crown Vic. Nervous. 6' 1". White. Glasses. Striped shirt. The guy came around the car, still talking.

"But what got me the most," the guy was saying to the movie star, "was when you said, 'You had my life planned out from the test tube.' You know, right after you slept with him, but just before you slashed his throat open?"

The movie star wanted out. Nodding like she was listening carefully, she retreated toward the set. "I forgot about that part."

The guy missed her body language. "And I thought, of course. Yeah. People have their lives planned out too much. It's like you said in *The Great Wind Race*..."

"You saw that, huh?"

She didn't make eye contact. Randy figured she'd rather this guy didn't bring it up.

"Sure did," the guy said. He nodded, like he was proud of it. "A friend of mine, he lives in LA. He sent me a tape. And it's like you said, 'My daughter deserves her chance. She may not have much, but she's allowed to make the most of it.'"

"Right, right," she said. Some movie crew flunky hovered behind her. "I've got to get going, Jerry." Randy's seen lots of lies in his time, and the movie star was lying. She could stand there all day if she wanted to. Jerry missed it. Climbed back in the Crown Vic. Drove off.

Randy widened his stance. Settled his sunglasses across the bridge of his nose. Tugged at his belt. Folded his arms. Midday traffic passed slowly. Warm for March.

"Get on with it," Chris muttered. Chris watched the cute skinny girl they called Debs run across the street with two coffees in her hand.

Randy looked him over. Nodded at the trucks parked up and down King Street. "First Paid Duty for a movie?"

Chris nodded. "Yeah. Figured my wife and I could use the extra hours."

"And the girlfriend too, right?"

They both laughed. "No thanks," Chris said. "One's enough for me."

"You gotta get used to the wait." Randy spit on the sidewalk. Watched the skinny girl run out of the restaurant the crew was shooting in, ducking past the lights on the sidewalk, and a bald black guy with a sewing kit run past her and inside. Chris watched him, too.

"Lotta fags in the movies, huh?"

Randy dropped his smile. Watched Chris from behind his sunglasses. Figured the guy was a real rookie. Shrugged. "Some on the force, too."

"I worked the Parade last year." Chris said. "Gay Pride Day. Man! Those guys are crazy!" He giggled. Shook his head. "Those chicks, too. Oh man!"

The movie crew radio barked out, "Picture's up. Lock it up, please, officers. Let me know when you're in position."

"Fucking time," Chris muttered. Trotted off to his end of the block.

Randy settled his sunglasses. Stepped out onto King Street. Gauging the eastbound traffic, he picked a Red Pontiac Sunbird, shiny clean like it got washed everyday. Made positive eye contact with the driver of the vehicle. Stuck out his hand. The driver halted. The traffic flow heading east stopped. Randy keyed his radio. "Eastbound locked up." Over his shoulder, hand still holding traffic still, he watched the westbound traffic slow and stop. Heard Chris on the radio. "Westbound traffic locked up."

"All right." One of the directors was on the radio. "This is for picture. Roll sound!" The radio went dead. Back in the alley, where some trucks were parked, he heard the yell, "Rolling!" Randy eyeballed the eastbound traffic. It wasn't going anywhere. He lowered his hand. The driver of the Sunbird, a short East Indian, late forties, stuck his head out the window.

"Excuse me, officer?" the man said. "Why is it we have been stopped?"

Randy walked over. Leaned in the man's window. "They're shooting a movie." He pointed over at all the lights shining into the restaurant's window. All the grips standing around. "The city has supplied them a permit to stop the flow of traffic for a period not exceeding three minutes. If you'll just be patient, you'll be moving in a minute."

"These fucking film crews!" the man yelled. "They are parasites. That's what they are. An infestation. Toronto is facing a traffic congestion crisis and everywhere we go we get film crews! You can't use the city parks all summer because of the film crews! Is this city a large backdrop for foreign entertainment monopolies, or a place where real people live and work, I ask you?" The man slapped his shiny red door.

Randy was trained in conflict situations, and recognized the challenge. "Sir, I'm asking you to please sit here calmly, with your vehicle at a complete stop, until I release you to go."

"What will happen if I do not?" Really angry now. "What will happen if I honk my horn? Will I ruin their precious photography?" His hand hovered over the horn.

"Sir, if you do that, I'm afraid I'll be forced to charge you with refusing to obey an officer in the course of his duties."

The hand wavered. "You'll arrest me?" Very surprised. "For ruining their photography?"

"Up to you, sir."

The guy hesitated, but didn't drop his hand. Randy thought he was going to go for it. He was bluffing, a little, making the guy think he could arrest him. Really, the best he could do was a ticket. Was the guy really going to honk?

"Cut!" burst out from the radio. "Cutting!" someone yelled from the trucks. "Officers, release traffic. Thank you." Randy stepped back from the Sunbird.

The man dropped his hand heavily on the horn. A grip turned and gave the guy the finger. He didn't notice, because he was yelling at Randy. "This is a police state." Breathless. "You don't enforce the law of the people. You enforce the law of whosoever pays your salary."

Randy waved the traffic forward. "Have a nice day, sir." He stepped off the road. Watched as the Sunbird sped away.

Chris came trotting over. "What was that about?"

Randy tugged at his belt. "Nothing. Thought I was losing my touch there for a second." Randy settled his sunglasses on his nose. Watched as the cute skinny girl ran across the street with two hot coffees. Randy figured she was good at her job.

"Going again," the radio barked. "Officers? Lock it up, please."

LIFE AND DEATH IN LITTLE ITALY
CALL SHEET

Italy Productions Inc.
Production Office:
345 Carlaw Avenue
Suite 317, Toronto, Ont. M4M 2T1
Tel: 416.463-1266 Fax: 416.463-1950
Set Cell: 416.526-3516

UNIT CALL: 0900
DATE: Thursday April 11, 2002

(see early/special calls on reverse)

Location: 17 Atlantic Ave.

Exec. Producer: Cathy Koyle
Producer: Renée Jato
Line Producer: Judy Nemeth
Director: Edward J. Nijar
1st AD: Allen Whyte

Shoot Day: 4
Lunch: 1500 @ on site
Weather: Bea-u-ti-ful
Hi: 18 Lo: 15

SCENE	SET DESCRIPTION	D/N	CAST	PAGES
74	BROTHEL Looking for Frankie	N	1,2,5,	2 3/8
88	BROTHEL Frankie talks to Candy	N	2,18	2 4/8

CHARACTER	ARTIST	P/U	H/W/M	BLKG	SET
1. Mario	Myles Day	0800	0930	0900	1000
2. Frankie	Ainsley Riordan	0730	0830	0900	1000
5. Tommy	Justin Walker	0800	0830	0900	1000
18. Candy	Janielle Michaels	1400	1430	1600	1700

PRODUCTION NOTES

TRANSPORT:
Hot and Ready @ 0730

CRAFT SERVICE:
Hot and Ready @ 0745
Early Breakfast X 10 @ 0830
Subs X 28 @ 1200

SPECIAL CALLS:
1st AD: 0830
2nd AD: 0800
3rd AD: 0745

HAIR/MU: 0900
WRDB: 0900
LOCATIONS: 0730

FIRST AID KIT / SAFETY GUIDELINE BOOK LOCATED AT CRAFT SERVICE
2nd AD: Walter Ho (H) 416.460-2929
3rd AD: James Watts (H) 416.534-3865
LOC. MGR: Morton Gibson (H) 416.699-2270
TRANS CAP'T: Roger Doyle (C) 416.566-1099

THE TRANSPORT CAPTAIN

"If there's a problem with one of my guys, I need to know what it is," Roger said.

Judy Nemeth said, "No, it's not a problem, really." They were standing on the sidewalk of Atlantic Avenue, which was lined with trucks. "It's just, the guys like Ainsley. Maybe a little too much. There's a lot of pressure on her right now."

"Watch your back," a voice called.

Roger stepped aside to let a couple of grips carrying a length of dolly track pass.

He said, "I can tell him not to talk." But the minute he said it he knew he'd never be able to get Jerry to be quiet.

The first week of principal and already this show was a mess. *Life and Death in Little Italy*, all tough-talking hitmen and mobsters and cops and hookers with hearts of gold. Sort of indie, but not really, like a lot of runaway productions: *Good Will Hunting* or *Virgin Suicides* or *Exit Wounds* or *American Psycho*. The vast middle ground of Hollywood that Roger had little time for.

"If you could just get another driver for Ainsley."

"Yeah, sure, okay." He'd do it for Judy. She was the line producer or associate producer, or whatever title they'd given her to come up here and tame the locals, the lowest ranking American on set. "I'll get someone started tomorrow."

A couple of electrics weighed down with overflowing tool belts came down the steps of the Craft truck talking loudly about tatoos. "Come on, if she's got that one on her belly, you *know* there's something further down."

"Yeah, I like that one on her back."

They walked past Judy and Roger and nodded a little at him, ignoring her.

Judy said, "Maybe you could take Ainsley home today and bring her in tomorrow."

"Yeah, all right."

"Great. Thanks very much." And she was gone before Roger could say anything.

"Canadian movies? Canadian movies suck. Slow, bleak, cold. We have summer, too, you know." Jerry'd been in the Craft truck for almost half an hour, talking the whole time. "Alienation is bad, tell me something I don't know. These artsy directors want to have their cakes and eat them too. They want to tell deep, important, literary, meaningful stories—novels basically—but they also want to go to parties with supermodels."

"Oooh, supermodels. Models by day, powerful superheroes by night."

"I was on that show. It was hell."

Four of them were crammed into the Craft Services truck pouring coffees and piling cream cheese and jam on toasted bagels. The main unit was set up shooting dialogue inside a house down the street. It was supposed to be a brothel or a massage parlour or something and the base camp was set up behind some apartment buildings.

No one was listening to him—Jerry was just a driver—but he kept talking. "You know, Canadian movies are basically short stories. They're not movies at all. They're those crappy short stories in literary magazines no one reads, where when you get to the end nothing really happened and you don't know why you bothered."

"I bother because I get paid."

"They're about the struggle, man. That's what drama is. The journey."

"Crap. I'd like to know what knobhead first said 'sad and lonely with boring shots of scenery instantly means deep and meaningful.'"

"I like it better when there aren't any actors. Give me beautiful vistas any day. Less stress on set."

"Bullshit. Movies are about people. All these young hotshot directors can talk the talk but they can't walk the walk. If I hear one more chain-smoking punk with a goatee go on and on about the symbolism of alienation and the dark side of character and irony—shit, irony… Nothing's so overused and as little understood as irony—and how film is a visual medium but he doesn't have the guts to even try and have a resolution because that would be emotionally risky, I'll—"

"You'll what? Do anything but get back to work?"

Jerry took an overly dramatic deep breath and was about to start again when he saw Roger.

"I'm waiting for the film from this morning."

"Yeah, well, they need some more AC in Make-up. Run the cable, Jerry."

"The pretties? Why can't one of the electrics do it?"

"Because I'm asking you."

Jerry stared at him for a moment, then sighed and started out of the truck. He stopped, though, and picked up another muffin. "Are there any more chocolate chip?"

Hillary said, "Just what you see there."

"And don't let them hear you calling their department that."

Jerry smirked and waved his hands, but did what his boss told him.

"Do you want a coffee?" This was Hillary's first show running Craft Services but she'd been an assistant for years. "Or would you like a cappuccino?"

Roger said, "No thanks, coffee's fine. Do you have enough heat in here?" The Craft truck was like any rental cube van with a logo on the side but instead of the rolling back door there were portable wooden stairs and a regular house-style door. Inside, the truck had been fitted with a kind of kitchen, complete with stove, fridge and fancy coffee machines.

Hillary poured the coffee into the Coffee Time plastic travel mug Roger had brought in himself. "Yeah, it's plenty warm enough in here, thanks. Cream?"

"No, just black."

"That's right, you're a real truck driver, aren't you?"

He looked up sharply, but she was being genuinely friendly. You could never be too sure on set. He pressed the lid into place and nodded at the other guy in the truck, the electric who had worked on the supermodel-superhero show. "Thanks."

There was a tattoo peeking out the top of Hillary's jeans in the front, some kind of design around her belly button. Roger couldn't see enough of it to tell what it was. When she turned around and bent over to empty the coffee filter he saw the other tattoo on the small of her back.

Roger stepped out of the Craft truck into the cold morning air. The first week of April and it was still more winter than spring. No snow, but the sky was grey. He walked along the row of tractor trailers: the dressing rooms and equipment trucks and the honey wagon. He knew each one would have a driver sleeping in the cab. Movie sets are a split shift for the drivers, showing up before the day starts and leaving after it ends for everyone else. Movie sets could be tough for truckers who were used to being by themselves for long hauls. Roger had worked with all these guys before, though, and they were good guys.

It was different with the guys driving the cars.

Driving cars, even star cars, is a real no-skill job that every producer and lawyer's nephew can do. Roger hated having guys on his crew he hadn't hired. That's why he'd given the movie star to Jerry. He'd hired Jerry himself and, except for the fact that the guy had opinions about everything, he was all right. He was always on time and always got the job done. He just wasn't as "Canadian" as people liked—he didn't suck up enough. Maybe that's why Roger had hired him.

"Locations for Transport." Roger pressed the button on the walkie-talkie's handset clipped to the collar of his jacket.

"Go for Transport."

"I've got the building super here. He says we're taking up way too many parking spaces."

"What's your twenty?"

"At the loading dock, in the back."

"I'll be there in five." Roger took his finger off the handset. He'd better deal with this in person.

A couple of hours later, when the last scene of the day had been shot and the actors were wrapped, the crew really got to work. It's hurry up and wait all day, but when wrap's called everyone's got lots to do.

Roger was waiting at the white Crown Victoria when Jerry walked up behind a couple of electrics, each loaded down with huge coils of cable over their shoulders and beers in their hands.

Jerry spread his arms and shrugged. "Can't help you now," he said to Roger. "I've got to get Her Highness back to the hotel before she turns into a human being."

Roger said, "You take my truck."

Jerry looked at the empty bed of the half-ton double-parked a couple of cars down. "You haven't got the signs yet?"

"I haven't got anything yet."

A couple of other drivers who hadn't worked for Roger before had gotten out of their cars to watch. The ones who had worked for Roger on other shows knew there'd be no scene, no drama, no raised voices; he'd just get it done.

Jerry said, "Why?"

"Because I have to drive this car." Matter of fact.

Jerry looked at the Crown Vic, the "star" car. "But I drive this car."

"I'm driving it now." No explanation, no story, nothing that would give Jerry the kind of confrontation he wanted.

Before it got too awkward, Ainsley Riordan, Judy Nemeth and an AD walked up to the Crown Vic. The AD turned and walked away immediately and Ainsley and Judy got into the back seat of the car.

Jerry said, "Oh, I get it."

"No you don't, so don't worry about it."

Jerry said, "I'm not *worried* about it. I just understand now."

Roger said, "Fine, okay, so you understand. Take my truck, get the signs and be here at five tomorrow morning."

Jerry said, "Yes massah, yessir, we do what boss-man Yankee say, yessir, yessir."

The other drivers laughed, more at Jerry's pathetic attempt at a southern accent than at his clumsy dig at his boss's authority.

Roger said, "You finished?" and before Jerry could say anything else, the back door of the Crown Vic opened and Judy Nemeth got out. She nodded at Roger as she passed him.

The drivers all stood looking at Roger but before he could even tell them to get back to work, Myles Day walked into the group.

"All right, gentlemen, where will the evening take us?" He was rubbing his hands together expectantly.

"Brass Rail?"

"Too classy. I don't think my guy would go there."

"Out by the airport?"

"No, my guy's more downtown. How about that cowboy place?"

"Jilly's?"

Myles Day snapped his fingers and said, "Jilly's it is. Mostly white chicks, right? My guy wouldn't really go for the Asians."

"Yeah, Canadian girls."

A movie star, but one of the guys. That's how Myles Day thought he came across, and if he wanted to use some method acting "in-character" cover to spend all his off hours in strip clubs, that was fine with the crew. After years of bad comedies and movies-of-the-week he'd finally gotten his own cop show, *Downtown Heat*. After it'd been off the air a few years he had a small "comeback" guest spot on *The Sopranos,* a good death scene that got him some real notice. Now he was getting those Harvey Keitel roles he'd always felt he deserved.

Roger waited till all the other actors had been loaded into the star cars and his drivers had their call sheets for the next day and he looked at all their eyes to see who was too stoned to drive—no one tonight, but it was only day four—then he finally went to the Crown Vic and got in.

"Tough day?"

He had expected Ainsley Riordan to tear a strip off him for taking so long. In fact he'd kind of hoped she would so he could go back to driving his truck, but when he looked in the rear-view there she was, all perky in the backseat.

He said, "Not particularly."

Ainsley nodded and looked out the window at the passing houses. One-and-a-half story, post-war brick. Small, well-kept yards and gardens.

"So, you're the Transport captain?"

Roger glanced in the rear-view again. She met his eyes. "Yeah." Was that it? She wanted to be chauffeured around by the captain?

She nodded again. Considering something. She looked almost like a teenager. She bit her lower lip a little—there had been collagen rumours on set but the lips looked natural enough to Roger. Her green eyes scanned the neighbourhood. A little cliché with her thick red hair, but she was undeniably sexy.

She said, "Tough day all right."

"Mm hmm."

"I'm really sorry about that other driver."

"It's okay."

"You know, I know it's a big deal for someone to lose their job, but I just didn't think I could take it for five more weeks."

"He didn't lose his job," Roger said.

Ainsley was surprised. "Oh. That's good."

"I moved him to Second Unit." Roger glanced in the rear-view and saw Ainsley looking right back at him. "You can't just hire and fire people all the time. It's one of the things I hate about working on set. There's always that threat of losing your job, getting fired for crap. Not on my crew."

Ainsley nodded. She looked like she was thinking about it. Or thinking about something, which surprised Roger.

"Okay, that's good. You're right. Shouldn't be so much stress. Do you mind if I ask you a question?"

"Okay."

"What do you think of this movie?"

This *movie*? That's all she wanted to talk about? Roger was relieved. He could bullshit for a couple of minutes and then she'd leave him alone. He said, "Well, there are a lot of unit moves, and a lot of downtown stuff, hard to get to and hard to get away from. Parking's always a pain."

"No, I mean…did you read the script?"

"Yeah."

"And…did you like it?"

He glanced in the rear-view. She was looking right at him, waiting for an answer. He really didn't want to spend the next half hour reassuring some insecure, anorexic actress. Everybody knows, don't say *any*thing to the movie star. You mention something you read in the paper about beef being recalled in Guatemala and the next thing you know every meal on set is vegetarian and the caterer's freaking out on you. Finally he said, "It's really hard for someone like me to tell from the script."

"What do you mean, 'someone like you'?"

"Someone who doesn't know anything about making movies."

"You work in the movie business, you know about making movies."

"I know about *making* movies, about being on set. Everyone asks me what a best boy does and I know that, but I don't know about making *movies*, you know, the storytelling stuff."

"Well, you've seen some movies, haven't you?"

"A few," he said, but he couldn't think of the last time he went to a movie theatre to see one.

"Okay, well, compared to the few other movies you've seen, what do you think of this one?"

It was taking her a long time to start asking about how great looking she was. Roger said, "I really don't know. I can't tell. You know, in the script it says, 'Frankie walks down the alley.' Well, I don't know if it's a long shot that makes her look small and vulnerable with soft sympathetic music or if it's a close-up travelling shot, a determined angry look on her face, harsh lighting, and a pounding techno beat."

"You can tell from the context."

"I can get a general idea but not...the real subtleties, the nuances..." He shook his head. "No, I can't tell."

"Sure you can. You think it's convoluted crap, bullshit, don't you?"

Roger wished he was back on set. Having a beer with the truckers, bullshitting about the tough-guy actors, telling the Winnie drivers where to get the cheapest propane. Man, he'd rather be working Locations, emptying garbage cans and picking up cones. Anywhere but here in this car with this girl.

But now, looking at her in the rearview, she didn't look so young. No make-up, her hair tied back, staring at him. She was waiting for an answer. What the hell, Roger figured, she wants to talk about movies, tell her the truth.

"Yeah, it's bullshit."

"All my movies are bullshit. How come?"

"Hey, come on. People love your movies."

"People love that I show my tits in my movies."

"Well, that doesn't hurt."

She nodded. "How come you tell me the truth?"

"What?"

"Everyone else tells me the movie's great, all my movies are terrific, I'm a wonderful actress, my 'craft' is developing. How come you say it's bullshit but my tits are great?"

"Well, just look at them."

"So why is it such bullshit?" She was still talking about the movie.

So Roger decided to tell her the truth. He said, "Because its reference points are all other movies."

"Reference points? What kind of a driver are you?"

"Hey, I'm the captain." But now that he'd started, he just kept going. "The thing is, it's not about real people, it's about characters in other movies." He turned his head a little and saw her nodding, disappointed, but also as though she'd just got some confirmation. "But you know, that can be hidden by really cool direction."

"Well, Edward sure thinks he's cool."

"Ever meet a director who didn't?"

She laughed. Then she let loose with questions: What was his name? How long had he been a driver? Was he from Toronto? He answered politely in as few words as he could, but now they just seemed to be talking, like friends.

He told her: Roger Doyle, ten years, two in the movies and no, he'd lived all over.

"Me, too. I've lived in five states, nine cities. Doyle, that's Irish, right? I'm Irish, too. Have you read *How the Irish Saved Civilization*?"

Roger nodded into the rear-view. "Not yet. I was planning to. I've seen it around."

"It's really good. You don't often see Irish and civilization in the same sentence."

"No."

"I am sorry about that other driver, you know. I'm glad you didn't fire him, it's just, I'm really nervous and he was always going on and on."

How could this chick complain about the drivers? She did all the talking. Roger wondered how Jerry got a word in edgewise.

"He *loved* all my movies, though. He knew all my lines better than I did. He seems to be basing his life on *Steel Shroud*."

"Was that the sci-fi one?"

"Yeah. I was a clone."

"I haven't see that one. It was a great short story, though."

"I didn't even know it was a short story."

"I remember reading it when I was a kid. What's it mean to be human? Who gets to decide? That kind of stuff. In the story some animals were given human genes."

"Yeah, that's right, not a clone, a GAL, a genetically altered lifeform. Of course, I was a cat that had become human. I didn't eat mice and cough up furballs, though, I wore a leather bra and slept with everybody. I can tell you, that's not what any of my cats do."

"I remember the poster."

"But you didn't see the movie."

"No."

She waited, but Roger concentrated on the road.

"Anyway, you know, tomorrow's a tough day for me. Six in the morning I'll be standing there at the lake in a miniskirt and six-inch heels and a bra and I'll have to cry and pout and then after lunch it's supposed to be night and I'm on a date with Myles and it's three months later and I'm wearing some fancy dress and a wig." She paused. "Then there's the goddamned sex scene on the roof. The roof. Who writes this shit?"

Roger had really only skimmed the script to get the locations. He nodded.

"Those are really different scenes."

"The crying's the hard part. I don't cry. I haven't cried since I was two years old. Oh well, they've got that stuff they put in your eyes."

And Roger realized for the first time she was nervous because of her work.

She shook her head, though, and forgot about it. "So anyway, what did you do before the movies?"

"Drove trucks."

"Like delivery trucks, like the UPS guy?"

"No, transport trucks."

"Those huge trucks on the highways?"

"Yeah."

"Wow. My uncle was a trucker a long time ago. Why'd you quit that?"

"A lot of reasons. You're away all the time." He saw her nodding in agreement in the rear-view.

She was leaning forward now, listening to him.

"And they're really squeezing the O and O's."

She tilted her head to one side.

"Owner-operators. Companies use what they call 'just in time' operations, so they don't have to pay to warehouse anything. You get paid to deliver, but if they're not ready when they're supposed to be, you can't unload. You lose more days that way. And, well, everybody's cutting their price to get work. Most months you can't clear enough to cover the payment on your rig."

She was listening. She said, "So, do you like working on movies?"

He was going to say sure and be done with it, but she looked as though she really wanted to know, so they talked about it all the way to the Sutton Place Hotel. She laughed when he complained about people who couldn't read a map and made some jokes herself about tough-talking producers who were scared of bellhops. At the hotel she thanked him for the ride, as if he was a buddy taking her home from a party, and jumped out. She waved as he pulled away.

On the drive home Roger figured that Ainsley was just a natural, a pro, a real actress, and all that friendly bullshit was just bullshit. He'd pick her up in the morning, drop her off on set and hire another driver right away. He hated being around the talent.

"He calls himself El Presidente, because of the uniform."

It was 5:45 a.m. when Roger had pulled up in front of the hotel. Ainsley was smiling and chatting with the doorman and had waited until he finished his story before she'd jumped into the front seat of the Crown Vic. She was wearing a baggy turtleneck, sweat pants and running shoes, and her hair was pulled back into a ponytail. She didn't have any make-up on.

She was still smiling and waving to El Presidente as they pulled out onto Bay Street and headed south. "So," she said, turning sideways in the seat and looking at Roger, "are you taking much action on the woody?"

Roger knew exactly what she was talking about. He said, "I'm sorry, what?"

She laughed. "Oh, come on. I've spent my whole life around actors. Don't think you can bullshit me. Which way is the action going?"

"You've got a lot of fans on the crew."

She laughed again. "Yeah, because of my *Playboy* spread, I'll bet. Imagine saying that at a party, 'my *Playboy* spread.' Could be worse, I guess. Could be my *Penthouse* pucker."

Roger nodded. "That would be worse."

"You bet. Oh well. It's tough on poor Myles, you know. If he gets a woody, I call him unprofessional and a creepy pervert. And if he doesn't, I make a scene and say, 'What's the matter? Don't you think I'm sexy?'" She paused. "Maybe I'll cry."

"I thought you said crying was hard."

"So you *were* listening." She slapped him playfully on the arm.

God. What a flirt. He wondered if it was a just habit or if that was how women got into the movies. He remembered seeing Ainsley on TV last month; she'd flirted with Letterman too.

"Well, before we have any fun, I've got to stand around in the freezing cold in my underwear. The things I do for a lousy million bucks." It was a punch line and she was looking at Roger to see if he was laughing. He wasn't. She moved on, though, and soon enough he was laughing. Something about a director and his incredibly convoluted attempt to see her naked. It wasn't the details, but the casual way she told the story, like they were old friends.

At the set, Cherry Beach, everything was in full swing.

Ainsley said, "What's the matter?"

Roger looked at her. "What?"

"You just suddenly tensed up. What's wrong?"

"Oh, nothing. I'm just usually here a lot earlier, before all this gets set up. Feels weird."

"Yeah, I never thought of that. It's always busy when I get in."

"And busy when you leave."

"Great, now I feel like a slacker."

"Well, you've got to stand in your underwear in the freezing cold. That's hard work."

"It is." She opened the door and got out. Then she leaned back into the car. "So, um, will you be back at lunch?"

"I doubt it. I have a lot of paperwork in the office and I have to hire another driver."

"Oh. So you won't be driving me home?"

"No, we'll have somebody by then. A deaf-mute, I think."

"Oh." She stared at him for a moment. "Okay, well, it's been great."

"Yeah."

She closed the car door and an AD appeared at her side, walking her to her trailer. After a couple of steps the AD looked back and winked.

Roger parked and checked to make sure Jerry had set up okay, then he headed to Craft for a coffee.

"Hey man, did she show you her birthmark?"

Roger said, "What?"

"She showed it to Conan O'Brien."

The truck was crowded and Roger felt everyone looking at him. Usually he slipped in and out unnoticed.

Karyn, the bald black woman from Wardrobe said, "Hey, Mr. Big Time."

Roger got his coffee and Hillary said, "I think it's great. Really Danny Moder."

Roger said, "Who?"

"Come on, he's the crew guy who married Julia Roberts."

"Not real crew," a grip said. "A camera girl."

Karyn said, "Yeah. Transport is much more of the people. Even if you are the captain." She looked at Roger and smiled. Everyone did.

He just walked out of the truck into the cold morning air, past the rows of trucks and Winnies, the busy crew, people going in every direction and back to the Crown Vic. He had no desire to be the centre of on-set gossip.

Driving along Eastern Avenue, Roger figured he'd get to the production office, hire a new driver, probably a chick, and get her to take Ainsley home. Then he wouldn't hear any more about it.

"Hey, Doyle, you banging Ainsley Riordan?"

Roger turned and saw Morton Gibson, the location manager, sitting behind his small desk in his tiny office. A guy Roger didn't know sat on the edge of the desk and laughed.

"Every chance we get. We're doing it in her Winnie on breaks."

"I wondered why it was parked so close to Craft."

Roger rolled his eyes and said, "MoGib."

The guy sitting on the edge of the desk said, "Oh, are we getting nicknames this show? What's mine?"

"Don't worry, you'll get plenty of nicknames," Morton said.

"Yeah, but they'll never be as cool as MoGib." He turned and looked at Roger. "I'm Garry Delisle." They shook hands.

"Garry's a scout," Morton said.

"Hey, I'm a filmmaker. Someday you'll all be working for me."

"As long as we're working for someone," Roger said.

Garry said, "I didn't catch your name."

Morton said, "Forget it, Garry. This is Roger Doyle. He's the Transport captain."

"Wow, a trucker without a beer gut. Where'd you come from?"

"No one knows," Morton said.

Garry was clearly amused.

Roger said, "I thought all the locations were locked."

"The last to know, that's us. The rewrites are coming in dribs and drabs and half of them have new locations. I think this is the writer's first time."

Garry said, "Be gentle."

"Did anyone tell you we're shooting at the airport?" Morton asked.

"Of course not. Why would they tell me? I've only got to figure out how to get the production there."

Garry said, "So, what's it like, banging a movie star?"

Roger started to walk away and said, "You know, you strip them naked and turn them upside down and they all look the same."

Garry spit coffee out of his nose and slapped his thigh. "Oh, you're precious, man, precious."

All right, Roger figured, file expense reports, fill out the insurance claim and hire a driver. Get this over with right now.

In the bullpen, Alice, a PA, was filling a coffee pot from the water cooler. She smiled at Roger as he passed. Tap water's just no good for movie people.

"Hey, Roger, get a look at this."

A driver and another PA, Greg, were standing in the director's office looking at something spread out over his desk.

Roger said, "What are you doing here?"

"I'm driving. Look. They had me pick up these from agents."

Roger saw the usual stack of headshots. These all seemed to be blondes, early twenties to mid-thirties.

The driver said, "We're ranking them."

"Yeah, hot, really hot and super hot. Who knew there were so many fine-looking women in this city?"

"That's what happens when you get into the movie business. The strip clubs score. But wait, look at this." The driver held up an envelope marked, "Confidential, for Edward Nijar only," and slid out a stack of pictures. "Thank God for digital cameras."

These seemed to be the same women, but instead of professionally shot black and white pictures of their faces, these were waist up, colour shots taken in brightly lit offices.

The women all had that deer-in-the-headlights look on their faces. They were also all topless.

"Okay, let's sort these. Strippers in this pile, hookers, I mean 'escorts,' here and the super-naive here."

"I guess the picture's really in trouble. It's going R," Greg said.

Roger started to walk away. "It was always R. This is bullshit."

"Yeah, what the local girls have to put up with to get into the movies. You think they do this in Hollywood?"

Outside the office Alice was still filling the coffee pot from the cooler. She smiled at Roger again.

"Feels like it's still prep in here. Location scouting, casting."

He said, "Yeah." And thought, and hiring drivers, too. It is prep. And production. At the same time.

Roger went into his office and sat behind his desk. Paperwork was piled high. Can't be a driver and the captain. Only five days into principal and already this show really was a disaster. Oh well, they always are and they always work out. Hire a driver, get back to doing one job. Never have to see Ainsley Riordan again.

He picked up the phone.

"Hey, Boss, I'll drive Ainsley."

"No way, man. I'll do her. I mean drive her."

Roger shook his head. The drivers were all standing around a couple of picnic tables set up near crew parking. The day had turned out to be sunny and quite warm. April weather, unpredictable as always.

"I think I'm going to have to hire a chick."

"You haven't found anyone yet?"

"Hire Vicki, man. She'd love it."

They all laughed.

"She's living with that chick who does the weather on CityTV."

"Ooh, the one with the blue hair and the really big tits?"

Suddenly everyone shut up at once. Roger had his back to the set and he figured Judy Nemeth was coming. He didn't turn around.

"How can you tell when the teamster's dead?" It was Ainsley Riordan.

Abe actually started to say something but Roger shook his head just enough for him to notice. The other drivers all had their mouths hanging open.

Roger said, "The donut falls out of his hand." He turned. Ainsley Riordan was walking through the mud of Cherry Beach towards him. She was wearing a long black overcoat, hanging open, and a black lace bra and leather miniskirt underneath. Torn fishnet stockings disappeared into high-top sneakers.

She said, "How many teamsters does it take to change a light bulb?"

"Four. You gotta problem with that, college boy?"

She stopped right in front of him. "I guess you've heard them all."

"Never from the talent."

She smiled and Roger thought, it almost looks like she means it. And then he wondered if she did mean it.

She said, "Yeah, how come actors are called the talent?"

"Because they have no useful skills."

And her movie star smile disappeared instantly. "What the hell's that supposed to mean?"

In all his years on set Roger had never spoken more than three or four words with an actor. Now this conversation had him all screwed up. He said, "Nothing. I didn't mean anything, I just meant..."

"Got you." She winked and walked away. "You missed a great lunch. Jerk chicken."

The drivers all burst out laughing. "If you could see your face, man."

"Yeah? Now you can all drop off your expense sheets at the office yourselves."

The drivers were still laughing and already telling each other about what they'd all just seen as Roger walked away. He started to think about how she said the word *jerk*. Did she mean him, did she mean it, "you jerk" or what? Man, she was getting under his skin. Well, that's what she does. That's all she does, every movie she's ever been in, every meeting too, probably, every interview for sure. She flirts. It's not personal. Forget it, it'll be over soon. Back to the office, hire another driver.

But she had walked all the way around the set till she found him.

"First rule of Transport, keys under the visor."

"No, the first rule of Transport is that it's Locations' problem. Talk to them."

Ainsley was sitting behind the wheel of the Crown Vic. The motor was running. She said, "I want to drive."

Roger said, "Move over."

"But I want to drive."

"You can't."

"Sure I can. Come on. I want to." Like a petulant child.

"Move over," Roger said. "I've got to do my job."

"I want to." She held the steering wheel and it looked huge in her tiny hands.

"Yeah, but I don't want to stand around in my underwear in the freezing cold and then make out with Myles Day."

Ainsley smiled. "He has the softest hands of anyone I've ever met." She slid across the big front seat. "It's kind of creepy, a man with such soft hands."

Roger got in and pulled the door closed. "Men can have soft hands."

"Yeah, sure," she said, "Keyshawn Johnson has soft hands, but he's a receiver."

"So?"

"So, they aren't literally soft, they're all banged up and mangled and bent and twisted."

Roger pressed on the gas and the big car slid soundlessly out of the parking lot.

"How do you know?"

"I gave him an award at the ESPY's last year. He's nice."

"That's good."

"That's the first question people ask when you tell them you met a celebrity. 'What's he like?' 'Is she nice?' People always want them to be nice."

"Or really, really not nice."

"That's right. What are you going to tell people about me?"

"No one's ever going to know I met you."

"Ha, you can't even stand the thought of someone else driving me."

"I tried everyone. There isn't a driver in the city who'll take you."

She looked hurt. Really, genuinely hurt. Roger waited for the *gotcha*. He waited and waited. She just looked out the window at the passing houses, kids playing road hockey.

"Are you kidding? They're lining up to Winnipeg to drive you."

"Really, but I got that guy fired."

"I told you, I moved him to Second Unit."

"Yeah, how come you can do that? I want a guy fired, he gets fired." She was back, but her voice lacked conviction.

"Second Unit is worse than being fired."

"Okay then, that's better." She looked at Roger and seemed happy again. He couldn't tell.

"So, how was your day?"

"Oh you know, another day, another 25 grand."

"No, seriously."

She looked at him for a moment, then looked away. "How was my day? Seriously? I don't know. I really can't tell. I'm hitting my marks and saying my lines. That's what I'm supposed to do, but I can't tell if it's working or not."

"I'm sure it's fine."

She nodded but didn't look convinced. Then she brightened. "Day off tomorrow. What are you going to do?"

"Laundry."

"Wow, what a coincidence. Me too."

Roger looked sideways at Ainsley.

"Okay, my assistant, or my assistant's assistant or somebody's going to do my laundry, but I'll be worrying about it all day."

Roger laughed and shook his head. Ainsley didn't say anything. She seemed like she wanted to, though, fidgeting on the seat and looking around. She looked a little frustrated. Finally she said, "Okay, seriously, I was thinking something silly and touristy, going up to the top of that big tower or something."

"Asking them how they wash the windows?"

"Yeah, and then a hockey game. Is there a hockey game tomorrow night?"

"There sure is. Montreal, a good one."

"Do you want to go?"

"To the game?"

"Yeah, sure. Do you want to go with me? And to the top of that tower, and anything else you might take some out-of-town visitor to see."

"Well, I, um…"

"Oh, come on, let's do it. You know the city. You won't bullshit me like all the yes-men they hire. Let's have some fun."

"I don't know."

"Okay, it's settled."

"That hockey game's been sold out for a long time."

"I'm pretty sure I can get a couple of tickets. *Hard Drive* did 100 million, you know. Where should we meet?"

"Why don't I pick you up here?" The car slowed to a stop in front of the Sutton Place Hotel.

"As long as it's not like work. You can't treat it like your job."

"I promise I won't put in for overtime."

"Okay. And you can't use this car."

"I'll have to."

"Why?"

He looked embarrassed. "I don't have a car."

"You're the Transport captain and you don't have a car?"

"I get a car from the production. I have a motorcycle."

"In Canada? What do you do in the winter?"

"I spent last winter in Costa Rica."

"Maybe I am in the wrong job. I spent last winter in Alaska making that dogsled movie. Okay, it's all set, 6:30. The game and then dinner." And in one quick motion she slid across the seat, kissed him on the cheek, slid back and was out of the car.

Roger watched her walk into the hotel without looking back or stopping to chat with El Presidente.

Back on set, Rahim handed Roger a beer and said, "Way to go, boss."

Roger didn't say anything. He took a swig from the bottle. It felt better to be back on set, watching wrap. Well, supervising, really, even though all the drivers knew what they were doing.

One of the grips said, "Hey man, no good can come of it."

"I think it's great."

They were all standing on Front Street, a block from the Novotel Hotel, in front of the Craft truck. The place was getting packed up fast.

The grip said it again. "No good can come of it."

Hillary was sitting on the wooden steps on the back of the truck. "No, it's great. Julia Roberts married below the line."

"Julia Roberts is nuts, though."

"What about that chick from *The X-Files*? She married an art director."

"Which one?"

"You know, the redhead, Scully."

"No, which art director?"

"Oh, I don't know. They're divorced now."

"And Sandra Bullock, she dated a grip."

"Grips are different," the grip said. "We know about tools."

The Wardrobe guy, Steven, put his hand on Roger's arm and squeezed. "It's sweet," he said. "Very endearing. You be nice."

"All right," Roger said. "Enough."

Everyone looked at him. He said, "Back to work," and walked away.

El Presidente came out from under the awning and shook his head at the filthy motorcycle. Then he looked more closely. "Wow, a Norton. Nice bike."

"Thanks."

"You do the rebuild yourself?"

"The whole thing."

The doorman leaned down over the bike. "Man, you had it down to the frame, didn't you?"

Roger had to make a real effort not to look at the goofy uniform the guy wore. Why do they put doormen in such ridiculous get-ups?

"Hey, General Noriega!"

They both turned to see Ainsley coming out of the hotel.

"Planning a coup?" She was dressed in biker-chick chic: leather boots, low-rider jeans, cropped T-shirt, and a leather jacket. "Nice bike. I was expecting a Vespa."

"Then you'd be a little overdressed, wouldn't you?"

She gave Roger the sexiest look he'd ever seen in his life and said, "Babe, if you know how to drive that thing, I won't stay dressed long."

El Presidente slapped his right hand over his chest with a loud smack and took a couple of steps backwards. Ainsley laughed and winked at him.

Roger said, "Sorry I didn't get a chance to clean it."

Ainsley carried a brand new black helmet, the short kind that bikers who hate helmet laws wear. "Looks good to me." She pulled on the helmet, left the chin strap dangling and jumped on the back of the bike.

Roger tossed the old helmet he'd brought to El Presidente and slowly walked around the bike and climbed on in front of Ainsley. He noticed the doorman and a couple of bellhops were staring at him. In fact, a small crowd had gathered in the hotel driveway and just outside the lobby. Everyone was staring at Ainsley and Roger prayed the bike would start first time. He flipped out the kickstart, jumped on it and felt the engine turn over. Ainsley put her arms around his chest and leaned tight against him.

They sped off, out onto Bay Street and south towards the Air Canada Centre.

The game was great. First round of the playoffs and the rivalry was back. Ainsley's tickets were right behind the Leafs' bench, the best seats Roger'd had for a hockey game in his life. She wouldn't say how she got them. He explained bits and pieces of the game to her but she was more interested in the people around them, the building, what hockey means to people in Toronto, that kind of thing.

Everyone had noticed when they walked in and guys whistled at her and shouted but almost no one approached them and Ainsley remarked how people were actually polite.

"I figured that would be another cliché that didn't come true."

"Hey, you're in the movies. You know the clichés always come true."

Towards the end of the second period a guy from Hockey Night in Canada asked Ainsley if he could interview her on air. She looked at Roger.

"What should I say?"

"What do you think?"

"It's a lot of fun, really fast. I like the body checks that rattle the glass."

"So, say that."

"Makes me sound like a dumb chick."

Roger said, "Yeah."

She shoved him. She meant it to be hard, to knock him back a bit, but her hands landed on his chest and stopped there. "What would you say?"

"Tell them anything can happen. It's not over till it's over."

"Like that's not a cliché."

"Sometimes clichés come true."

The noise from the 20,000 fans seemed to disappear as they stared at one another. After what seemed like a long time Ainsley nodded and smiled.

When the TV camera was in place and Ainsley started talking, Roger was amazed how relaxed and friendly she seemed. She even said a few things about the Leafs' ability to get the puck out of their own end quickly and use their speed.

The CBC guy was very impressed, and when they were off-air and starting to leave, he looked at Roger and said, "Are you in the movie, too?"

Ainsley jumped in, grabbing Roger by the arm. "No, he's my date."

The CBC guy was way more impressed with that than by her knowledge of hockey.

Mats Sundin put it away with three minutes left and people flooded out of the ACC. Roger asked Ainsley if she wanted to leave but she said they might as well stay to the end. A lot of people who walked by their seats waved at them and plenty of guys gave Roger the thumbs-up. Finally, after the three-star selection they got up to leave.

In the corridors under the stands, that odd combination of brand new high tech with TV screens everywhere and exposed pipe and concrete utilitarian that new sports arenas seem to love, the crowd had thinned out, but a few guys still stood at the brew pub bar in the lobby. They all noticed Ainsley Riordan as she passed and some of the comments were loud enough for her to hear.

Roger looked at her and said, "You want me to kick their asses?"

"You're so gallant."

"Well, I didn't think Leonardo DiCaprio could do it."

"No, when we go out he usually hires someone to do it for him. Doesn't want to bust up his manicure."

Outside the evening had gotten cold and Ainsley zipped up her leather jacket.

"You really came prepared on this shoot."

"What are you talking about? I sweated for hours today shopping."

The bike was parked under the Gardiner Expressway at the base of a support pillar. It was dark and cold and even though cars passed by steadily on Lakeshore it was surprisingly quiet. Roger put the key in the ignition and looked at Ainsley. She was standing beside him, staring, looking very serious.

"What?"

She grabbed his arm, pulled him close and kissed. Soft wet lips. She kept pulling him closer and for a moment he didn't do anything and then finally he put his arms around and held her tight and kissed back.

A very long moment later she pulled away slightly and moved her mouth up to his ear. "For a minute there I thought you weren't going to kiss me back."

"Took me by surprise."

"You think I've been faking this? I'm that good an actress? Don't you read *Movieline*?"

"I told you, I don't really like movies."

She pulled away and looked him right in the eyes. "I like you more and more all the time."

She kissed him again and this time he was right there kissing her back. She pressed so hard against him, he had to push back. She grabbed the back of his head and kissed his face, licked his ears, kissed his neck. He slid his tongue over the smooth skin of her neck and crouched down a little, picking her up off the ground. He sat her down on the motorcycle and again found her mouth. She lay back and wrapped her legs around him, pulling him on top of her. Her hands moved over his shoulders and chest, she pulled his shirt out from his pants and touched his skin.

Roger still held her, his arms tight around her body.

"Ouch, hang on."

"What?"

"There's something here, jabbing me."

"That's the gas cap. Sorry."

"It's okay, here." She pulled him down on top of her again but quickly pushed him up. "Now that hurts. You know what? This would be a lot better at the hotel."

He stepped back a half step and she sat up on the motorcycle facing the back of the bike. He looked at her, flustered.

"Nice big bed, clean sheets, room service."

"In the movies this would work. It would be hot and sexy."

"It would take eight hours to film and it would hurt. Come on, let's go back to the hotel."

It was great in the nice big bed with the clean sheets.

The next day they slept in late, had a room service breakfast, watched a little TV and made out. In the afternoon they went for a walk.

On Yonge Street, Roger asked Ainsley if she wanted to go shopping and she said, "I thought you knew me."

They walked over to Cabbagetown instead and went to Riverdale Farm. She thought it was so weird to see a farm, cows, horses, pigs, chickens, the whole thing, and a four-lane expressway a few feet away. "This is such a weird city," she said. "How come it never looks like this in the movies?"

"Nothing looks like it really is in the movies."

"That's true," Ainsley said, "Sylvester Stallone looks tall in the movies."

Back at the hotel the nice big bed was great again.

In the morning there was a loud knock on the door. Ainsley sat up in bed and yelled, "Who is it?"

"Tracy."

She dragged herself out of bed and pulled a blanket around herself on her way to the door. Opening it a crack, she saw the cheery fresh face of one of her young, efficient assistants. "What time is?"

"Five thirty. Your driver will be here in 30 minutes. Do you need anything?"

"No, I'm fine, thanks. I'll see you on set."

"I was hoping to catch a ride with you. I need to see Judy today."

"Take your own car. I need to study these new lines."

"But Ainsley—"

She closed the door on her and went back to the bed. With a quick two final steps she jumped into the air and landed hard on the mattress.

Roger rolled over. "Wh-what?"

"You're supposed to be here in 30 minutes."

"Oh shit."

"I've got to take a shower. Care to join me?"

"No, I better get going."

"That's not what you really want to do."

"No?"

She pulled the blanket away and grinned at his bobbing penis. "No, it's not."

"Every man wakes up like this. It's just because I've got to piss."

She reached out and wrapped her slim fingers around him. "But that could wait."

"I guess it could, yeah."

She crawled back into bed with him, never letting go.

When Ainsley joined Roger in the bathroom afterwards, Roger thought how it would take the pretties two hours to get her looking the way she did, hair falling around her face, puffy lips, eyes sparkling behind half closed lids. Easy on wardrobe, though, still naked.

Roger said, "I have to go get the car."

"Let's take the bike to wherever the car is and go from there." She started running the water.

"Oh yeah, that'll work."

Ainsley switched the water flow to the shower, turned around from the tub and stood up straight. "Join me?"

"I've got work to do."

"Yeah, and apparently you have to pee again."

"Ainsley."

"Come on," she said, holding him again, barely touching him, moving just close enough for him to feel the warmth coming from her body. "We've got time."

They stepped into the shower.

No good could come of it.

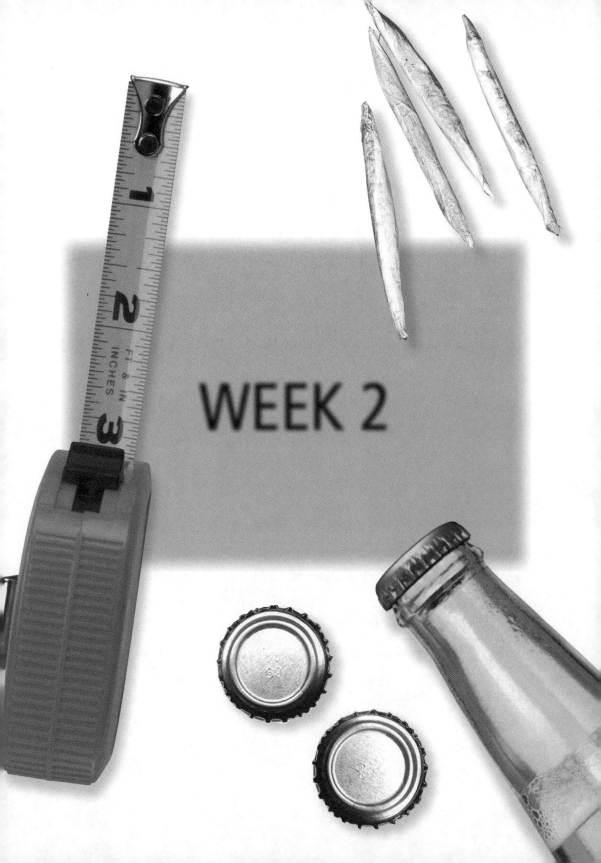

Deal Memo – Employee

Life and Death in Little Italy   Italy Productions Ltd.

Employee: _____

Address: _____

City: _____ Province: _____

Postal Code: _____ Phone Number: _____

S.I.N. ____/____/____   Date of Birth: ____/____/____

Tax Withholding Information (please attatch your TD1 to ensure accurate deductions)

Net claim code: _____   Net claim dollar amount: _____

Do you want to increase the taxes that are withheld?   YES / NO

How much additional tax do you want deducted from each pay?: _____

Start Date: _____   End Date: _____

Department: _____

Position: _____

Rate of Pay: _____ Expected Hours to be worked per week: _____

Rental Fees: _____

Guarantee: _____

Credit: At Producer's Discretion

Accounting dept only: G/L account #: _____ Fringe Account No: _____

Approvals:

Employee: _____ Date: ____/____/____

Production Manager: _____ Date: ____/____/____

Executive Producer: _____ Date: ____/____/____

I was resident in Ontario on the 31st of December, 2001 and my address at that time was as noted above, or as follows:

THE SET DRESSERS

"If I could do anything I wanted right now…" Andy said, as if David hadn't even spoken. His lips didn't move, his face pointed limply up at the truck's roof. The joint curled down from Andy's mouth, breathing ash into the thick smoke. "…anything I wanted? I would be smoking this jay at home, with Jerry Springer on the tube, and a big-ass pile of porn on the couch beside me. I know it's just a daydream, but someday I could make it happen."

The cold air whistled through the bad seal above David's door. The heater was on full, hot air howling from the dashboard. David shifted in his seat and stared at Andy. "Didn't you hear what I said?" David held up his cellphone, somehow proving his news. "Lenny and Bruce just quit."

Andy held the smoke in his lungs and passed the joint to David. "Things aren't too busy. Boss'll get someone else. What about you? Anything at all? What would you be doing?"

David ashed on the floor. "Running this show."

It was freezing cold for April. Not winter cold, but the smell of it was still in the air. The driveway started at the stonework gates, and took its time through the artificial mounds of landscaped nature before circling a baroque fountain and ending where the rented truck idled in front of the house. Five years ago, David had done a spot on this house for one of those home and garden shows. The voiceover had echoed the real estate listings. "…this lovely palatial estate…" Since then it had changed hands so many times its current owners were hidden in bankruptcy filings and corporate holdings. Now, it was on the market again, news that produces a measurable rise in Toronto's productivity index and draws location scouts like an underage fashion model draws married producers at an open bar industry party. The only thing that ruined the magazine layout perfection was the cube van blackening the driveway with exhaust fumes, the Heritage Ford logos covered with graffiti tags—illegible street names and turf claims.

Nothing moved for twenty minutes.

David opened his eyes as a car burst through the gates. A white Ford Escort wagon, it hugged the corners, and came to an unreasonably solid stop beside the van. Andy carefully put the roach in his pill box. "Here's the boss."

A mass of red curls exploded from the Escort, and the rest of Cathy followed. "Next time you give me directions, David, it would help if you knew what you were talking about." The guys hopped out of the van and rolled up the cargo door.

David shrugged. "I got here fine."

"Yeah." Andy slapped him on the back. "After I reminded you that the 401 is north of Bloor."

Cathy sat on the tailgate of the van, her legs dangling and ankles hooked together. "I got some news," she said, short fingernails trying to untangle her hair.

David nodded. "Lenny called me."

Andy smiled and slipped on his tattered gloves. "You worry too much, boss. Someone out there wants the work."

Cathy pulled a pack of cigarettes from her purse. Empty. It seemed to make sense to her. "Markie's already called in her own guys. A favour to her." Cathy's thin lips tightened around that word—favour. "A few more favours like that and the three of us will be looking for a new show."

Andy tossed his cigarettes to Cathy and grinned. "I bet they'll be great guys."

David's jaw waggled from side to side before he turned on Andy. "Have you even been on the same show as the rest of us? Markie kept Lenny and Bruce at the warehouse all night redressing that set. So they quit."

Cathy lit her cigarette and stuffed the pack deep into her purse. She stood up and stepped deeper into the van. "Oh, for fuck's sake, guys!" She stomped her foot, and her eyes rolled up at the dome light. "Don't smoke up in the fucking van. It gets in the upholstery. People can smell it, and I get in shit."

"Sorry, boss," David said, but he was smiling. Andy snickered. Cathy spun around. She eyed them silently from under her heavy curls, and then groaned and laughed along with them. "Okay. New rule. We're not going to do anything that's going to help get Cathy fired. Okay?" Cathy turned and grabbed the cases of paintings piled up against the other furnishings filling the truck. She handed them down to her guys and reached for the straps holding the pool table upright.

"Whoa!" David yelled. Cathy jumped back from the pool table and threw her arms up over her head. When nothing fell on her, she looked up.

"What?"

Andy peered up at her. "We're not going to load in the pool table ourselves. It took four guys just to get it on the truck."

Cathy shook her head, and for a moment her hair was a red cloud hovering above her. "We have to get this set in tonight."

"It doesn't play for a couple of days," Andy protested.

David pulled out his shooting schedule. "Tomorrow's that new picnic scene."

"Don't you guys read the call sheets?" Cathy demanded. "This set is the snow cover."

"*Snow?*" Andy and David laughed together. Cathy waited for them to stop.

"Come on, Cathy," Andy said. "We're not going to hand bomb a full-sized mahogany pool table up to the third floor!"

Slowly, deliberately, Cathy nodded at him.

David eased into the discussion. "When are Markie's guys coming?"

"Not for an hour," Cathy told him.

"Okay. We wait on the pool table until they get here." David got a nod from Andy. Reasonable enough.

Cathy's hair went flying again. "Those guys are not going to tell Markie that I couldn't handle a simple load-in. We're bringing up the pool table. And we're doing it before they get here."

Andy looked from Cathy to David. "Why?" When no one answered him, he raised his hands in surrender and climbed up into the van. "Tell me again why I didn't become a mover?"

"Because you have aspirations," David gently reminded him.

Cathy steadied the table while Andy pulled the straps.

"I do?" Andy asked. "Are you sure?" And the pool table came loose. They maneuvered it onto the tongue dolly, and eased it down the rolling ramp. Andy leapt out of the truck as the pool table picked up speed.

"Slow it, slow it!" David called out. Cathy dug her feet in as the pool table hit the smooth cement driveway, heading for the fountain. Andy and David got in front of it and eased it to a stop.

"Are you sure you want to do this?" David asked.

"Are you sure you want a job tomorrow?" Cathy shot back.

"Not completely," David muttered to Andy. They caught their breath and wheeled over to the mountainous front doors. Cathy cursed until her purse spat out the keys. The dolly slid smoothly over the threshold and into the empty, echoing front hall. A majestic sweeping staircase rose from their left and ascended 29 steps to the second floor.

"Twenty-nine hand-carved oak steps," David repeated to them.

"Shut up." Cathy squeezed out from the other side of the pool table. "Nobody cares that you did some five-dollar cable TV EFP here 10 years ago."

"Here's something," Andy said as the top-heavy load wobbled over the tile flooring. "I'm just a buyer on this show. I go out. I buy things. Table lamps. Coat trees. How come I'm doing heavy lifting?"

"Because," David grunted, "Every dollar we save—" They pivoted the pool table and positioned it at the first of the 29 oak stairs. "—goes straight into Judy's and Renée's pockets."

They paused, breathing. They looked up. The staircase spiraled above them to the seemingly unreachable heights of the second floor. Cathy pushed her hair back from her face. "You know what, Andy? You knew what the job was when you took it."

They all got into position, Andy on the dolly in front and above, Cathy and David each to a corner behind and below. David gritted his teeth, "When I took the job I didn't know it was politics and lifting pool tables by myself."

Andy's voice drifted around the thick table to him. "I'm here."

Cathy locked eyes with David. "Now you know. You don't like it, you can quit."

"On three," Andy called, a standard joke.

They all yelled, "THREE!"

Their grunts flooded the hallway, and the pool table lifted four inches off the ground. Each stair was six inches high.

"Down!" choked Andy. "For the love of cheap booze, down!"

It took almost as much effort not to drop it.

"We just need to get a rhythm," Cathy told them.

"Tell me again…"

"Shut the fuck up, Andy." Cathy growled. "On three."

"THREE!"

"Mother of fuck!" someone shouted. Muscles jerked. Tendons strained. The dolly rolled up and over. They made the first step. Twenty-eight to go.

"Keep going," Cathy squeaked.

"One," David counted.

"UHG!" echoed around the marble hall, and they were on the second step.

"Two. Say," David panted, "what exactly went wrong last night?"

Cathy grunted out, "Nobody told us… UHG!… the scene had changed." Three.

Andy snorted. "Big fucking surprise on… UHG!… on this fucking show." Four.

"Isn't that your… UHG! Five. Isn't that your job, Cathy?" David asked, as he shifted his feet on the narrow side of the steps.

"UHG!" Six. They were getting their rhythm. Cathy locked her jaws. "Nice, David. I didn't get the damned… UHG!" Seven. "…damned rewrites until this morning."

Andy spoke from around back of the pool table. "You guys even… UHG!" Eight. "…even read the script?"

"What's the point when… UHG! Nine," David counted, "…when they change it every… UHG! Ten."

"Near as I can figure…" Cathy gasped between breaths. "UHG!" Eleven. "…these crooked cops run a brothel and Frankie, the one cop's… UHG!" Twelve.

"The mafia doesn't want her there because... UHG!" Thirteen. "She saw the cops kill someone and... WHOA, GOD!" The pool table tipped dangerously overhead. Cathy could think of nothing but the new guys—Markie's guys—finding them broken and bloody at the bottom of the stairs.

"I got it." David's gloved hands wrestled the pool table back under control. "My foot slipped on the... I'm on the inside, for fuck's sake."

"Take it up with your union," Cathy told him.

"You think I won't?"

"Let's go!" Andy called. And the pool table resumed its ascent. "UHG!"

"Fourteen." David said.

"Way I read it..." Andy said, "UHG!" Fifteen. "...wasn't the girl, but her sister... UHG!" Sixteen.

"There's a... UHG!" Seventeen. Cathy choked out the rest. "...there's a sister?"

"There's no fucking sister." David told them firmly. "UHG! That's eighteen."

"There's a sister," Andy said. "That's what... UHG!" Nineteen. "...the whole first scene is about."

"The first scene in the hotel? UHG! Twenty."

"The first scene on the strip board is in the car... UHG!" Cathy sounded quite sure as David counted "Twenty-one."

"The first scene in the... UHG!" Twenty-two. Andy kept going, "...the first scene in the fucking alley... UHG!" Twenty-three. "...with the sister! UHG!"

"There's no sister. UHG! Twenty-four."

"I skipped that one... UHG!" Cathy said. Twenty-five.

"You... UHG! Twenty-six." David said. "...you skipped it? You're the lead dresser."

"So?" Cathy said. "I'm not the... UHG!" Twenty-seven. "I'm not the fucking decorator. I don't need to... UHG!"

"Twenty-eight." David said. "You've got to know the... UHG! Twenty-nine. You've got to show the... UHG!"

"Stop!" Andy screamed. "Stop fucking stop. We made it! We're here!"

"Thank god," Cathy and David said, and let go of the pool table.

The sudden full weight of the pool table pushed Andy backwards; his 100-dollar, steel-toed, thick-soled workboots useless on the marble tiles. Oxygen deprived, Cathy and David watched as the pool table rolled away from them.

"Whoa! Whoa! WHOA!" The pool table yelled, and thudded heavily into the wall. It rocked back on the dolly tongue and tipped to one side. Not quite balanced on one corner, it continued to tip...

Cathy and David rushed over to the table and hoisted it upright.

"Andy?" Cathy called. "Are you all right?"

"Fine, Mom," Andy said as he slipped out from behind the table. "Just resting."

David fingered the fresh chip in the marble window ledge. He shook his head and helped pull the table away from the wall. They eyed it suspiciously. It took them a moment to convince each other that it wasn't going to tip again. Andy massaged his elbow.

"If that's the worst thing to happen today, we'll be lucky." Cathy nodded at David. Andy scowled at them while he massaged his ankle.

"Oh yeah? You take the dolly this time, Dave."

"I'll take it." Cathy stepped forward, but Andy shook his head.

"Too heavy."

Cathy shoved a hand on her hip, and glared at him under her hair. "Screw you. I'll take it."

"Look, Cathy." Andy held his hands up. "This isn't a man-woman thing."

"It is so a man-woman thing!" Cathy fumed at him.

"It's really heavy, boss," Andy said. "Really heavy."

Cathy was angry. She took a deep breath.

But David cut in. "Can't we just do this?"

Cathy turned on him. "I don't want to be shoved aside because of the chick thing."

David buried his face in his gloves. "Cathy… Markie's guys'll be here in half an hour."

Cathy nodded. "Fine. You men do it. I might break a nail."

"That's the spirit!" David clapped her on the back, and moved around to grab the dolly handle. Andy took one corner, and Cathy the other. This part was easy. They rode the pool table on the overexerted dolly's low riding wheels and headed for the back stairs to the third floor.

There they stopped. They looked up from the pool table at the narrow staircase and the tight landing.

"No way," Andy said.

"Shit!" Cathy beat her fists against her legs. "It won't fit."

"Goddamn Locations." David sank to the floor, and Andy dropped beside him. "Goddamned Mo fucking Gib. No one scouted these locations? No one carries a tape measure?"

Cathy stalked around the pool table, eyeballing the stairs. "It'll fit up sideways."

"What?" David asked.

"We'll…" Cathy made a point of not looking at them. "What we'll do is we'll carry it."

"It's not a long staircase," Andy allowed.

"There's no way, Cathy." David pointed at the sharp landing.

"You guys think they build a 20-million-dollar house and don't make a staircase big enough to move furniture?" Cathy measured the clearance with her arms.

"What are we doing this for, Cathy?" David wanted to know.

"I told you," she shot back. "Rain cover. Snow cover. Whatever. Because it's our job."

"Technically, it's not…"

"Shut up, Andy." Cathy cut him off. "It's our job now. Because if we don't do it, the company'll have nothing to shoot tomorrow."

This got to David. He nodded at Andy, and they got to their feet. The three of them gingerly eased the felt-covered giant onto its side. David grabbed one of the legs; he'd be the first up the stairs. Andy took the whole inside edge; he'd negotiate the corner. Cathy found her place at the back and grabbed a leg of her own; she'd keep the whole thing moving. They breathed and looked at each other over the pool table. Everyone knew their job. And no one wanted to be there.

"On three," Cathy said, and they all got their grips.

"THREE!"

Backs and legs strained. Wood creaked. With an effort more mental, even spiritual, than physical, the pool table rose into the air.

"Okay," David grunted. "Okay, okay. Up the stairs."

The pool table lurched forward, its weight giving each step a momentum of its own. The first step was under David's foot. "Let's go, let's go…"

And they were up it. The second one went by. Andy braced himself against the wall, and felt a wave of exhausted euphoria lift him. The pool table, almost on its own, moved.

"The landing," Cathy said. "Andy, get under it."

Andy got under it, hoisting it high over his head. David got under the leg, twisting it around the corner. It was going fast now. Sweat poured, limbs trembled, and joints popped. But they were set dressers, goddamn it, and nothing was going to stop them from dressing their set.

Until something slipped. It might've been Andy's ankle, or David's glove, or Cathy's back, but something slipped. They could all feel it at the same time. That loss of control over something much more powerful than you are. With their three screams of terror, the pool table fell.

On Andy.

The bottom corner hit first. The top flung itself over, throwing all of its weight back toward the landing. There was a wall-shuddering thud and then quiet.

Cathy looked up from the bottom of the stairs. The pool table had wedged itself on the landing. "Andy?" she called up. "You okay?"

There was no answer.

David tried to pull the pool table away from the wall. It wouldn't budge. "Andy? You alive back there?"

There was a rustling sound. A metallic clink. And a cloud of pot smoke wafted out from under the pool table.

Cathy let out a sharp laugh of relief. "Jesus, Andy, I thought we'd killed you."

"Yeah, almost." Andy's voice came out from the corner.

"Don't panic, Andy," Cathy told him. "We're going to get you out."

"That would be good."

"You get him out," David said. He stepped lightly on the pool table and hopped over it.

"What?" Cathy stepped back as David jumped down and headed away.

"I quit," he called over his shoulder.

"What, like…now?" Andy wanted to know.

"You can't bail on me." Cathy followed after David. "You can't quit."

"You can't quit now!" Andy called.

"Watch me," David yelled at both of them. Cathy sprinted around in front of him, stopping him at the top of the 29 stairs. "Look. I know this isn't what you had in mind when you agreed to work for me…"

A pounding came from behind the pool table. It sounded like Andy's head. "I want to go home."

"Andy! Shut! Up!" Cathy yelled up at him.

Andy yelled back, "I have porn I haven't read!"

David pushed past Cathy, and onto the staircase. "David, listen. It's just a pool table!"

David paused, and took one step up toward her. "No, it's not." His voice was raised.

"Things are getting out of control here," Andy remarked.

Cathy clutched her hair in her hands. "You're right. It's the whole show. It's cursed. There's a curse on this show. But we can make it work."

"Things aren't cursed," David told her. "Things are mismanaged. Things are fucked up! And we won't make it work. That's the problem with this whole show. Everyone's just trying to make it work, and no one thinks ahead, and things like this happen!" David tossed an angry hand toward Andy and the pool table. "This show is…fucked! That's what this show is! Fucked! This is your first show as lead and Markie's first show as decorator, and this is the most disorganized show I have ever been on. I'm done. I'm done carrying pool tables up two flights of stairs. I'm done picking up couches at 3:00 in the morning. I'm done working with you." And he turned and resumed his descent. Cathy followed behind him, shouting at his back over the hand-carved oak railing.

"You think this is the way I like to work?" she screeched. "Do you think I don't know how fucked up this show is? I don't need to be told how poorly this show is being run. I live it. I fucking live it. Every morning I wake up and think about how fucked this show is. And I know you could run this show in your sleep, but you're such an asshole, who's going to hire you?" David reached the floor, and crossed the marble hall. Cathy stopped where she was, halfway down, her voice shrieking and almost incomprehensible. "But I think we are all tired, and we just need to CALM DOWN!" She screamed this last part at the empty doorway. David was gone. She sank down to the steps, and put her face in her hands.

"What's going on?" Andy called down. "Hello?"

Cigarette smoke drifted in from outside.

Cathy stood up. Squaring her shoulders, she climbed down the stairs, crossed the hall, and went outside.

David was leaning against the cube van, smoking. Cathy marched up to him.

"You're not going," she told him.

He looked surprised. "I said I was."

"And I say you're not. You're not going anywhere unless I fire you." David was silent. "You're right. You could run a better show than me. But you're not. I'm lead dresser. When things go wrong, I take the shit. I take the shit for you, I take the shit for Andy, I even take the shit for Markie. And instead of waiting for me to fall on my ass so you could say I told you so, you could have given me some help."

David thought about that. "So are you going to fire me?"

"Not yet."

"But soon?"

"Very soon," she promised, and reached into his jacket and helped herself to a cigarette. A pounding echoed through the open mansion door.

David gave Cathy a light. "Do you remember the last time we had a fight like this?"

She nodded. "You moved out."

"I'd like to try again," he said. "The cat misses you."

"I miss you." For a moment, there seemed to be nothing else to say. They both smoked their cigarettes and watched as a red Escort wagon turned into the driveway and made its uncertain way past the dry fountain.

"Markie's guys," David said.

"Yeah."

"I'm sorry I walked out on you."

"Thanks. I'm sorry I called you a cocksucker."

David turned to look at her. "You called me a cocksucker?"

"In my head."

The red Escort pulled up to an easy stop beside the cube van. Cathy rubbed her arms against the chilly air. Three guys got out. "Hi," they said.

"Hi," Cathy said.

The three guys looked at each other, nervous, and then back at Cathy and David. "We're Markie's guys," the one guy said. "You're Cathy, right?"

Cathy nodded, but didn't help them out. After another awkward pause, the one guy spoke again. "We wanted to see if you still needed us."

"What do you mean?" David asked. "Didn't Markie send you down?"

"Yeah, but…" The one guy looked at the other two and went on. "Now that she's been fired, we didn't know."

The cigarette dropped from Cathy's mouth. Her hair floated above her head until she could finally say, "Excuse me?"

"Yeah," the skinny guy stepped forward. "You didn't hear? Markie said you'd be decorator now."

And Cathy started to smile and couldn't stop.

"First we heard about it," David told them.

Andy was pretty happy to hear the news. He was a hell of a lot happier when they pulled the pool table off him, and got it up into the rec room. With the other three guys, even with Andy sitting out for the first few hours and Cathy heading back to the office to sort things out, it only took them until midnight to bring up the rest of the furniture, hang the paintings, put up the shelves, arrange the plants, and change the curtains. Exhausted, they all stumbled out into the cool night air. The skinny guy, Benny, grabbed the beers out of Cathy's Escort Wagon, and they all sat around the back of the cube van. Andy sparked another joint, and passed it around. Then Cathy spoke up.

"Sleep in tomorrow, boys. I don't need you until 8:00 a.m.!" There were handshakes and back slaps all around and the three new guys drove off. Cathy tossed her keys to Andy. "Take the Escort home tonight," she said. She had her arm around David. Andy shrugged and did what he was told.

He hopped into the Escort, lit a cigarette, honked goodnight, and drove off.

With Cathy's mix tape loud in the radio, the car swam through the deserted streets and onto the Don Valley Parkway, headed north, headlights catching the first few flakes of snow. It took Andy only a few minutes on the empty highway to make it to the 401, and hands drumming on the wheel, he headed east and got off at McCowan. He turned north, where the light was just turning red.

He didn't wake up until after the car had stopped. Cathy's mix tape was screaming in his ear, and under it he could hear the engine racing. He took his foot off the gas, and shut off the car. The car pinged at him until he turned the lights off. He opened the door. The pavement was lower than his feet remembered. He hopped out, slammed the door, and took stock.

"Shit."

The car was up on the sidewalk on the wrong side of the empty Scarborough street. He thought that the hubcap across the street was one of his. There was at least one more missing. The front fender was wrapped around a bus pole. His eyes followed the tire tracks in the fresh snow. Fifty feet behind him, the light turned red again.

"Shit."

Well, he was awake now. He opened the door and grabbed his cellphone. He knew the right thing to do here was to call the Transport night numbers. What was the captain's name? It was there on the call sheet. It would be the right thing to do. The kind of thing they expect you to do when you sign the deal memo.

Andy thought about his day. He'd been up since the 3:00 a.m. pick-up. He'd been yelled at. Assaulted by a pool table. Twice. Left for dead. And almost killed in a car accident. All in all, Andy figured that was a pretty full day to give the show, and he was ready for bed. Right after he dealt with this situation.

Andy put his head down and ran.

THE TRANSPORT CAPTAIN

They were supposed to be shooting exteriors, a picnic scene that no one had seen script pages for, but here it was April 14th and it was snowing. The whole week was looking like a disaster. Nijar was stomping around pissed off at the world because the script wasn't working. He was getting new scenes from the writer in LA every day and even writing some himself.

Even the grips could tell it wouldn't cut together.

Roger dropped Ainsley off on set. He was walking back to the Crown Vic when Abe, one of the truckers he'd worked with a few times before, stopped him.

"I think I'm going to have to quit."

"Why?"

"This show is such a fucking mess, I can't take it."

"What do you care?"

"What do you mean, what do I care? We never know where we're going next."

"You get a call sheet at the end of every day. It tells you."

"The schedule is just so fucked. Some days we shoot an eighth of a page. We're picking up actors in the middle of the day. Shit, they're still casting. I don't even think they're going to finish this piece of shit movie."

"Come on, they're all shitty and they finish them all. You know as well as I do, once a movie starts, it doesn't stop."

"There's just so much tension on this set, so much stress."

"Not in Transport."

"It's just so fucked."

"Look, Abe, it's only the second week. We don't usually have this conversation till the fourth. Hang in there, okay?"

"Okay."

Roger drove back to the production office. Man, week two and already the place was coming apart.

There was a message for him on his desk. As Roger was reading it he noticed Judy Nemeth standing in the doorway.

"Hey."

"Hey. What's up?"

Roger said, "Some set dec guy working at the Cormier Mansion last night."

"Oh yeah," Judy said, "the snow cover," like it was the most ridiculous thing in the world.

"Says his rental car was stolen."

"A lot of four-year-old Escorts get stolen in this city?"

Roger crumpled up the note and tossed it close to the garbage can. "First one I've ever heard of. Maybe when his hangover's gone he'll remember where he left it."

Judy nodded. Then she said, "You're spending a lot of time with Ainsley."

"You keeping track?"

"Come on, Roger. You know nothing can come of this."

"You mean, nothing good can come of this. I know. A grip already told me."

She smiled at him. Patronizing. "It's just, well, there's a lot of movie left to shoot and this…romance could be a distraction."

Roger said, "This is maybe the most fucked-up production I've ever been on. You've got plenty of real distractions to worry about."

"The production's fine. But it would help if Ainsley was a little more… focused."

"I didn't see anything in the deal memo about who I could date."

"You know, if you had told me you were going to go out with her I would have said fine, be discreet, but you have to show up on *Hockey Night in Canada*."

"That's mighty white of you."

"Okay, we are under a lot of pressure here. This is serious. This show could go down."

"Now? Two weeks into principal, that much money spent? Never going to happen. Look, you know as well as I do that on a movie set people have no other social life. They don't see any other people for a couple of months. There are on-set romances all the time and they end when the shoot does."

Judy said, "Well, I'm glad to hear you've got such a handle on things. I just wish Ainsley did."

"What do you mean?"

"I've worked with Ainsley on three films. This is the first time she's ever had a sleepover."

"What?"

"You think she does this all the time?"

"No, I just thought, you know, she flirts with everyone and…"

"No, it's not like her. She must really like you."

"I really like her."

"Good, because this could screw her up."

"She's not a child."

"Worse, she's a movie star. Be careful." She turned and walked away.

Man, Roger thought, this show really is in trouble.

BREAKDOWN
IN THE FRAME CASTING

PROJECT:	LIFE AND DEATH IN LITTLE ITALY
TYPE OF PROJECT:	THEATRICAL FEATURE
UNION:	ACTRA
PRODUCER:	RENEE JATO
DIRECTOR:	EDWARD NIJAR
CASTING DIRECTOR:	DEE PRIEST
CONTACT INFO:	TEL: 416.505.7024
SHOOT DATES:	LATE APRIL, TBC
SHOOT LOCATION:	TORONTO
AUDITION DATES:	APRIL 24-26, 2002
AUDITION LOCATION:	96 SPADINA, IN THE FRAME
DELIVERY INSTRUCTIONS:	VIA R.D.O. WEDNESDAY, APRIL 24, 2002

SYNOPSIS

When Frankie, a down-and-out prostitute, witnesses two crooked cops commit a crime, she is forced to turn to a mafia hitman for protection. What she doesn't know is that one of the cops is her estranged sister's ex-husband, and a high-profile pimp. With millions of dollars at stake, the crooked cops go on a rampage and Frankie, the hitman, her sister, her sister's young son and her father get caught in the crossfire. The entire neighbourhood is threatened. Is there a way out? That's LIFE AND DEATH IN LITTLE ITALY.

CHARACTER DESCRIPTIONS

PERFORMER   **MELODI**   **AGE: EARLY TO MID 20'S**

Melodi is a hard-working street walker just trying survive the only way she can. She's soft and tough, strong and vulnerable. Even though she's a victim, she's still a person. She is tall, blonde, sexy and confident. The role involves simulated torture and possible nudity. All ethnicities welcome.

PERFORMER   **MURIEL**   **AGE: LATE 30'S, EARLY 40'S**

Muriel is a student at the same school as Frankie. She has returned to University after an abusive marriage ended. She's been through a lot, but her love for her kids keeps her going. She's tall, blonde and athletic. This actress will be seen topless in a bathtub. All ethnicities welcome.

NOTES

We are casting for various smaller parts. More roles will become available in the near future, and we will be casting them out of these auditions. Other roles include: female police officers and prostitutes. Dancing experience an asset.

THE LOCAL TALENT

All right, Anne-Marie decided, she'd give the casting guy one blow job if he could guarantee a speaking role. And it had to be with one of the stars, not just a bunch of extras standing around and one gets a line. She was getting serious about this acting business.

She walked down Spadina towards Front Street, checking the addresses on the old dark brick buildings. The street signs claimed it was the "Fashion District" and there were a lot of so-called designers and art galleries and fur coat stores, but they were mainly sweatshops filled with stocky immigrant women hunched over sewing machines. Fashion comes at a price.

Okay, maybe she'd sleep with him once, but it'd have to be in the casting office because she wouldn't go to some sleazy welfare motel out on Kingston Road with him. And it'd have to be straight intercourse, no doggie. Okay, maybe her back to him would be better, but no anal. These guys watched way too much porno. She saw the building, 96 Spadina, and pushed open the door.

In the glass door of a designer denim store across the lobby she caught her reflection and stopped. Blonde streaked hair to her shoulders, smooth white skin, crimson lips, dark eyes, perfectly trimmed eyebrows, long thin legs. She knew she was good looking. Sunshine Girl, March 5th, 2000. She hadn't made the calendar but she had refused to go to the "private photo shoot" for a no-pay gig. She shook her head a little from side to side and pushed her hair back over one ear. Good but not great. She could lose a few pounds. Why wasn't this movie in May or June when she'd be down to bikini weight? In April, it's still practically winter.

She looked at the old creaky elevator and decided to walk up the three flights of stairs. In the wide concrete stairwell she rummaged through her shoulder bag and fished out her portfolio, the one from Barry's agency, Starz, with the professional head shots and almost entirely made-up résumé. As she pulled out the thin binder she glanced at the other portfolio, the digital pictures Barry took himself. The ones that looked like topless mug shots. A couple of full-body nudes, even a couple from behind. Barry insisted that only the director would ever see them; they'd be sent directly to him. The horrible lighting and lousy framing of those cheesy tit shots always made her appreciate the 300 bucks she spent on professional head shots.

The second floor of the building was almost completely open and empty. A scaffold stood in the middle of the room and the ceiling was pulled away to expose some rusted pipes and beams.

A couple of construction workers were sitting on the window sill looking out at Spadina. Anne-Marie smiled at them as she passed and one of them smiled back. She heard the other one say, "It's a fucking parade today," and the one who smiled, who was wearing a clean T-shirt and shorts that might have been from Eddie Bauer, said, "Let's get back to it," and they tossed away their Coffee Time paper cups and headed back towards the scaffolding. The clean guy picked up a welder's mask and a torch.

On her way up the final steps to the casting office on the third floor she could almost hear Barry's voice saying to her, "This is such a great chance, Annie. The whole movie was cast and they started shooting but they've had a lot of problems with the script. The writer is coming up from LA and they're making changes at the last minute and they have to cast a bunch of new roles here. Good roles. Big, beefy, juicy roles. This is such a great chance, a really terrific opportunity." Even as he had said it she was waiting for the "but." Or in Barry's case the "There's just one thing." She wasn't some nineteen-year-old star-struck kid from Brampton. She lived in the real world.

"There's just one thing. The reason I was able to get you in there is because I have a bit of a relationship with the casting director. Normally they wouldn't see anyone without a lot more on-camera experience than you have, but the thing is, this person can be persuaded." She had almost said to Barry, right there in his office, "Do I have to fuck him, or will a blow job be okay?" but she played along.

Barry thought he was running a big-time talent agency. He thought he was going to move up the ranks and be a player, maybe join Great North or even The Characters. Barry had ambition.

So, the casting guy could be persuaded and that'd get her a one-on-one with the director, some spoiled rich kid from New York who'd made some music videos and had all the right connections. It really was a great chance, a real opportunity. Linda Grigette was in this movie, this *Life and Death in Little Italy*. Of course, Ainsley Riordan was the star, the flavour of the month, some chick younger than Anne-Marie. Everyone knew what a stuck-up bitch Ainsley Riordan was.

But Linda Grigette was someone Annie had watched on TV her whole life. A lot of that was in reruns of the seventies show *Fashion Fuzz*, supermodels going undercover to catch drug smugglers and arms dealers. It started to get replayed in the nineties as "irony" and there was even talk of turning it into a big budget action movie after *Charlie's Angels* hit. Wouldn't that be great? She'd get to meet Linda Grigette on this movie and then maybe even get a shot at *Fashion Fuzz: This Year's Model*.

Maybe she'd go to a nice hotel and do the guy more than once if he wasn't totally creepy.

The third floor looked like a brand new office building with fluorescent lights on the ceiling, fresh paint on the walls and clean tiles on the floors. But it was in the "fashion district," after all, so the office doors were like smaller versions of the steel warehouse doors on rollers that slid to the side instead of pulling open. Must have been custom-made. The door to In the Frame was already rolled open.

Anne-Marie paused for a brief moment, took a breath and walked into the casting office wearing her most confident smile. It faded fast. There were at least fifteen other women in the waiting room. All the chairs were taken and she had to push her way past a couple of women to get to the reception desk.

One woman stood talking into a cellphone and wouldn't move. She had blonde streaked hair to her shoulders, smooth white skin, crimson lips, dark eyes and perfectly trimmed eyebrows. She was tall with long thin legs. "No, we can't leave Friday afternoon. The 400 will be a parking lot. It'll take us two hours to get Barrie, for God's sake. Let's leave in the morning… But I want to go to the cottage this weekend. The Martins are having their party. It's always fantastic."

"Excuse me."

The woman on the cellphone moved about an inch, enough of an opening for Anne-Marie to push the rest of the way to the reception desk.

"Hi, this is for *Life and Death in Little Italy*, right?"

The receptionist nodded. The woman on the cellphone raised her perfectly trimmed eyebrows and looked away.

"Or Thursday night. Well, take Friday off. Or I can meet you there. I'll take the Land Rover up Thursday."

The receptionist looked at the portfolio and said, "Anne-Marie Robinson?"

"It's a little boring, I know."

"That's you, right?"

Annie was about to make a sarcastic remark, something along the lines of "You're looking at the pictures, honey," but she bit her tongue. "Yes."

"Have a seat, find a piece of floor, whatever." The receptionist dropped the portfolio on a pile with a few others.

"How long will it be?"

"As long as it takes."

Another woman had just come through the door and she was pushing her way past Annie to the reception desk. "Excuse me." She had blonde streaked hair to her shoulders, smooth white skin, crimson lips, dark eyes, perfectly trimmed eyebrows and was tall with long thin legs.

Annie made her way to a clear piece of floor between the front door and a door to the inner office. As she was leaning back against the wall the door to the inner office opened and a woman came out. She looked pleased with herself and confident. She smiled to the whole room and wove through the bodies to the front door. She had blonde streaked hair to her shoulders, smooth white skin, crimson lips, dark eyes, perfectly trimmed eyebrows and was tall with long thin legs.

But that wasn't what Annie noticed. She recognized the woman but couldn't place her. She watched the woman as she made her way to the front door of the office and stepped out into the hall.

The woman turned her head slightly, her blonde hair sweeping gently over her shoulder and she glanced back with a much less confident look on her face. Not unhappy, maybe wistful. No that's not really a look, no one could make a wistful face on command. Regretful? Worried? No. She gave the women in the room a quick once-over and stopped when she saw Annie. Did she wink? Then she turned and walked out.

"I'm going to Stratford in a couple of weeks. Do you know when this shoot is over?"

"Stratford? Hey, congratulations."

"Yeah, I'm pumped. I know it'll be mostly walk-ons with maybe a line here and there, but it was my first audition for them, so it feels great."

"I heard it's a bit of an assembly line there now."

Annie glanced at the two women who were talking. Didn't take long to get catty. They both had streaked blonde hair, their white skin was smooth and their eyes were dark. It was hard to tell how tall they were because they were both sitting down, but Annie had a pretty good idea.

"It's a lot of work, yeah, but this year will be a great start. You can move up pretty fast. Did you audition?"

"No, I want to concentrate on film and television."

"Really? You don't like theatre?"

"It's not that I don't like it, it's just, you know, you always work nights. While everyone else is out *going* to the theatre you're working."

"Well, I had such a good time at Queen's. The drama program is excellent. I wouldn't want to waste all that."

"Oh no, I mean, I really benefitted from the studying. McGill is a terrific program and I did a show at the Centaur while I was there."

"Really? Which one?"

"*A Moon for the Misbegotten.*"
"O'Neill is soooo depressing."
"It's wonderful theatre."
"Oh yes, of course."
"So you won't be up at the cottage much if you're going to be in Stratford?"
"No, not this year."

Annie scowled openly. Four years in university to study acting. Acting. It was just playing dress-up and pretending. Six-year-olds win awards for their acting.

The door opened again and all eyes were on a young, short, slightly overweight man with thick glasses who came out and went to the reception desk.

Wow, Annie thought, I hope he's not the casting guy Barry was talking about. He looked like he could be persuaded all right, but she doubted it would be by a woman. She certainly wasn't going to get into any role-playing for a lousy one-line hooker scene.

But there was that longer scene Barry had showed her. His "relationship" meant he got to see a few new scenes as they came up from LA. It was a hooker scene, but it had some oomph to it.

The guy with the glasses picked up a stack of head shots with résumés on the backs and read the name off the bottom one. "Deirdre Smith." At least they seemed to be going in order.

The woman beside Annie, the one who wasn't going to Stratford because she wanted to concentrate on film and television, got up and disappeared behind the door to the inner office.

As the door closed, Annie suddenly remembered where she'd seen the first woman who'd come out of that office. She'd been in Barry's office at Starz a few weeks ago. She was another client of the same agency. Annie was more pissed off than surprised because it probably meant the other woman had also been told that the casting guy could be "persuaded." Or had she? Barry wouldn't tell everyone. He wouldn't tell any of these college girls with drama degrees who played Shakespeare all summer, would he?

They wouldn't persuade anyone. Would they?

No one had taken the chair vacated by Deirdre, so Annie sat down. She pulled the "sides," the scene they sent out to casting agents for auditions, out of her bag and unfolded the fax paper. A few half-page scenes of cops talking to hookers. "Do you know this woman?" That kind of thing. "Piss off, asshole." How many ways could you say "piss off, asshole"? Well, actually, if Annie's experience was anything to go by, quite a few.

Then there was the other scene Barry had given her. He had told her it was a rough draft of a new scene and the dialogue would probably change, but the gist of it would be the same. It was a scene she could really play.

Another woman came through the front door of the office. She had blonde streaked hair which came to her shoulders, smooth white skin, crimson lips, dark eyes, perfectly trimmed eyebrows and was tall with long thin legs. She stood in the doorway and looked around the room.

"This looks like a promo shoot for Hot Blonde Babes Dot Com," she said in a rough, downtown, uneducated kind of accent. "We should start a union, hold out for better working conditions." She laughed at her joke and pushed her way to the reception desk. The woman beside Annie, the one who was going to Stratford, who loved the drama program at Queen's, made a tsk tsk sound.

The one who had just come in would certainly persuade someone. How ironic is this, Annie thought. These chicks go to drama school for years and then all the parts they go up for are hookers and strippers. She smiled and looked around the room. Blonde streaked hair to her shoulders, smooth white skin, crimson lips, dark eyes, perfectly trimmed eyebrows, tall with long thin legs. They all wore miniskirts and platform boots. She stopped smiling. Who went to drama school?

Annie looked back down at the script pages.

```
EXT. AIRPORT—NIGHT

As one plane lands another takes off in a
different direction from a different
runway. Red lights disappear into the
darkness.

Small trucks pull numerous trailers
overloaded with luggage across the dimly
lit tarmac.

                    GRISS
                    (VO)
          There she is.

                    TREY
                    (VO)
          Which one?
```

                    GRISS
                    (VO)
          The blonde getting out of the
          cab, with the legs all the
          way up to her ass.

                    TREY
                    (VO)
          That's where legs usually go.

                    GRISS
                    (VO)
          What we want to know is whose
          head these ones have been
          wrapped around.

The plane that just landed has taxied to the terminal.

EXT. AIRPORT HOTEL—NIGHT

Taxis, limos and buses cut one another off as people weighed down with shoulder bags and pulling suitcases on leashes weave their way across the four lanes dividing the airport terminal from the hotel.

Two men, GRISS, a stocky white guy in his late forties, and TREY, a tall black man in his early thirties, get out of a nondescript four-door sedan which sits idling in a no-parking zone in front of the hotel.

A tall blonde woman in her early twenties is leaning back into a taxi paying the driver. Her miniskirt is pulled so tight across her round behind that businessmen coming home exhausted from long trips suddenly wake up and stare at her.

INT. TAXI—NIGHT (CONTINUOUS)

The cab driver, a young dark-skinned man wearing a turban, nods his head quickly up and down as he stares at the ample, and quite exposed, bosom of the blonde paying him.

                  MELODI
    Is that enough?

                CAB DRIVER
    Sure, yeah, okay, enough, enough.

                  MELODI
         (smiling)
    You sure?

                CAB DRIVER
    Plenty. Is plenty.

She winks at him and stands up. For a moment she stares at the hotel and her happy face fades into sadness for a brief moment.

EXT. AIRPORT HOTEL—NIGHT (CONTINUOUS)

Melodi takes a step from the cab towards the hotel but suddenly Griss and Trey are on either side of her, whisking her back to their car.

                  MELODI
    Hey, what the fuck! Let go of me!

                  GRISS
    Shut up.

She struggles, but it's only a few feet and they easily overpower her and shove her into the back seat of the car. Trey gets in beside her and Griss jumps behind the wheel.

INT/EXT. CAR—NIGHT (DRIVING)

Without looking at the traffic, Griss pulls away from the curb. HORNS blare.

          GRISS
  Eat shit, asshole.

In the back seat Melodi continues to struggle, but Trey holds her wrists tightly. The headrest of the front passenger seat is raised and Trey shoves Melodi's fingers between it and the seat.

          MELODI
  What do you assholes want?

Trey slams the headrest down as hard as he can.

          MELODI
  Owww! Fuck!!!

She struggles to pull her hand away but it's trapped between the seat and the headrest.

          GRISS
  Will you shut up, bitch.

          MELODI
  Ow, that hurts. Who the fuck
  are you?

Griss has been driving very fast, cutting from lane to lane and suddenly he turns the wheel sharply and the car screeches around a corner and into the parking lot of an industrial area.

EXT. PARKING LOT—NIGHT (CONTINUOUS)

The delivery companies and rental car outlets are all closed and the parking lot is quiet and dark.

                    GRISS
          I'm asking the questions,
          honey.

The car slows to a stop in the loading dock area behind the building. It's very dark.

Griss turns around in the passenger seat and looks at Melodi. He holds up a mug-shot-style picture of a young woman with red hair and too much make-up.

                    GRISS
          Who's this?

                    MELODI
          How should I know?

Griss shakes his head sadly and looks at Trey.

                    TREY
          Tell the man what he wants to
          know.

                    MELODI
          I don't know the chick.

Griss leans forward and opens the glove compartment. The light inside the small space shines on the small plastic tool kit he takes out.

He opens it and removes a pair of long-nosed pliers, then slams the compartment door closed and sits back up.

                    GRISS
          I'm not an evil man by
          nature. Please tell me the
          name this woman uses when she
          works with you.

                    MELODI
          I don't work with her. I
          don't work with anyone. I'm
          an independent escort. I--
          HOLY SHIT!!!!

Griss has grabbed hold of one of Melodi's bright shiny fingernails on her hand trapped under the headrest and pulled it off.

                    MELODI
          Owww, owww, ouch fucking
          ouch!!!

She flails around in the back seat, but can't get her hand out. Trey puts an arm around her to hold her still.

                    GRISS
          Now, as I was saying, I am
          not an evil man by nature,
          but… I am in a hurry.

Blood is flowing from the first nail. He gets a good grip on the next nail.

                    GRISS
          This time I won't pull the
          nail so quickly. I'll pull it
          slowly, bit by bit. It'll
          help you remember.

He starts to pull on the pliers and the edge of the fingernail comes away from the skin.

> MELODI
> Ow, ow, please stop. Please, I swear, I don't know anything. I'm begging you, please stop, it hurts, please.

> GRISS
> It's too late to beg. All you can hope for now is that when you tell me, and you will, I may leave you one nail. I can't promise I won't cut open your skanky nose.

Melodi is suddenly calm and glares at Griss.

> MELODI
> You fucking bastard. You like this.

Griss merely stares back. He pulls the nail a little more.

> MELODI
> Amber. She calls herself Amber. Sometimes Abigail… I think her real name is Frankie McCall. We've done a couple of duos together and an orgy in some boardroom.

> GRISS
> Where does she live?

> MELODI
> I don't know. We're not close. You know, we don't socialize.

> GRISS
> You just fuck each other.

                    MELODI
          It's better than your job,
          asshole.

Griss yanks the fingernail off.

                    MELODI
          Ow!!!!!! Oh God!!!!!

                    GRISS
          All right, this one will be
          slow. How did you get hold of
          her?

                    MELODI
          Raquel set it up. She
          arranges the parties.

                    GRISS
          Lace Escorts?

                    MELODI
               (nodding. Her eyes fill with
                tears)
          Yeah, she calls me sometimes.
          She uses a few independents.

                    GRISS
          And Frankie is an
          independent.

                    MELODI
          Yeah. She's, like, part-time.
          She goes to school or
          something.

                    GRISS
          Right, you chicks are the
          best educated broads in town.

By now Melodi has run out of energy and
the pain in her fingers is too much.

She's slumped forward and talks barely above a whisper.

> MELODI
> Fuck you.

Griss looks at the pliers on her fingernail and then at Trey. Trey shrugs.

> GRISS
> You know any of her school chums?

> MELODI
> Yeah, we're in the same sorority. We go skiing in Aspen together.

Trey leans close to Melodi.

> TREY
> We're serious here. This is important.

Melodi raises her head slightly to look at him.

> MELODI
> After the orgy, we took a cab together. She got out on Hudson Street by the college. Some other girls recognized her and they all went inside that old library building.

> GRISS
> She went to the library?

> MELODI
> I told you, she's going to school.

Melodi looks up at Griss.

>   MELODI (CONT' D)
>   We are real people, you know.
>
> Griss looks unconvinced, but it's all the
> information he's going to get. He takes
> the pliers off her fingernail and motions
> to Trey.
>
> Trey raises the headrest as gently as he
> can and reaches over to open the car
> door.
>
> Melodi starts to say something but stops
> and gets out.
>
> EXT. PARKING LOT—NIGHT (CONTINUOUS)
>
> Melodi stands beside the car and Trey
> gets out of the back seat. He hands her a
> white handkerchief and stares at her for
> a moment, then walks around the car and
> gets in the passenger door.
>
> The car drives away as Melodi wraps the
> cloth around her bleeding fingers.
>
>   **FADE TO BLACK.**

Yeah, Annie thought, I could do a lot with a scene like that. It had great emotional range, from bitchy and aggressive to crying and defeated, all in a few pages. It could be memorable. It would be better if it was with Linda Grigette. After *Fashion Fuzz* faded, Annie remembered seeing her in a few TV movies. The first couple were crappy *Dynasty* rip-offs, all pilots, really, for more night-time soaps, but then she played a single mother who got raped at work, by her boss. No one believed her, the usual stuff, but Linda Grigette was great. It was the first time Annie remembered seeing her look less than glamorous.

What if she ended up in a scene with stuck-up Ainsley Riordan? The bitch probably wouldn't even stay for the reverses of Annie's close-ups. If the big star even let anyone else have close-ups.

Barry had told Annie not to get her hopes up, anyway. They weren't casting that scene now and they might be flying someone in for it, some singer trying to break into the movies. The director, Kneejab or something, had a lot of contacts in music. In fact, everyone who talked about this movie said what a great soundtrack it was going to have. So the hooker scenes were going to the usual Britney Spears wannabes.

Annie was really up for one of the small parts. Little half-page scenes, cops—they were the bad guys in the story, a nice twist, they thought—talking to students and a few other hooker scenes. She remembered reading once in *Entertainment Weekly*, one of her favourite actresses, Illeana Douglas—she was so great in *To Die For*, and that had been shot in Toronto—said that a woman in Hollywood being asked to play a hooker was like a man being asked to play Hamlet. It was a great compliment.

Being asked. Yeah, right. Being given the chance to "persuade" was more like it. Everybody in Toronto loved it that Hollywood came to town, but nobody wanted to look too closely at what really went on.

A few other women had gone in and out of the inner office while Annie was reading, and now the short guy with the thick glasses called her name. She stood up and tried not to look at the other actresses as she walked towards the hall.

"Hi, I'm Kevin."

"Oh, hi, I'm Anne-Marie Robinson. Annie."

"I know." He waved her head shot as they walked down the hall.

"Oh, right."

"Don't be nervous. This is just preliminary, a few questions. It's more about your general personality than your acting skills."

"I studied all the sides they sent Barry."

Kevin stopped in front of a closed door and looked at Annie. He had a sly smile. "Barry, right." He opened the door and stood aside. "Okay, don't be nervous."

Annie nodded and walked into a large room. One wall was covered by a thick black curtain and in front of that was a small table. A man and a woman sat behind the table.

The woman was talking on a cellphone, turned sideways from the guy.

Kevin dropped Annie's headshot on the table in front of the guy and said, "This is Anne-Marie Robinson. Barry Sherman from Starz sent her over."

The guy smiled big time. "From Starz? Well, hi, Anne-Marie. That's a beautiful name. Is it French?"

Oh shit, what a moron, Annie thought. Yeah, this guy could be persuaded. "Yes."

Kevin walked past the table to a video camera set up on a tripod and sat behind it on a stool.

There were no other chairs, so Annie just stood in front of the table.

"Great, Anne-Marie, that's great." He said it again like he was trying it out. "I'm Mark. This is Dee." He motioned to the woman on the phone, who glanced over her shoulder. "And you met Kevin."

Annie looked at Mark. He wasn't that bad. He was probably in his late thirties or early forties. It looked like he went to the gym once in a while. The hair transplant was a bad idea but it looked like he wasn't bothering to keep it up.

Okay, Annie thought, it depends on the scene. If it's one of these half-page cop scenes it depends on who's playing the cop. Griss seemed like the Joe Pesci type but she hadn't seen his name in Rita Zekas' "Star Gazing" column and this movie was already shooting. Chris Rock was in town, but it didn't seem like he'd play a sidekick like Trey at this point in his career. That might be Omar Epps. If Griss was being played by a big enough name, doing Mark might be worth it.

"Kevin's going to read with you and tape this little conversation, if you don't mind."

"No, not at all." They weren't even going to wait for the woman to get off the phone. She must be the one up from LA, probably not very interested in these roles, the small parts they dole out to the locals to keep them quiet.

"There are a few parts to be filled, but we won't ask you to read for all of them. We'll go through a couple of things, okay?"

"Sure."

"Why don't we start with the first one?"

"Sure."

Kevin turned on the camera and said, "What's her name, bitch?"

Anne-Marie raised her eyebrows and looked at Kevin like he was scum. "Screw you."

Mark said, "Try it again, but you're a little scared."

"Scared? Okay." She waited, then realized she was just supposed to say the line again. "Screw you?"

"It's not a question."

No, she thought, it's not. "Screw you."

"A little more emotion, though."

"Screw you."

"Not as annoyed."

"Screw you."

"No, these are cops. They're big, intimidating guys."

"Screw you."

This is what Barry's always on about, she realized. Actor, be an actor, play the role. She knew she was letting this Mark guy get to her. She was pissed off at having to fuck him for this one line. And this California chick who was still on the phone, not even listening. The whole scene pissed her off. This parade of women, most of them willing to do anything for a part.

This was just like the strip clubs are now, Annie thought, since they've been bringing in chicks from Romania and Slovakia and the new "White Third World." Those women would do anything for almost nothing

"Let's try the next one."

"She's going to put this all on you if you don't tell us first."

"That bitch."

"Not so angry."

"That bitch."

"More sad."

"That bitch."

"A little more disappointed."

"That bitch."

"Yeah, um, not so annoyed."

"That bitch."

"That's good," Dee said.

She'd finally finished her call and flipped the phone closed.

Annie had no idea how much of the reading Dee had heard.

"You've got a good edge."

Annie didn't say anything. She almost said, "Shit, you people and your fucking 'edge.'" Everything's edgy. Of course those college girls had no edge. But she didn't.

"Where did you study?"

"I didn't study drama at college. I took a few courses, Acting for the Camera, Scene Study, Laura Tooles, that kind of thing." Not bad, made it sound like she studied something else at college.

Annie could see the tension between Mark and Dee. She knew this didn't have anything to do with her. This was all about Mark getting his balls in a knot because some woman flew in from LA and pulled rank on him. Annie knew as soon as Dee started to show some interest in her that she was done. Mark wouldn't give her a line in this movie.

"Have you done any dancing?" Dee asked.

Yeah, right, Annie thought, but she just said, "Yes, some."

"Musical theatre?" Dee looked right at her and Annie couldn't tell if she was being serious or not.

"Well, there was music."

Mark said, "Well, that was great. Thanks for coming in."

"Just a minute," Dee said.

Annie watched Mark look at Dee. He tried to stay in charge. He said, "Okay, why don't we try one more? Let's go with... Kiss my ass?"

Annie flipped her script to the next page but she didn't look at it, she looked right at Mark and said the three words very slowly and deliberately. "Kiss. My. Ass."

Mark said, "Okay, that was great."

"One more, please." It was Dee again.

Annie said, much more playfully, "Kiss my ass."

Dee laughed.

Mark harumphed. "Okay, that was great. Thanks for coming in."

Why, Annie? Why'd you have to treat the guy like the petty jerk he is? She kept looking at him, knowing she'd blown it. She'd have to tell Barry that she had been willing but the guy had just pissed her off and Barry'd say, "Of course he did. That's what always happens with you."

"I have this other scene—my agent gave it to me. You know, I've played prostitutes before and I really think this is a good scene."

Mark wasn't happy. "Your agent? Oh right, Barry. Well, we're not casting any other scenes today. Thanks."

Dee said, "You have the Melodi scene?"

"Yeah."

"You think it's a good scene?"

"I think there's a lot of range to it. I think there's a lot going on. It's very emotional."

"You want to try it?"

"I'd love to."

Mark flipped papers on his desk. "I don't have that scene. What scene are you talking about?"

Dee pulled some fax sheets out of her big leather bag and handed them to Mark. "Read it with her."

"Kevin can read it with her."

"No, you read it."

Mark grabbed the pages and flattened them out on the desk. He made a big production of it.

Annie smirked at him. What was the point now? She had no chance. He'd never be "persuaded," even if she brought along three Romanian chicks and a midget. This whole thing was now just the LA woman putting the snowback in his place, showing everyone who was boss.

Okay, Annie figured, she's trying to teach us all our place, but I'm going to give her something to think about.

Mark said, "Will you shut up, bitch?"

"Ow, that hurts. Who the fuck are you?"

They ran through the scene. Mark read the Griss and Trey lines as badly as he could. Usually the person reading lines just does it in a monotone, but Mark was even worse.

Anni,-Marie though, was terrific. She was a scene stealer. She was defiant and tough and vulnerable. All those things hack screenwriters put in the stage directions without thinking through how someone is going to get across such subtlety with such bad dialogue. But Annie did it.

"We are real people, you know."

"Very nice," Dee said. "Very nice."

"But," Mark said, "we're not casting that part today."

Dee said, "No, you're not."

Whoa, Annie thought, nice one.

"All right. Well, thanks for coming in."

Dee looked right at her and nodded. It was like she was supposed to get something from it, but she didn't know what. She was glad to help out, putting a jerk like Mark in his place, but she still wasn't getting anything out of it herself.

"Thank you," Annie said and left.

She walked down the hall towards the waiting room. Just as she was about to turn the handle Kevin came after her.

"Anne-Marie," he called as he came quickly down the hall. Thirty feet and he was almost out of breath. "Hang on a sec. Look, um, they were wondering, well, just one of them, really..."

Shit, Annie thought, the sleazeball is still going to try to get laid out of this.

"Um, the thing is, um, Dee thought you did a great job, but there were a lot of distractions in there, you know, and she thought maybe you guys could get together again, because, um, she thinks you did a really great job."

"Dee?"

"Yeah, um, she was wondering if you might be able to meet her later, say around 8:30? Um, she'd be happy to buy you dinner."

Barry's relationship is with Dee? Annie almost laughed out loud. That prick. Really, though, she was impressed. Barry actually knew someone who worked in LA. Or maybe he was full of shit, and there was no persuading anyone to get her to see the director. Maybe they were all really professionals and Dee just wanted to be thorough, get the absolute right person for the part. Maybe she took her job really seriously.

"Um, she'd like to be a little more relaxed, so instead of coming here, could you, um, go to her hotel room at the, um, Sutton Place. Have some room service."

Oh yeah, really seriously. Barry, what a shit. How desperate did he think she was? For what, a five-page part with the two movie stars? A little torture? Might even be in the trailer, on the TV ads, might be the scene everyone talks about?

"Sure. Eight-thirty."

"Great. Thanks." He started to walk away and stopped. "You were really good."

When Annie walked through the waiting room there were only three Hot Blondes Dot Com left to do their auditions. Well, she thought, at least she'd made the first cut.

She might have slept with Mark. It wouldn't have been the first time she'd slept with some guy to get something. She remembered the old line, would you sleep with me for a million dollars? Of course. How about for ten bucks? No way, what kind of a woman do you think I am? We've already established that. Now we're just haggling over price.

Everything comes at a price. How high was the price on this one? One night. How much would it change her life to get this part?

It would lead to more, for sure. She might be able to dump Barry and get in with a real agency, like Characters or maybe The Core Group, those snobs who wouldn't even talk to her now. That would get her parts on lots of movies shot in town, or at least in Canadian movies and TV shows, *Blue Murder, Da Vinci's Inquest, The Eleventh Hour*, or better yet, something fun and tacky like *Relic Hunter* or *Stargate*.

She could move to a better apartment, maybe a loft, maybe even buy a small condo. She could stop dancing and not be tempted to escort every time she needed cash.

It certainly seemed she was that kind of woman, just haggling over the price. Hell, she'd seen plenty of girl-girl shows in the clubs. It didn't always look awful and this Dee was kind of cute. She could be like Anne Heche, suddenly start sleeping with women. What did Woody Allen say? Bisexuality just doubles your chances for a date.

She stopped short on the stairs when that word flashed in her head. Bisexual. Don't think about it like that. Then she heard voices, or at least one voice, and she stopped and peeked around the corner.

The construction worker, the clean one, the one wearing a T-shirt, was talking on a cellphone. Now it was awkward because she'd stopped walking and, without the sound of heels clicking on the concrete steps it was so quiet. It would sound like she was eavesdropping, but if she started walking again it would confirm it.

"No, I can't make it... Because I have somewhere to be. Well, because I said would and I can't just go back on my word... You mean lie?"

What the hell. She started walking again, quickly, and almost ran him over in the stairwell.

"You can talk all night, but I said I would and I will. Bye." He clicked the phone shut and looked right at Anne-Marie. "Some people."

"Yeah, some people."

"If people can't take you at your word, what are you worth?"

"Nothing."

"Nothing, that's right. They think they can buy anything. How desperate do they think we are? Some people."

"Some people."

He walked back across the empty second floor of the office building to his tools which were still strewn on the floor. She watched him for a moment, then continued down the stairs.

It was almost 6:00. If she was going to get changed and get to the Sutton Place by 8:30 she'd have to cab it home. She stepped off the sidewalk and held out her hand, waving at one of the yellow cars on Spadina. She hoped she had enough cash to cover the fare.

THE LOCATION SCOUT

"When was the last time anyone shot at Jilly's?"
"The strip club?"
"*Detroit Rock City*, '98."
"*Angel Eyes*, 2000."
"*The Widows*, 2000. But it was a pilot, didn't go anywhere."
"What about *House of Lancaster*?"

Garry was searching the stacks of the Ontario Media Development Corporation Locations Library, row after row of red legal-sized folders filled with pictures of every bar, restaurant, hotel, motel, park, subdivision and street corner in the city.

The other location scouts, Fred and Barbara and a couple Garry didn't know, were sitting at a table going through files.

Garry said, "The TTC will give you directions in 140 languages and the UN calls this the most multi-ethnic city in the world, so why is it that every single scout I do is for bland and generic?"

"No, Garry, they just say generic. You bring the bland to it all by yourself."

Garry walked out from the stacks and looked at Fred, the frumpy guy in his late forties who had scouted *Detroit Rock City* and said, "I'm a lot of things. I'm never bland." He dropped a pile of red files on the table and sat down.

"You know, I understand that every freaking inch of this city has been in some movie, always disguised as something else. I'm just wondering if we should be so proud of it."

"What are you on?"

"*Life and Death in Little Italy*. Piece of crap gangster movie by that video hack, Edward J. Nijar."

"Aren't they, like, halfway through shooting?"

Garry opened a file and looked at yet another apartment building claiming to be "so New York" because it had a canvas awning. "They have no idea what they're doing. Look, look what I have to deal with." He pulled out a few fax pages. "New scenes every day. New locations. These idiots gave Myles Day script approval. And now they've cast some local actress they really like, so suddenly the hookers are all students."

"We shot *Searching for Bobby Fischer* at St. Veronica's. They were cool."

"We don't have Larry Fishburn."

Fred smirked. Larry.

Barbara stood up, slung her camera over her shoulder and said, "Who shot at the El Mo?"

"I did." Fred again. The guy was everywhere. "*Hendrix*. But the place has new owners now, remember."

Garry said, "Try the Filmore, or the Gladstone. We shot *New Jersey Turnpikes* in both." Then he shook his head. "Shit, we can't make movies of our own. Why do we have to bend over and grease ourselves up everytime an American walks into the room?"

Fred said, "That a fantasy of yours?"

"Yeah. With you, Fred. Then your mom walks in."

"You going to make a movie?" Barbara asked.

"I sure am," Garry said and stood up. "And it'll be set in Toronto and it'll have the Tower in the frame and people will walk on Bloor Street and they won't be ashamed."

"Will they be ashamed to go see it with the raincoat crowd?"

"Oh, you wound me, Freddie. You cut me deep."

Bev, one of the librarians, said, "I heard Rita Zekas has a picture of Ainsley Riordan and some grip she's screwing."

"Rita Zekas is screwing a grip?" Garry said, all innocent and wide-eyed.

"No, you idiot, Ainsley... oh, I get it, ha ha. They were at Riverdale Farm looking at the sheep. It's supposed to be awful."

"Aw, poor Ainsley Riordan, might look bad in a picture in the paper." Fred was really on today.

Garry signed out his files and left.

East on Bloor, over the viaduct. Cars on the DVP. Garry saw the best way to shoot a chase on the expressway. In tight, from another car with a wide angle and then from above. Was there a place where the cars could hop the median and drive into oncoming traffic? Maybe a construction site, some debris could make a ramp. It would be cool to see the skyline of the city in the background. Would the chase be into town or away?

Garry pulled his old Volvo station wagon onto the Danforth. Street signs in Greek. Sidewalk cafes, even the few chain places, a Starbucks and a Swiss Chalet of all things, looked good. A neighbourhood this cool should be in the movies and on TV all time. Garry couldn't remember the last time he'd seen it. Well, *My Big Fat Greek Wedding*, sure, but it was supposed to be Chicago. Had Nia Vardalos ever even been to Chicago?

The vast expanse of Scarborough. Okay, even Garry admitted it would be tough to make it look good, but a slow pass of some of these tiny post-war, one-and-a-half story houses on a long lens, a 75mm or 85mm, with all their little additions and lawns and struggling flowers could sure strike a few emotions—as long as you didn't linger too long and went inside quickly to some people. No worries for Garry.

Then it was Garry's home turf—seventies bungalows, the heart and soul of suburbia. And Garry was the guy to prove it had a soul. He could shoot subdivisions. Not all Todd Solondz *Happiness* dark and twisted. No, that would be too easy. Everyone who grew up there hated the burbs. Not all silly like *Wayne's World*, even though that really was Scarborough. No, Garry had plans.

Today, though, it was *Life and Death in Little Italy* shooting inside a farmhouse north of Pickering. Acres of land had been expropriated for an airport years ago and now a couple dozen houses sat empty. Prime movie locations.

Garry found MoGib in the Craft truck, talking to Hillary. He handed the files to him.

"Here you go, boring houses, nondescript office buildings and hospitals."

MoGib said, "Thanks, Garry. Have you met Hillary?"

She said, "You want something?"

Garry noticed the tattoos disappearing below her hiphugger jeans. "No thanks, I'm fine."

"So now they're talking about something on the waterfront, something industrial, docks where big ships get unloaded."

Garry said, "What city does this movie take place in?"

MoGib said "New York," at the exact same moment Hillary said, "Philadelphia."

A grip filling his pockets with chocolate bars said, "I thought it was Chicago."

"It doesn't matter," MoGib said. "We only have one set of docks in Toronto, so that's what they get."

"Do they want a big ship being unloaded with a big crane?"

"Probably."

"But they'll shoot it so tight and dark that we could actually be at Cinespace or some warehouse."

"Right."

Garry sighed. "Every time, you tell me it'll be different. You say, 'these guys are really creative, they're looking for something new.' Every time you say it."

"How's your script coming along?"

"My script is done. I got some Harold Greenberg Fund money for another draft, which it doesn't need, and now I'm getting Telefilm development money. What I need is a producer." He looked at MoGib.

"What?"

"I heard a rumour you were back on track."

"Don't believe everything you hear."

Garry opened the door and said, "Oh but I do, I do."

"What about some of your Film Centre pals? They have a producing program."

"This is a generation that thinks *Back to the Future* and *Ferris Bueller's Day Off* are the greatest movies ever made. Not exactly *Citizen Kane*, you know."

MoGib said, "Where are you going now?"

Garry turned around and started down the steps of the truck, pushing past a couple of electrics and a PA and said, "I'm going to take a proper picture of Ms. Ainsley Riordan and our very own Roger Doyle."

MoGib laughed. "You doing beauty shots now?"

"Every picture I take is beautiful."

Garry jumped his way around the puddles on the gravel road. He could see the huge lights way up on the tops of the cranes surrounding the tiny farmhouse a mile off in the distance. Good, he thought, keep a few grips trapped up there all day.

An AD walked by listening intently to her headset walkie, but not saying anything. Garry stopped her.

"Hey, is that Ainsley Riordan's Winnie?"

"Who are you?"

Garry held up his camera. "Her personal photographer. Didn't anyone tell you I was coming?"

The AD looked very worried. "No, I don't know anything about that."

"Is that her Winnie?"

"Hang on, I'll get you someone."

She started to press a button on the walkie, but Garry said, "That's okay. I see it."

Up ahead, just past the camera truck was the row of Winnies. Garry pointed to the nicest one.

"No," the AD said. "That's Renée Jato, the producer."

"On set?"

"Every day."

"Man, you guys are in trouble."

"It's that one." The AD pointed to the fifth Winnie in line, furthest from the set.

Garry shook his head. "And I heard she's sleeping with the Transport captain. You'd think he could get her a better parking spot."

The AD said, "Parking is Locations'—" But Garry was already walking away.

He saw half a dozen people standing beside the Wardrobe truck. Someone, it could have only been a grip, said, "If she was gonna go slumming, why couldn't it have been with me?"

Then Garry saw Roger Doyle push his way past the others and start to walk away.

A tall, thin, very good-looking black guy stepped up beside him and said, "Roger, I just wanted to let you know that Rita Zekas is going to run a picture from Riverdale Farm."

Roger stopped and looked at the guy. He didn't understand.

"In *The Star*? On Sunday? 'Star Gazing'?"

Roger said, "What are you talking about?"

"He is so precious."

The black guy looked at Garry. "Hello?"

Roger said. "Hey, Hollywood." The new nickname for Garry.

"Ouch. That one's going to stick, isn't it?" He looked at Steven. "Hi, I'm Garry Deslisle."

"Oh, hi. I'm Steven. Wardrobe."

"I heard about 'Star Gazing,'" Garry said.

"On the farm?" Steven said. He looked at Roger. "What were you thinking?"

Roger said, "It wasn't my idea."

Garry held up his camera. "I thought since they're going to run a picture anyway, we might as well give them a good one."

"Well, aren't you thoughtful?" Steven said.

"Just looking out for my man BJ and the Bear here."

Roger said, "What the hell are you guys talking about?"

Garry and Steven were already talking about the best place on set to shoot the pictures.

"You think Ainsley will go along with it?"

"Ms. Riordan is wonderful," Steven said. "A real trouper."

"Okay, let's go get her."

Steven said, "Let's get her some decent clothes."

"Great." Garry looked at Roger. "What are we going to do about him?"

Steven laughed. "He's fine. You can't fake genuine. At least not on our budget."

Ainsley said, "You guys are so sweet," and thought she caught a look between Garry and Steven. "Is it too cold for the Dior?"

Steven said, "It's never too cold for Dior," and handed her a see-through blouse.

Garry watched him as he went through the Wardrobe truck looking for accessories and said, "I'll go get Roger."

Steven came back with a pair of leather boots in his hand and said, "Here you go."

Ainsley shook her head.

She said, "If you think you can get him to change for pictures, you try," and she and Steven laughed. She took the boots. "These are great. Where do you want to do this?"

Garry said, "We can do it right outside here. With the trees in the b.g. It'll be nice, rustic."

Ainsley winked at Steven and jumped out of the truck. She called back, "I'll get the trucker. He may need some convincing."

Garry looked at Steven, who was smiling after her like a proud big brother. Garry said, "Why do people say she can't act? She's doing pretty well now."

Steven said, "You don't really know her."

Garry rolled his eyes.

Steven said, "Starlets. It's tough, you know. Everybody wants something from them. They don't have any friends."

Garry said, "Huh."

"They have pretend friends, imaginary friends. Make-up, Hair, even Wardrobe. We're their deepest, most intimate friends till we wrap and then they go make new ones on the next set. It's not an easy way to go through life."

"Do we always have to suck up to the big-shot Americans and forgive them everything? What the fuck are we afraid of?"

Steven stepped out the back of the truck. "I don't know, getting to know them? Getting to know ourselves?"

They stood very close to each other for a moment. A long moment. Garry didn't have a snappy comeback.

Roger was still annoyed when Garry showed up with Steven and Ainsley. Of course, she thought it was a hoot. She insisted on posing for a couple of glam shots and then they went outside and she pretended to be hiding from the camera behind Roger and pushing Garry away.

Garry said, "Say, Rog, could you try and look a little pissed off?" and Steven burst out laughing.

Roger said, "Watch it, Hollywood."

Ainsley and Steven were like old friends and Garry seemed to fit right in. They were laughing and joking and posing and giggling so that when Nijar and Judy Nemeth walked up they didn't even notice.

"What the fuck is going on here?"

Judy quickly said, "Ainsley, we've got another new scene. Come see your lines."

Nijar said, "No one takes pictures on my set but me. Give me that fucking camera."

Garry stared at him. Steven moved closer to Ainsley.

Roger said, "Calm down."

Nijar, all red in the face and wound tight, glared at him. "Who the fuck are you?"

Roger said, "Go back to your Winnie."

Nijar stared at Roger but he didn't say anything. Then he looked at Steven and said, "We're gonna need new wardrobe right fucking now." He walked away.

No one said anything for a second and then Ainsley stepped up to Roger and said, "My hero," and everyone laughed. After a minute, so did Roger.

"Fucking movie sets," he said.

Ainsley kissed him and said, "I can't wait to see the new scenes. Think there'll be any nudity?" She winked and walked away.

Steven stood watching Ainsley for a moment and then said to Garry, "I'd like to see those pictures."

"Sure. I'll bring them by at wrap."

Roger walked away, looking for a truck or some tools, something he understood.

City of Toronto
Code of Conduct for Film Crew and Cast

Film and television production are all guests in residential and commercial areas and should treat all locations, as well as the members of the public, with courtesy. It is the responsibility of each production company to ensure that crew and cast comply with the Code of Conduct. Please observe the following accordingly.

To the Public: If you find this production company is not adhering to the Code of Conduct, please call the Toronto Film & Television Office at 416.392.7570, Monday to Friday between 8:30 a.m. and 6:00 p.m., or

Judy Nemeth	of Italy Productions	at (416) 744-7728
Line Producer	*Life and Death in Little Italy*	*Telephone number*

1. When filming in a neighbourhood or business district, proper notification is to be provided to each merchant or resident directly affected by filming activity (this includes parking and meal areas). The filming notice should include:
    - name of production company, title of production
    - kind of production (ie. feature film, movie of the week, television series, etc.)
    - type and duration, and description of activity (ie. times, dates including prep & wrap)
    - company contact; in this production:

        Morton Gibson   Leanne Merriweather
        Location Manager   *Assistant Location Manager*

    This Code of Conduct should be attached to every filming notification which is distributed in the neighbourhood or business district.

2. Production vehicles arriving on location in or near a residential neighbourhood shall not enter the area before the time stipulated on the permit. Production vehicles shall park, turning off engines as soon as possible. Crew and cast vehicles are not covered by location filming permit and shall observe designated parking areas noted by the Location Manager. Filming in residential neighbourhoods takes place between 7:00 a.m. and 11:00 p.m., unless residents are surveyed and have given approval.

3. Moving or towing of any vehicle is prohibited without the express permission of the owner of the vehicle.

4. Production vehicles shall not block, or park in private driveways without the express permission of the driveway owner.

5. Pedestrian traffic is not to be obstructed at any time. All cables and similar items are to be channelled.

6. Do not trespass on residents' or merchants' property. Remain within the boundaries of the property that has been permitted for filming.

7. No alcoholic beverages are permitted at any time on any set or location.

8. Crew and cast meals shall be confined to the area designated in the location agreement or permit. Individuals shall eat within their designated meal area during scheduled crew meals. All trash must be disposed of properly upon completion of the meal. All napkins, plates and coffee cups used in the course of the work day should be disposed of in the proper receptacles. All catering, craft service, construction, strike and personal trash must be removed from the location, ensuring all locations are returned to their original condition.

9. Observe designated smoking areas and always extinguish cigarettes in proper containers.

10. Removing, trimming and/or cutting of vegetation or trees are prohibited unless approved by the permit authority or the property owner.

11. Film crew shall not remove City street signs. This must be done by City staff (City Works Services).

12. Every crew and cast member shall keep noise levels as low as possible at all times. Crew and cast will refrain from the use of lewd or improper language.

13. Production employees shall wear appropriate clothing while on location.

14. Crew members shall not display signs, posters, or pictures on vehicles that members of the public may find offensive or objectionable.

15. Every member of the crew shall wear a production pass/badge when required by the location.

16. The crew and cast shall not bring guests or pets to the location, unless expressly authorized in advance by the company.

17. The production will comply at all times with the provisions of the filming permit. A copy of the filming permit shall be on the location at all times with the location department.

To the Crew and Cast: The production company appreciates your cooperation and assistance in upholding the Code of Conduct. Failure to comply with this Code of Conduct can result in disciplinary action by the production company or your union, guild or association.

Italy Productions Inc.
Toronto, Ontario

THE GRIPS

"Quiet, everybody. This is a take."
"Roll sound."
"Speed."
"Camera."
"Frame."

Then nothing happened. It was always the same, that dead air pause while the director was deep in thought. It seemed to stretch on forever, before he finally whispered, "Action."

The grip turned down the volume on his walkie and said, "You ever been on a show that went down?"

"You mean, like, they had everything together except the financing?"

"Course not."

One guy was sitting on the back of the grip truck, winding gaffer tape around a piece of two-by-two about three feet long.

"Then, no, not once shooting started." The other grip came to the back of the truck and dropped a few more rolls of gaffer tape.

"Well, have you ever seen script pages this colour? I don't even know what it is."

One of the gaffers had just walked up, a cup of coffee in his hand. "Taupe. This show is such a mess the rewrites are now in their third shade of beige."

"But you think the show will finish? We'll get the full six weeks?"

"Definitely."

"Absolutely."

"For sure."

"You're sure?"

"Once shooting starts, you can take it to the bank," the gaffer said.

"And that's why, because it's the bank's movie now."

"Cut," came faintly over the walkie.

"But it's such a mess. No one knows what this fucking movie is about."

"It's about Ainsley Riordan in fishnet stockings and a push-up bra."

"And out of the bra."

"It doesn't matter. Making movies isn't about telling stories, it's about making deals. When the deals are all made, shooting starts. What happens after that doesn't matter."

"So I'm getting five more weeks' pay?"

"Yes."

"Absolutely."

"For sure."

"I can count on it? Even if it's this big a mess?"

"All right, everyone, first positions. We're going again."

"Why don't you turn that off? They'll be shooting this same set-up for hours."

He turned the volume down, but not quite off. "Is it Ainsley in her underwear?"

"Yeah, she's trying to say some lines. It'll take all day."

"You think she's dumb?"

"She's a movie star, isn't she?"

"Yeah, but look at all this crappy dialogue. She only got the stupid taupe pages this morning."

"So, all she has to do is say these lines."

The grip looked at the sides, the scenes they were shooting that day, stapled to the back of the call sheet. "Yeah, but look at this. It's pages and pages of this crap."

"It's not like she has anything else in the world to think about."

"So this show will keep going?"

"I just told you, you're looking in the wrong place. You're looking at the script, the casting, the production. That's not what it's about. The producers get paid if the movie goes. The lawyers get paid, the bankers get paid. They get nothing if the movie doesn't go. Doesn't matter if the script makes any sense."

He started rolling up a wad of gaffer tape and then rolling more over it, squishing it down as hard as he could.

"So why do they keep rewriting it?"

The other grip looked at the gaffer.

The gaffer said, "It's a game. Look, Edward Nijar cares, Myles Day—does he *ever* care, pain in the ass lighting him—some of the producers care because they're like you, they love movies. But the people who decide if they get financing, they don't like movies."

"They don't like movies?"

"They just don't care about movies one way or the other. It's just a product. It would be *nice* if it was a huge hit and made millions, but like I said, they already made their money making the deals so they don't *really* care."

"It's like Kraft Dinner," the other grip said.

"What?"

"Do you think the big shareholders in Kraft, the CEO of Kraft, the Board of Directors, those guys, do you think they ever eat Kraft Dinner?"

"I doubt it."

"Okay, but it's important to them that it gets made."

"Yeah."

"Well, that's what this is. The movies are Kraft Dinner. It might be important to you, but you know what the Barenaked Ladies said, even if they had a million dollars *they'd* still buy it. They like it." He dropped the tightly wound ball of tape on the ground and started rolling up another.

"So, like, Nijar and Myles Day, they're like the Barenaked Ladies. They'd still make movies. But the people who decide what gets made, all these people on the fax list at the end of the day, they're just deal makers. Could be movies, could be Kraft Dinner, doesn't matter, they'll never see it, or eat it."

"There you go."

The gaffer said, "Unless they want to meet Ainsley Riordan. You don't get that with Kraft Dinner."

"That would be cool, though, if you got something with Kraft Dinner."

"Like a movie star?"

"Or a picture even. A really hot picture of Ainsley Riordan."

"In Kraft Dinner? Are you fucking stoned?"

"So this show will definitely go the six weeks?"

The third gaffer tape baseball was ready. "Yes. Now, where's your glove?"

"In the truck."

"Give me the bat."

The two-by-two was covered in the shiny silver gaffer tape, skinny at one end and then bulging out. Not a perfect baseball bat, but pretty close. It must have taken three rolls of tape. He swung it.

"Nice."

The daily ran up to the truck, out of breath. "Wh-what's the matter with your walkies?"

"Batteries must be dead. Why?"

"They needed you guys on set five minutes ago."

As they started out of the truck, one of the grips said, "We're busy here, you know. If we go over into lunch, someone's going to fucking hear about it."

THE TRANSPORT CAPTAIN

"So now it's summer," Ainsley said. She closed the door to her Winnie and dropped onto the couch. "Changes so fast. Is that why everyone's so obsessed with it?"

Roger said, "They brought you the new pages."

Ainsley untied the blue checked shirt she was wearing and started to unbutton it. "Picnic scene. No one had any idea what it was about. Nijar spent an hour playing with the dishes on the blanket."

"Be glad that's all he played with."

She took off the shirt and unclipped her bra. "I've never seen so much rewriting during shooting," she said. "It's a whole different movie. If it's even still a movie."

Roger was reading the pages as she dropped them. "What colour is this? Goldenrod?"

"We've been through every colour I've ever seen," she said. "Twice."

He said, "Usually revisions during production are just dialogue changes and they don't really matter—"

"Excuse me?"

"But for this one, we're getting new locations, new cast members, new everything. Did they even have a script when they started?"

"I'm pretty sure my agent read something. Where are we now?" Ainsley sat up and looked out the window. "Looks like the middle of nowhere."

"It's a little further north than that. They call it Vaughn."

She got a sweatshirt from the cupboard above the couch and pulled it on. "I bet Eddie is having a blast casting these new scenes. Every one has a hooker in it."

"Student hookers."

"There weren't enough clichés. Now all the hookers are college students."

Roger said, "What does Linda Grigette play, the professor?"

Ainsley pulled down the Daisy Duke shorts and found a pair of sweatpants. "You know, I completely forgot she was in this movie."

"She gets here tomorrow."

"That should calm Eddie down a little."

"You call him Eddie to his face?"

"I didn't used to. But man, you start screwing below the line, things just fall apart."

Roger said, "It'll be over soon."

She sat down beside him. "Are you kidding?"

"Are you?"

She said, "You are, aren't you? You're very good, you know." She stretched out on the couch, her head on his lap. "You ever thought about being an actor?"

"No."

"People in the movies," she said, "think everyone else in the world wants to be in the movies."

"I've noticed that."

"You see some woman, she's a doctor, a scientist, she's working on a cure for breast cancer, people say, 'I wonder what her screenplay's about?'"

"You think they're compensating?"

"For what?"

"I don't know, grown men getting up in the morning, putting on make-up, playing make-believe."

"Now I know you're kidding. You've got good delivery, though."

"I moved around a lot, always the new kid in school. It's a defense thing."

"Me too. Keep people at a distance, don't get too close 'cause it'll be too hard when you leave. Psychology 101, right? When I do my Barbara Walters I'll tell her I can't be a tree; I've got to be a potted plant so it'll fit in the moving van."

Roger said, "Moving van, wow, you had it made."

She looked at him. "You know, a couple of hours ago I was really stressed. On set, everyone looking at me, I don't know my lines 'cause I just got them five minutes ago, Eddie's screaming at everybody. My stomach all tied in knots. I feel pretty good now."

"Yeah. Me too."

LIFE AND DEATH IN LITTLE ITALY

345 Carlaw Avenue,
Toronto, Ontario, Canada M4M 2T1
Tel: 416.463.1266 Fax: 416.463.1950

IMMIGRATION - What's it all about?

There are no exceptions. Everyone must go through Canadian Customs upon entering the country. It is essential that you carry two pieces of valid identification: a passport, driver's license, birth certificate, some type of photo identification is preferable.

Just to let you know… before your arrival a request was made to the Canadian Consulate to obtain a work permit for you to come to Canada to work on the feature film *Life and Death in Little Italy*. Your flight details, port of entry and other personal details were submitted and logged by Canada Customs - they are expecting you!

Upon entering Canada be specific about your stay in Canada; if you are just visiting then let them know you are just visiting. If you are coming into Canada to work and need to obtain and pay for your work permit then please follow the directions below.

At your port of entry into Canada please let Immigration know you are coming to Canada to work on the feature film *Life and Death in Little Italy* and require your work permit. *Note: With your travel memo, or attached to your airline tickets you will have a copy of the letter from the Canadian Consulate General which contains your authorization for temporary employment in Canada. In this letter there will be a file reference number and an authorization number*. Please deliver your letter of authorization so they can locate you in their files, pay the $150.00 permit fee and step through Customs to where your driver will be happily awaiting your safe arrival and will take you to your accommodations.

The fastest way to process the permit fee is to put the cost on your credit card. Then, submit the receipt to production and we will reimburse you. (There are alternative methods for paying the fee. If you prefer to pursue a different form of payment please let me know and I can run through the options.)

Thank you so much for taking the time to read through this document. If you're aware of the process involved then all you have to contend with are the line-ups.

Many thanks, and best wishes for safe travelling.

Anne Richardson
Production Coordinator

THE PRODUCTION ASSISTANT

To Greg, being a PA was a breeze once he figured out one simple rule: it's all about finding the slack. He'd been at it for over three years. Three summers and all last winter, working around town. His paycheque was up to a $650 weekly flat. That was top dollar for PAs. The other PA on this show, Alice, was only making five and she was totally stressed. Always running around, always apologizing. This was her first show, so Greg was trying to show her the what's-what and what's-not, but it was clear to him that she was not going to make it. She was headed for a breakdown, wound up that tight. And Anne, the Production Co-ordinator, had a work ethic that Greg could not get behind, so he spent as much time as he could on the road.

It was hot out, finally. He had the windows down, the air on max. He was cruising along Broadway on the top of the city. One of the things all PAs figured out was how to get around traffic at any time of the day, and it usually involved speeding on the side streets. On every job, Greg's co-ordinator fed him some bull that they would rather he was late than drive unsafely. It was some sort of unwritten legal requirement, and Greg never bought it. Broadway was one of his faves. It took him from Bayview to just north of Yonge and Eglinton and he used it every other day. Being on the road all day got Greg sick of the radio. He had his Nirvana tape, booming. He tried to blow the speakers out from every rental car they gave him. He usually succeeded. Those were the things that Greg loved about PAing—the free wheels, gas paid for, and the petty cash flow. The accountant was Greg's best friend, or worst enemy. Only a dumb PA wouldn't suck up to the accountant. Greg knew plenty of ways to make money off the petty cash float. He'd be nuts not to take advantage of it, with the shitty money they gave him.

He pulled up to a stop, and waited for the hick driving the blue Ford pick-up to go through. Nothing. No signs of life. Greg finally honked, and the pick-up jumped forward. Greg hit the gas and passed just behind it.

His pager went off. He was doing almost 100 in a 40 zone, and of course, when he finally squeezed the pager out of his pocket and under the seatbelt, and took his eyes off the road to look at it, the scrolling text read, "Where are you? Call in! Anne." Did she think he'd fly there? It was the middle of rush hour. Greg shrugged it off. Like he told Alice, no co-ordinator has the time to find a replacement once production has started. They can't fire anyone.

Greg tossed the pager onto the seat beside him, saw the chicken place, and he was at Yonge Street. He pulled into his usual parking spot under the No Parking sign, and jogged the two blocks north to the Cell Shoppe.

The Cell Shoppe was small, just a front room with cellphone paraphernalia on the walls. The eye candy behind the counter was with someone, so Greg grabbed the phone.

"Production," Alice answered.

"It's Greg. Anne paged?" The phone went dead, and he was on hold. Quickly Anne came on.

"Greg!" Anne accused him.

"Yeah." He was careful. "I just got to the Cell Shoppe." There was a pause in the conversation that had nothing to do with Greg.

"Linda's waiting for her phone," Anne finally told him.

"I know." He smiled to keep his voice pleasant. "It's rush hour. I can't really get around."

"That's why you were supposed to get the phone and head to set before rush hour." Greg could tell she was not smiling. "You're going to Ajax. Now it's going to take you two hours to get there."

"I know." Greg said, the smile slipping. "I had to do all the other stuff you gave me."

And that was just wrong. Greg had to complete a minute-by-minute rundown of his afternoon. The eye candy behind the counter finished with the customer and smiled hello at him. Greg felt the traffic getting heavier every second.

"I gotta go," he broke in. "The cellphone's ready."

"Just come right back after you drop it off." Anne said. "The bank run will have to wait until tomorrow, but I still need two scripts dropped off to the cops' players." Greg knew the characters she was talking about—they didn't play until next week, but Anne wanted the scripts to go out now. It meant that Greg would be working until after 10:00 p.m. Anne was going home at 6:00.

"Sure." It was all he could say.

"And Greg." Anne raised her voice. "Check the damn phone before you leave this time." And hung up.

Greg shook his head at the world. Once you lose the slack for good, you end up like Anne. He'd seen it happen before. He smiled at the eye candy and tried to remember her name. He flirted, got the phone, and he was out the door.

He didn't really mind sitting in traffic. He aimed the air vents at his face and cranked his Smashing Pumpkins tape. He edged forward along with everyone else, holding his place and cursing the old man who kept him from changing lanes. The whole fucking way there.

Ajax was a tiny suburb of Toronto. Dull. Boring. Greg thought of the Courtney Love lyrics, which went something like, "Everybody dresses the same, everybody fucks the same." Greg passed rows of identical tract homes surrounding huge strip malls, like something out of a fifties ad for nuclear energy. The failed dream of the nuclear family. The suburbs, the breeding ground of apathy, intolerance, and dull listless kids turning into dull listless consumers. Where cinemas first became entertainment complexes. An odd chemistry flowed through the suburbs, and Greg blamed them for twice voting Mike Harris into office. He had to blame someone, and he didn't vote. Greg hated the suburbs. It was where he grew up.

The set was just north of Ajax, and Greg checked the call sheet map and passed through the small town like an undigested piece of corn, headed for Highway 7 and the forgotten dirt concession roads around it. He followed the traffic cones that some location PA got paid to put out at every turn. That was one job that Greg would never do.

He turned onto a dirt side road with a whole bunch of cars parked nose to ass on the side of the dirt road, nowhere near the "crew parking" square on the map. He knew he had found the set.

Still following his crude map, he headed for "Honey Land," the euphemistically over-descriptive name for the trailers that held the toilets, and where the Winnebagos were parked. They belonged to the talent and to what Greg liked to call his lords and masters, those American producers and directors that flooded into the Toronto hotels and film sets every summer, looking for a low dollar and film crews eager for whatever work got tossed their way.

He parked his car in close to the Winnies, and rushed out before Transport told him to move it. Like anyone who worked in film, from the movie stars on down, Greg knew the first rule—no matter what, you leave your keys behind the visor so they can move your car if they have to. Greg dropped his keys in his pocket. If they needed his car moved, they could come and find him.

The Winnies were parked up tight in what was once a grassy field and was now a wash of mud and peeling cardboard walkways. Greg cruised up and down the narrow alleys between the trailers, looking for Linda's Winnie.

Linda Grigette was big in the seventies as one of the babes in *Fashion Fuzz*. Not one of humanity's shining moments. In fact, for the most part, Greg felt that way about the whole decade. He just couldn't believe in space-happy, neo-hippie, love-and-peace alien conspiracies because they would have taken one look at the Earth during the seventies and packed it in. But Linda Grigette, she was *it* for about two years there, while she was on that show. She left it for a film career, and she was still looking. She'd had more than her share of *Playboy* spreads, and she had hit the talk shows from time to time. On this show, she was playing Margaret, who was the mother to the hooker with the heart of gold played by Ainsely Riordan. Greg had the tent pants for Riordan, but she was fucking Roger in Transport. Greg thought Roger was a good guy, but he just couldn't see her going for him.

He found the Winnie with "Margaret" written on the back of some old call sheet. He knocked on the door. He waited.

The door was kicked open, and Greg almost took it full in the face. A guy about Greg's age, but better dressed, stood there, blinking down at him, a cellphone to his ear.

Greg stared at him, and he stared through Greg.

"Yeah, well, just fax me the waybills and I'll take care of it," he said. Greg was about to tell him he didn't have any waybills, when it percolated through his brain that the guy on the cellphone might not have been talking to him. He motioned Greg inside.

He turned to Greg. "Yeah?" He shut down the cell. Greg's brain was fried from sitting in traffic for an hour and a half.

"What's with you people?" he demanded of Greg. "You guys're the fifty-first state, but going through your Customs is like shipping to a third world country."

Greg immediately disliked him, and it was made worse by the fact that Greg had no answer for him. Plus, Greg wasn't sure if he expected one.

"I give up," the American assistant said.

"What?" It was the first word Greg said to him, and Greg was not proud of it.

"I have no idea why you're here," he blurted. "I can't guess. You'll have to tell me."

"I'm looking for Linda," Greg said, and he tried to give it a "who the fuck are you?" kind of tone.

"Yeah, well, she's got other stuff to do than wait for some flunky to do whatever it is you do." He said it like he and Greg were pals. Like he hadn't just insulted Greg ten different ways. "All these trucks here? We're making a movie, José."

Greg had never realized that conversations had winners and losers, but he wasn't coming out ahead in this one. He held out the box with the phone in it.

"I have her phone," Greg said.

"Oh!" he said. "Her phone! The one she was supposed to get three days ago when we made the mistake of flying into this tarted-up small town." He grabbed the box from Greg, ripped it open, and started to spill the contents over the little dining room table. He talked the whole time. "Are you the phone boy?

The phone guy? Executive in charge of phones and sundry phone-related items?" Greg just stared at him, as completely and hopelessly lost as a Richmond Hill teen on a downtown pub crawl.

He looked up at Greg. "Speak," he said.

"What?" Greg asked.

"Good boy." He returned to the phone. "Now roll over."

"I'm a production assistant, from the office." Greg hoped this would give him some much needed credibility.

"A PA on a Canadian film crew. Your mother must be so proud," he said, but more to himself while he finished checking the phone. "No earbud. Linda needs her earbud. Some jerk told her cellphones gave you brain cancer."

"Oh," Greg said. "I'll let Anne know."

"Forget it," he said. "I'll let Anne know." He picked up his cellphone and speed-dialed the office. Greg took his chance and quietly slipped out.

"That fucking American jerk," Greg thought. He leaned back against his car, and his cigarette lighter agreed with him. His cigarette did too, and he used it to calm down. One of the things Greg hated about PAing was dealing with the Americans, both the ones who came here and the ones who stayed home. There were two types of Americans in the film industry in LA: the rude "why are you bothering me?" type and the dumb "what's a zed?" type. Greg suspected that there were nice people in the States, but they didn't work in film. The two types combined in the ones who protested the runaway productions that came up to Canada to shoot. Even though Greg had heard you couldn't shoot in LA because they burned every location worth shooting in. For the time being, Greg and the rest of the city welcomed the billion dollars a year the Yanks spent on filming in Toronto. The thought of his job reminded Greg that Anne was going to be pissed at him. He could hear her already—"I told you to check the phone, Greg." "You're making me look bad, Greg." Greg wasn't going to rush back. Those bit-player cops could get their scripts tomorrow.

"Hey, PA!" It was Linda's assistant. Greg jumped into his car, and fumbled for his keys. The American came over to the open window.

"Hey," he said. "There a Starbucks near here?"

"Yeah," Greg answered. "In Ajax."

"I don't know where the fuck that is," he said as he came around the car. He opened the door and dropped inside. "Let's go."

"Go where?"

He twisted to face Greg, one arm over the headrest. He spoke slowly, watching Greg's face to see if he understood. "To the Starbucks." He sat forward again. "I gotta get some real coffee, or as close to it as you guys get." He swayed his head side to side and snapped his fingers. "Let's go," he chanted. "Let's go. To the Starbucks. Let's go. Let's go."

"Anne wants me back to the office," Greg informed him. "I gotta drop off some scripts."

"No," he chanted. "You don't. To the Starbucks. Let's go. Let's go." He turned back to Greg. "I told her I needed you for a few hours."

"What did she say?"

"I don't fuckin' know. I told her I needed you for a couple hours. It wasn't a public survey. If I had sled dogs and a map I'd go myself. I don't know my way around the tundra. That's why I need a native."

Greg was out of arguments. He really had never wanted anything in life so completely as he wanted to be away from this jerk, but the prospect of catching slack in a coffee house was pretty enticing. Greg fished out his keys and started the car. The jerk went back to swinging his head and chanting.

"Let's go. Let's go. To the Starbucks. Get some coffee. Let's go. Let's go."

Greg pulled out off the dirt concession road onto Highway 7 and headed for Ajax. A phone rang, and Linda's assistant pulled out the smallest cellphone Greg had ever seen and flipped it open.

"Carmen. Go," he said. It was the closest Greg got to an introduction. He could hear someone yelling on the phone, cutting in and out.

"What?" Carmen yelled. "I can't come meet you." More yelling on the other end. "I'm in Canada. Canada!" Greg could very clearly hear laughter. "Fuck you, man. You think I came here of my own free will?" The yelling on the other end was divided by longer periods of silence. "I can't hear you," Carmen said. "This fuckin' Canadian reception is shit." He listened, and after a few more *what*s, Carmen said, "For a week," and more laughter. The conversation went like that until they pulled onto the main drag in Ajax, when the phone went dead.

"Fuckin' Canadian reception." Carmen tucked the phone back into his pants. "You know what terrifies me? You guys are the early warning system for transpolar nuclear launches, and you can't get a cellphone to work."

The Starbucks was in the main strip mall, like 96% of Ajax's local economy. The evening crowd was lining up outside The Gravy House, and Greg could hear the loudspeaker announce, "Will the party with Norma Snockers please mosey on up to the front? Your table is ready. The party with Norma Snockers." Yeah, Ajaxians knew how to have fun.

Greg's car cruised through the six acres of parking lot and pulled up right in front of the Starbucks. Two teenage girls were sitting on the lame-ass patio out front, really just an umbrella between two lawn chairs in the reflected heat of the asphalt and concrete. Greg stared at them as he climbed from the car. Maybe they were young, but he would fuck them. They were wearing Barbie doll T-shirts that were so last year in Toronto but Greg loved them. He smiled at them as he walked past. They smiled politely back.

Once inside, Carmen started up again. "Fuck, I would love to give it up the ass to the two of them. Yeah. Make them bleed. Yeah. Show them why they call me The Horse."

This Starbucks was not on its own, but was actually part of a Chapters bookstore. It was the lounge where easily manipulated bibliophiles could sit, enjoy a coffee, and quietly read a book they had no intention of buying. Some were doing that now, some housewives unwinding by having an overpriced coffee and reading to their kids. Carmen, blind to it all, was doing the pelvic thrust, and talking loudly about molesting the underage girls outside.

"Yeah," he repeated. "I'll make them give me a rim job. Oh, yeah."

"Look," Greg told him, "there's kids here."

Carmen looked around, and saw them for the first time. He looked pained for a second, and then muttered, "Fuckin' Canadians too polite to say anything, anyway."

He looked up at Greg. "Now I was in LA, and did that? I'd get shot." He gave Greg a look for a second, and Greg realized that it was meant as some sort of apology.

"Come on, wage slave." Carmen crossed to the cash. "I'll buy you a coffee."

Over coffees, Greg told him about Roger and Ainsley and the hockey game. How the day after, they got so many phone calls from LA the office got shit done the whole day. Carmen told Greg about his family. His dad was an AD, his mother a Hollywood party girl whose claim to fame was that she slept with Spielberg and Lucas on the same day at Margot Kidder's beach house. But his grandfather—he was on his way to being a big star, except he got squeezed out by the talkies. Carmen talked about his grandfather with the same mix of reverence and missed opportunity that A&E always used for the silent film era.

In the middle of his story about his grandfather's exploits, which had a lot to do with studio heads that everyone in Hollywood must know by first names, his phone rang.

"Carmen. Go," he yelled into it. Greg heard laughing. "Yes, Canada," he yelled at them, and proceeded to spend the next half hour yelling into the phone, punctuated by *what*s at regular intervals.

Finally, he finished on the phone, and Greg drove back up to set to drop him off. He got out—without a thank you or goodbye—and he was back on his phone.

Greg got back to the office easily enough. By now it was almost 7:00, and Anne had gone home. The Assistant Co-ordinator, Kelly, made Greg go out and drop those scripts off, and of course they were on the other end of town, and of course no one was home at the first one, and of course Greg wasn't done until well after the crew had wrapped. He didn't get home until almost 11:00, thinking, "Why do I do this job?"

Kelly asked him the same thing. It was the next day. Greg had more scripts to deliver, but Kelly got shit for him being out of the office at wrap, leaving her to stamp the call sheets with "the push," the time changes the Second AD called in. That meant Greg was sitting around doing nothing, waiting for wrap, so he could do all the things he normally had to do at wrap, and then go out to deliver four scripts. He was bitching about it to Kelly, while in his mind he was banging the fuckin' life out of her on Anne's desk—Greg always had a thing for redheads, ever since Justine in grade 11.

"Why do you do it?" Kelly asked him.

"Dunno," Greg said. "For the chicks." She laughed. That was another reason why he liked her. He couldn't believe she was fucking married.

"How long have you been a PA?" When he told her three years, her jaw dropped in shock. "What do you want to do?"

"What do you mean?" he asked her.

"Produce? Direct? Co-ordinate? What?"

"Not really," he said. "It's just a job, you know."

"Most people become a PA in order to get a start in the industry." She paused to smoke, and ashed in an old soda can they kept hidden under her desk for just that duty. "I started as a PA only a year ago, now I'm an Assistant Co-ordinator. Nobody stays being a PA for three years."

"Look," he told her. "I'm not some ass-kissing wannabe. My buddy offered me a gig on a commercial, and from there I moved into features. That's it."

She looked at him, strangely, probably fearing for his sanity. "Why don't you get a real job then?"

"What? Like a nine-to-five, middle management, inter-office memo, paper-pusher job? No thanks."

The phone rang, and he answered it, "Production."

"We've wrapped." The Second AD, Walt, said. "Stand by for a push." And then hung up.

"Wrap!" Greg yelled. "We're waiting for a push." Kelly nodded and smoked. Greg wondered what time he'd get home.

THE LOCATION SCOUT

Garry knew that on any given day, there were between 18 and 40 productions shooting in town. Toronto's Film & Television Office had issued almost 4000 permits in 2001, giving over 1,200 projects permission to shoot on location.

Now MoGib was telling him they needed a meat-packing plant. How could those cliché-loving Hollywood hacks have missed that in the first draft of their mobster movie?

He had the shots of Ainsley and Roger in his camera bag. They'd had a good time taking the pictures even though Garry was still miffed at Steven. Imagine a Wardrobe guy talking to him like that. But Ainsley really did seem to like the guy and when Garry'd asked Roger if he could "look a little pissed off," Steven had laughed hard. Ainsley was great. They'd been having a lot of fun until that video jerk, that prick Nijar came along and got all snotty.

Still, Steven had asked if he could see the pictures and Garry had agreed. In fact, he wanted an excuse to see the guy again.

It was just the two of them in the back of the Wardrobe truck, Garry and Steven. Everyone else was busy with wrap. It had been a big day at the airport. Huge load-in, full dress, and for what? Four lines of dialogue while a couple of tough guys waited for a plane and loaded their guns.

Garry said, "I couldn't believe it. What an asshole: 'No ones takes pictures on my set but me.' And demanding, *demanding* my camera."

"You were going to give it to him."

"I was not."

Steven looked at him sideways and shrugged.

Garry said, "If Roger hadn't sent him to his room, I would have."

Steven looked doubtful, but then he let Garry off the hook. "I can see what Ainsley sees in him."

"She really is into him."

"She keeps saying that I must know it's real, because she's not that good an actress."

Garry shook his head. "She doesn't seem like a bitch at all."

Steven finished looking through the pictures and handed them back to Garry. "She's not. It's this show. The whole thing is fucked. It's one big dick contest. With these tough guys compensating all day, how's she supposed to compete?"

"With Myles Day? I think she has a really good shot."

Garry was standing at the back of the truck, holding on to a clothes rack and kicking a little at the wood floor. He was trying to be casual, cool, but he knew it wasn't working.

Steven said, "These are great pictures."

"Thanks."

"You said you were going to bring them by yesterday."

"I got sent on more scouts. You wouldn't believe the changes they're making."

Steven looked around the Wardrobe truck. Row after row of black suits and white shirts. A couple of cop uniforms and way in the back small dresses and thigh-high boots. Gangster movies.

He said, "Sure I would. Every day they add new characters, put them in more scenes. They watch the dailies and Nijar gets all *inspired*. Luckily, it's almost always more hookers wearing leather."

"Challenging."

"With the budget I've got, it is."

"What about Linda Grigette?"

"She's bringing her own."

"This show has enough in the budget to bring in Wardrobe people?"

"Just the clothes. I'll still have to fit her."

"Without telling her that she's gained weight."

A PA stuck her head in the truck and said, "You guys want a beer?"

They sat in the Wardrobe truck, drinking from the bottles. Steven asked if Rita Zekas would really print Garry's picture instead of the one she had and Garry said sure she would, she wouldn't want to piss off the sexiest woman in Hollywood. They talked a little about old-time Hollywood gossip and fan magazines. They talked about movies they'd both worked on and Steven wondered why they hadn't crossed paths before.

"Because I try to avoid these Yankee pieces of crap."

"But with very well-dressed people in them."

"Yeah, of course."

When the beers were finished Garry said, "So, um, I was wondering…"

"Yeah?"

"I have this script I wrote. I got some development money for another draft, and well, there's some stuff about fashion in it, and I don't really know anything about that, so I was wondering, could you maybe read it?"

It wasn't what Steven was expecting, but he said, "Sure, bring it by set tomorrow."

Garry looked pleased, more than he wanted to, and said, "Okay, that'll be fine," and jumped out of the truck.

Steven watched him go, then went back to work.

Garry spent the day taking pictures of parking lots—*parking lots*. This one was used in *Exit Wounds*, that one in *Bless the Child*—what was Michelle Pfeiffer thinking?

Okay, so Steven must be close to 40, Garry didn't dare ask. He was 27. That wasn't too big a difference. Right?

```
EXT. HOCKEY ARENA—NIGHT

A sign in the parking lot welcomes "25th
Annual Men's League Tournament of
Champions—Good Luck, Guys!"

The old arena sits just off centre of a
small town. The parking lot is filled
with pick-ups, minivans and a couple of
Japanese sports cars.

The sounds of a hockey game are heard: a
player being slammed hard into the
boards, sticks against glass, skates on
ice, pads on pads and a loud grunt.

              JULIE
              (os)
     Okay, okay, the big question.
     Despite his enthusiastic
     efforts, you haven't achieved
     an orgasm. Now you're
     exhausted and would rather
     just roll over and go to
     sleep.

INT. ARENA—ICE SURFACE
```

A fierce game is being played by two men's league teams—guys range in age from their twenties to their early fifties.

A player, RALPH, is being slammed into the boards. His face is pressed against the glass and the much bigger guy checking him gives him one more shot before skating away.

As Ralph falls to the ice, the nearly empty stands can be seen.

INT. ARENA—THE STANDS

A group of five women sit together about halfway up the stands. In the centre of the group, a very pregnant JULIE is reading aloud from a magazine on her lap.

          JULIE
What do you do? Say, "That was great anyway," and mean it? Let him keep trying—it's worth the effort? Tell him it might be your fault—maybe you're not in the mood? Fake it just to get it over with, then roll over and go to sleep?

The women around Julie are not watching the game at all. VERONICA, early thirties, is a tall thin attractive woman wearing a long overcoat, TERI's in her mid-twenties, attractive in an athletic way, wearing jeans and a sweatshirt under her leather jacket. JENNIFER, also in her mid-twenties and pretty, wearing a skirt and blouse, and CAROL, in her late forties.

          VERONICA
My fault?

                    JENNIFER
            Lie to him?

                    TERI
            I am so tired of faking it.

Just then two well-dressed men carrying silver coffee thermoses walk into the stands and sit down nearby. Julie glances at them and looks at Carol.

                    CAROL
            What's an orgasm again?

INT. ARENA—ICE SURFACE

On the ice, the game continues. The action is fierce.

INT. ARENA—THE STANDS

Jennifer has looked up at the game long enough to see a player get driven into the boards. He gets up slowly.

                    TERI
            That's him.

                    JENNIFER
            Which one?

                    TERI
            The one getting up.

                    JENNIFER
            He looks dazed.

                    TERI
            Cute, though.

Jennifer considers this for a brief moment, and nods in agreement.

                    JENNIFER
          So is this typical? This is
          what it's usually like?

                    TERI
          Well, no one's been taken off
          on a stretcher yet, and I
          don't see any blood, but
          yeah.

Julie flips a page in the magazine.

As she reads the next question, the game
continues. It is very hard hitting, fast-
paced, action-packed. None of the women
really notice.

                    JULIE
          Okay, okay, next question. You have a
          burning desire to be stroked in a
          particular place in a certain way. So
          far, he hasn't found your magic
          garden. Do you: show him the way with
          your body and hands? Plant the seed
          by stroking him just the way you
          would like it? Explain in detail
          exactly what you want? Or feel
          terribly unsatisfied and resentful?

                    VERONICA
          Why wouldn't he know?

                    JENNIFER
          Feel resentful?

                    TERI
          I got so tired of telling
          every guy what to do, I
          printed up complete
          instructions with diagrams,
          the right order to follow,
          length of time to spend in
          each place.

One of the guys behind them laughs.

Julie turns to look at them.

> JULIE
> You guys not playing?

One of the guys, CONNOR, shakes his head.

> CONNOR
> The cheering section. We've never been to one of these tournaments before.

Carol suddenly realizes something.

> CAROL
> Oh my God, are you guys gay?

All the other women shush her and make faces and look embarrassed.

> CONNOR
> Was it the outfits?

Carol looks at the ice. One team is completely dominating the other.

> CAROL
> You mean THAT'S the gay team?

Connor and the guy beside him both nod.

> CAROL (CONT'D)
> Oh my God, Jerry's going to freak. We heard there was going to be a gay team, but he said they wouldn't show.

Julie looks at the scoreboard.

                    JULIE
          They're beating the crap out of
          us.

                    CONNOR
          Sorry about that.

Immediately the woman are apologetic and
reassuring.

                    JULIE
          Oh no, I didn't mean it like
          that. Sorry, no. It's just,
          the guys… oh wow.

Connor nods, understanding.

                    CONNOR
          That's a beautiful coat. Is
          it Italian?

                    JULIE
          Yeah, it is, thanks. It was
          way more than I could afford,
          but once in a while, you
          know…

Connor nods. He knows.

Behind them, on the ice, the gay team
scores another goal.

The women shake their heads, worried, but
also a little amused.

Connor and his friend look a little
worried.

"So they bond over fashion?"
"They don't completely bond, but yeah, it's the in. The wives and girlfriends and the partners in the stands, they start to talk. I need the coat to be by some designer, but I don't really know any."

"To a hockey tournament? Could be Hilary Radley."

"Clinton's wife?"

Steven couldn't tell if he was joking or not. "Might be a rights issue, but there are plenty. Hell, make it Armani."

"Not really the suburban wife designer."

"So you know some?"

They were sitting in the Starbucks on the Danforth. Steven had read Garry's script right away and agreed to tell him what he thought. Garry had said to be "brutally honest," and Steven said, "I always am," but then wondered if he really was.

"And you got money for this?"

"I'm in development hell. Kickbacks, hush money. In this country there are a lot of people making money off cable TV and off distributing American movies and they have no interest in making Canadian movies, so to shut up all those people who say 'If we're going to protect your monopoly, you've got to give us something back,' they run these programs to develop scripts and then they just claim none were any good."

"But people do make Canadian movies."

"Yeah, the same people make the same movies over and over. Or new people make the same movies. I can't even tell anymore. Someone said Canada is all about loneliness and alienation and inability to communicate and cold and bleak and distant and that's what we do."

"If you have an inability to communicate the least you can do is shut up about it."

Garry laughed. "That's good. Can I steal that?"

"I did."

"So, I went to film school and I went to The Canadian Film Centre—don't get me started—and I'm going to be the one who does it. I'm going to make a big mainstream hit movie in Canada."

"A fag hockey movie?"

Garry looked at him.

Steven said, "You certainly have a lot of energy."

"What did you think of the rest of the script?"

"It's funny. A lot of it is really funny. Touching. You're sure not afraid of emotion. Schmaltz. I've never seen anything that mixed *Slapshot* with *Queer as Folk*, I have to say."

"You'd go see it?"

"Who's going to play Darryl? Yeah, I'd go see it."

"I don't want to make weird marginalized movies that only cool, downtown festival people see. I think Guy Maddin and John Greyson and the gang have that covered."

"I don't think anyone would mistake this for one of theirs."

Garry nodded. "Actually, I met John Greyson and he's really cool. I'd like to get him the script."

"You need a producer."

"I sure do."

Garry started to say something else, but he noticed Steven nodding.

"You know one?"

"I didn't say anything."

"But you do, don't you? Oh my God, you know a producer. Will you give him my script?"

"Slow down, relax." Steven drank some of his latte. "You don't think it's a little cliché when the kid on the bad boy team comes out?"

"Cliché? You think there's something cliché in a gay hockey movie?"

"I don't mean like that. Just, you can kind of see it coming."

"You think it needs another draft?"

"I think in this business you have to get used to criticism, to input. Lots of people give it; you have to be able to take it. How good your work is is part of it, and how well you play with others is another part of it."

Garry was rocking forward on his chair, starting to get tense. Usually in this kind of scene he'd be a lot more aggressive, he'd defend himself more and then even go on the attack, but Steven was so calm, so careful and so... Well, he was taking the time on his day off. "Maybe I can work on the pacing."

"You don't have to do anything right now. You just have to be willing to talk."

"Okay."

They walked along the Danforth and through Riverdale and went to dinner. They talked movies, of course—what else does anyone talk about?—and they gossiped about the on-set romances: Roger and Ainsley, and Hillary in Craft Services and that guy in the camera department.

"I heard a rumour that the casting agent from LA is making the hooker chicks sleep with her for speaking parts," Steven said.

This seemed like very confidential, high-level gossip and Garry appreciated it. "Wow, a casting couch. I feel like Hollywood now."

"I could never be a casting agent."

"They don't get a lot of credit, but the right cast means a lot."

"And the wrong one, too." They shared an insider's smile over that. "Turning all those people down, breaking so many hearts. I couldn't do it. I'd want to hire everyone."

"So you're the reason Heather Graham keeps getting work."

It was dark when they left the restaurant and Garry's stomach was all tied up again. He didn't know if Steven would flag down a cab or say good night or what. They walked back through Riverdale until Steven stopped under a big willow tree in front of a small house.

He said, "So, getting me to read your script and getting together to talk about it? Was that just a way to ask me on a date without having to ask in case I said no?"

"You got me. I write whole screenplays just to avoid asking for dates."

Steven smiled. "So you do care what I think?"

Too quickly Garry said, "Yeah." Then he slowed down. "I mean, sure. You know, you work in the movies, you know movies."

"I know Wardrobe."

Garry didn't say anything. They looked at each other. Inside, Garry felt like he wanted to scream and yell and jump up and down and pound his fists into car hoods.

But he stood there, perfectly still.

Steven pulled him close, gently, and kissed him on the lips. They wrapped their arms around each other. They pulled out of the kiss slowly and Steven whispered, his mouth so close to Garry's ear that his hot breath tickled, "Okay, so let's call this a first date."

Garry stood on the curb watching Steven walk up the short path to the front steps of the house and disappear behind the door. He waited for a moment, till a light came on inside and then he turned and started walking down the sidewalk. His face felt strange. Then he realized that it was because he had such a huge grin on his face. He started to run. He jumped as high as he could and ripped some leaves off a maple tree. He spun around in a circle when he hit the ground and kept running.

Three blocks later he realized he had no idea where he was. He started laughing. The best location scout in the city, the guy who can find anything you need, any alley or storefront or sleazy motel room or mansion or library or hospital or you name it—this guy knows every inch of the city and now he's lost!

Yeah, lost maybe, but not alienated or lonely or unable to communicate. This is no Canadian movie.

THE CAMERA TRAINEE

In her inner movie—free from compromise, collaboration, and audience—he slipped through space in luxurious slow motion and into the doorway, against her. His body, masculine energy and weight, pressed her into someone's rusty mailbox. It had been weeks, every second of it. Her eyes closed, watching inside, kissing wet and dry, his stubble at her cherry lipstick, tongues electric. Her perfume tangled with his cologne. Orange fingernails tugged at his shirt. Short, jagged ones dug for her nipples through the jacket she bought three years ago at Le Chateau. The one she had tried to patch when she was high. It had been weeks, and his cock grew inside his only clean pair of jeans. Eyes closed, soft smile, she watched in close-up as her hand left his ass and cupped his dick. He broke off. Breathing hard. Eyes open. He smiled.

"Wanna go to a party?"

The corner of her mouth twitched into a smile. "I thought that was the whole point."

There was a stream of people, dressed up and down, coming both ways along Richmond Street, coming up to the heavyset guy with the light wand waving them past the DGC sandwich board. There was an official name for the biannual Directors' Guild of Canada event, but to all the accountants, art directors, production managers, assistant directors, picture editors, sound editors, location managers, and yes, even directors, who are all members of the Guild, the party was referred to as FREE BOOZE. And tonight, and tonight only, they came. From the suburbs and beyond. From all the trendy low-rent parts of town. With names like Parkdale. The Annex. Young and Eg. College Street. They filled the subways and the highways and the sidewalks. Meeting in groups at the Second Cups and the Chapters, and since Future's Bakery had become a fern bar, the last of the self-conscious anti-corps found themselves in the Queen Mother, Friar and Firkin, or the Tequila Bookworm. An hour before the time printed on the counterfeit-secure invite, you couldn't find parking closer than Bathurst. And this was a Wednesday. Nellie and Simon joined the flow, her inner movie sweeping them along with a breathtaking overhead crane shot of the crowd. In one immaculate take past the checkpoints of waving light wands at the alley's damp mouth. It was now or never and you were past the warehouses and offices whose outsides were a hundred years older than the Ikea lighting and iMacs inside. Adrenaline heartbeats of drum and bass rose from a pulse of anticipation to a deep throb, guiding the way to a nameless nightclub so hip you could never find it on your own.

The crowd pressed Simon against Nellie. She didn't mind. She tugged at her skirt hem with one hand and Simon's elbow with the other. The invites were checked with black light by two thin girls. Perfect casting, the type of girls who hated their bodies enough to want to be models but couldn't play the game. Through the door, still in one smooth camera move, past the keening coat check line. And the world opened up into a single dimension of nightclub.

The nightclub air—that mix of drunk, sweat, and cigarette—washed over them. They hadn't gotten far when their momentum stalled against the flood of people around the nearest bar. Flirtation sparked everywhere. Meaningful glances between strangers as skin brushed skin.

He left her. She caught eyes until he returned with the booze, two Melon Balls held safely above his head. There was music cascading through her soul— dragging her body and therefore Simon into the trembling flesh of the dance floor. Dancing blended with foreplay.

"Don't forget your pager." Simon's voice was a buzzing in her ear. She flashed him her pager, plastic neon in her palm.

"When did he say he'll call?" Simon shook his head and leaned in closer.

"What?" she screamed in his ear.

Simon grinned a helpless shrug. "Just keep an eye on your pager." She never heard him. Instead, she stepped into a break in the crowd behind her. Eyes closed. Hands, head, body, waist, hips, legs helpless in the music and the cocaine buzz.

Wonderfully lost.

Simon pulled Nellie back to him. He pointed to a girl, unnaturally thin, who smoothed out a ripple of female challenge on her sequined dress. Strapless, it hung on her small breasts and tightened itself around her waist before allowing her anemic legs to drop to the floor. Deep black hair shining in the half-light danced over her face. Clutched at her shoulders. Deep blue nails held a drink to her cosmetically wet lips. "This is Debs," in Nellie's ear. "She's the TAD on set." Debs' eyes flashed hello. "This is Nellie," in Debs' ear.

"Hello, Nellie," Debs screeched. Her eyes rolled and laughed at dance floor introductions. "This is my boyfriend." Glitter snowed onto the dance floor, stars lost in the indoor sky. The crowd cheered, and his name was lost forever. He joined the list of people known only as "so-and-so's boyfriend" to Nellie and "that guy she's fucking" to Simon. Debs turned to her boyfriend. "Simon's the Second Art Director on my show," into his ear. He nodded tightly and everyone knew he wasn't in the industry.

Debs smirked at Simon, and leaned in close. Simon shook his head, pointed Nellie at the bar. "There's our Location department." Nellie had heard the stories. The tall older guy she tagged as Morton. Called himself MoGib. The gay guy beside him, dressed up in his mesh shirt, must be his scout, What's-His-Name. Simon waved his beer bottle, and shouted in Nellie's ear.

"They have no idea we're making a fucking film. Gave me a long speech about 'check with me before you do your graphics.' 'Cause no, we don't want to piss off our locations. Maybe if he didn't use the same locations in every Hollywood movie he wouldn't be so worried about their goodwill. You know?"

Nellie watched the little group at the bar. The older guy, Morton, looked a little out of place, but the younger mesh shirt guy and the girls beside him looked like they were having a good time with their white wine.

"The chick with the short dark hair is Lenore Halmen. She's the commercial director hack they got for second unit." Simon turned away, and laughed with Debs about something, and Nellie was sick of wasting her high on this office gossip shit.

"Wanna hit the bathroom with me, Debs?" Nellie invited Debs with a tilt of her head. Debs was shrugging to her guy as she slipped off after Nellie.

The music assaulted the bright, white quiet with waves of wall-shaking bass. The bathroom was packed. Nellie grabbed at Debs. Pulled her into a stall. Slammed the door in the face of the next-in-line to the girl's "What the fuck?"

Debs smile was unsure. Until Nellie pulled out the powder and the playing card. Debs laughed. "I came to pee."

"Oh, come on." Nellie's eyes were on the coke. "Eighties retro is back."

Debs stuffed a hand deep into her tiny backpack, and lit a ciggy with a skinny lighter. "You gonna join us on set?"

"I'm waiting for the call." Nellie pulled the snipped-down drinking straw from her jacket, held it out for Debs. "My big break."

Debs considered the straw. "At least that fuckup Carl is gone." She took the straw. "I haven't done coke since high school." She leaned over the john and took the line easy in one smooth motion. She pulled at her nose—the smile hit her face. She was gorgeous when she was high. Her eyes lit up, and her skin went flush, and Nellie took the rest thinking, that's why. Why Simon was so eager to hook up with Debs here. They left the stall with Debs' ciggy floating in the bowl.

Upstairs, the crowd had its back to sofa chairs tucked in a corner. To Nellie's eyes the special skills extras parted to let the camera float through them on a Steadi-cam handheld rig; the edges of the frame floated like they should. Bloody light shimmered from sculpted candle flames. Beer bottles, empty glasses, and dead cigarettes covered the liquid table between them. Debs handed out another round of precious Camels. The nightclub's acoustics allowed for conversation here.

"I really really really hope I get it." Nellie sucked deeply on her American cig, the nicotine sharp on her tongue and between her teeth, then delicious in her bloodstream with the booze and the coke. She talked on the next inhale. "To work with Franz fucking Woceski? My fucking god."

On the chair across from Nellie, Debs bobbed her head. "They screened *The Ways of Man* at Ryerson when I was there."

"Did you see it?" Simon's smirk made Nellie giggle. Knowing what was coming.

Debs' laugh spit out her ciggy. "Are you kidding?" She reached limply for the cigarette. "It's over three hours long!" She got her cigarette and spilt her drink. "Shit…" The funniest thing any of them had seen and there had been lots of that.

"Three hours?" Debs' guy forced out.

"Over…" Debs lost it and snorted. Even funnier.

Nellie recovered. Yelled, "Okay, go!" Four drinks went down, ice vanished over cheeks and onto the floor. Nellie was last, and that made her Drink Girl.

Debs' boyfriend crunched his ice. Pointed his stir stick at Nellie. "Did you see this guy's movie?"

Nellie knew Simon was laughing at her. "Everyone says how good it is."

"But not one person has seen it!" Simon was triumphant. He had been pushing this joke since pre-production.

"Fuck off." She pushed him back into his seat.

"What?" Like he was surprised. He knew her well enough. "Anyway, don't you have drinks to get, Drink Girl?"

Nellie stood. Stepped into her balance. Drifted off towards a memory of the nearest bar. Behind her Simon said, "Did you tell him about the driver that's fucking Ainsley Riordan?" Another of Simon's favourites.

Nellie compared the guys at the bar to Simon. They parted to let her belly up. When the drinks came, she was still talking with her hand on the arm beside her.

Then there was someone else behind her. Simon. "What are you doing?" She leaned hard on her drunkenness.

"Talking."

The guy beside her. "Hey, buddy…"

"Whatever. Where's your pager, Nell?" It all left her. Her hand jumped up to her mouth, and her stomach rotted. Her inner ear wanted the floor to keep still. Through her nausea and vertigo Simon held her pager to her face. "It almost jumped off the table when it went off. You're lucky to have such a kind, considerate..." He stopped in time. "Date."

Her eye glowed in the pager's light. "I need a phone. Omygod I need a phone."

"Calm down, Nell."

Wild now. The floor dropped out from under her. The chasers and strobes and mirror balls and smoke revealed nothing but the guy beside her laughing. The bartender shrugged and swept her tips into her apron with peppermint fingernails. Debs was behind Simon. "You need my cell? Here, use my cell."

"Thank you, thank you." Nellie snatched the phone.

Debs waved for drinks. "You better call soon. First one in gets the gig." Sipping her martini, she missed Nellie's "no shit, Sherlock" smirk.

The phone took its time. She squinted at the sickly green digital hieroglyphics. "No service."

Debs' boyfriend offered his. Nellie stabbed the power button. Now she would have to get his name. From the phone an angry beep. "No service!"

The guy Debs is fucking was confused. "Really?"

A guy at the bar twisted unnaturally. Sticking to his bad boy lean. "The metal." He stroked the air above with an outstretched finger. They followed his point to the trendy, unfinished I-beam ceiling.

"Nellie!" Simon called after her. She was long into the crowd. Through conversations and things more physical. The next day at slow, mid-afternoon brunches all over the Golden Horseshoe she was going to be that crazy girl with the braids. An arctic icebreaker spilling drinks and ruining dresses. Through the crowd. Across the mezzanine. She made the stairs. Halfway down. She hit the dance floor edge, where the uncool and the too-cool mixed on the fringe. She stalled. Simon caught up. There was a pair of speakers dangling from black chains overhead. Talking was wasted and she could feel the lack of signal. A tingling of absence. An alternative sense that film couldn't do. The air was hot—stale. Hard to breathe. Outside was fresh air. Outside was cell signal. All you'd ever want. CN Tower broadcasted wireless digital coverage. By the time she saw the shock on Simon's face she was already in mid-air.

Part of her would always be there, frozen on that single frame of 35mm Kodak 800 "S" Vision T, not a hint of grain, deep focus, a colour timer's boner as he played with the balance of the hues and the density of the shadows. Composed in full aspect, TV safe zones ignored. Nothing compromised to the pale electronic reflection of video. Only the chemical accident of light reacting with silver and salt, as if etched on time itself. Suspended in jelly. Perfect. Forever.

She came down on shoulders, cigarettes, booze, beer, shouts. She hit hard. Debs' fucking boyfriend's cell slid from her numb hand. A hand closed on her, then she was dangling from the grip.

"Are you crazy?" The bouncer's mint-fresh breath choked her. "What's with you people?"

Around them people recovered. Rubbing tomorrow's bruises and smoothing clothes. "She should pay for my beer."

"It's already free," the bouncer yelled. The crowd laughed, pleased to have a new victim. The bouncer headed for the door. Nellie suspended from his grip.

"My phone!" The feet it vanished into receded.

"I'm never working one of these Guild parties again." Another bouncer joined them, and helped carry Nellie. They were through the dance floor. Past the coat check. And out the door into the night.

"Go home." She was dumped into the cold cement of the worst night of her life. She stumbled out of the twisting alley. Through the trickle of late arrivals. Out on Richmond. Her skin goosebumped in a baptism of cold and microwave cellphone signal. Leaning out over the nightclubs, offices, condos, restaurants, movie theatres, was the Tower. Blinking at low-flying aircraft and Nellie. Central hub of the cellphone network. Without a cell, she spun. Thinking violently of a pay phone.

And there was Simon. In her inner movie a wind machine ran its invisible fingers through his hair. Slow motion. Confident. Heroic. The music cue was the one that sold the sound track album. Behind him the cross-armed bouncers were blurry. Beyond the narrow field of focus. Just Simon, with two jackets, a smile, and a cellphone.

It just took a second to dial and a sleepy voice answered, low and French. "Oh," the First Camera Assistant said. "I had almost given up on you, and gone down the list. Sorry it's so late."

"That's okay, that's okay. It's not late. That's fine. Yeah."

"Simon talked to you?"

"Yeah, fine. Simon. Fine." What the hell? Her face was hot.

"You've done commercials?"

"And music videos."

"C'est ça. You want the job?"

"I'll be the best trainee you ever had."

"Just be better than that fuck-up Carl." He yawned. "Simon's got a call sheet, yeah? Don't worry about the pre-call, unless you want breakfast. I know it's late, can you be there by eight?"

She looked at her watch. Almost 1:30 a.m. She was drunk. High. An hour from home. Simon had brought a change of clothes. And she was looking down the barrel of her big break into the majors.

"Fuck, yeah!"

THE TRANSPORT CAPTAIN

Linda Grigette's arrival had no effect on the production. Week four, and it was still a mess. Any crew member who could get work on something else took it.

Roger thought about doing it himself. He'd been offered a three-month job that would take him right through the summer. Big period piece, shooting mostly up in Muskoka. Driving her back to the hotel, he told Ainsley he was considering it.

"What?"

"Get me right through the summer."

"Sure, but... I thought you didn't like the big shows, same people week after week."

"That's right, I said that, didn't I?"

"Yes."

"It is getting a little awkward here, though, isn't it?"

"Why, because there's gossip? That bothers you?"

"No." They pulled up in front of the Sutton Place.

"Maybe it's the trucker in you, makes you restless."

"How do you know? Oh yeah, your uncle was a trucker."

"That's right. You remembered. When I was a kid he used to bring me gifts from truck stops. Salt and pepper shakers in the shape of cactuses."

"I think I've been to that stop."

"He could never settle down."

"I don't think that's it."

"No?" Ainsley got out of the car and walked into the hotel.

What was it then?

Back at the production office the place was nearly empty, just a couple of PAs sending faxes and MoGib sleeping on the couch. Roger walked down the hall towards his office and slowed as he heard voices from Nijar's office.

"Because this shit doesn't work." Tough guy Myles Day. With the soft hands.

Nijar said, "It works fine. It just needs to be tightened up a little."

"It could be as tight as your asshole, honey, it wouldn't help this crap."

Roger stood in the hallway and thought, actors, they're soooo tough. The door opened and Charles, the technical advisor, came out. He nodded at Roger and kept going.

Through the open door, Roger saw the producer, Renée, nod at Myles Day. Then she looked at Edward Nijar and said, "When Spellman gets here, honey, he'll clear this up in no time."

Roger felt a tap on his shoulder and turned around to see Judy Nemeth. She led him away and waited until they were a ways down the hall before she said, "We'll need another driver. The writer's coming to town."

He said, "Okay, no problem," although he knew for a fact that it'd be a problem. The whole city was crewing up and everyone who was any good was already working.

"What is it?"

"What do you mean?"

"You look worried about something."

"No, just… How experienced does the driver have to be?"

"Hell, not at all. It's just the writer."

"Okay, fine. We'll need another Crown Vic."

Judy laughed. "I said it was the *writer*. We're only getting him a driver so he won't get lost. Get him a Focus." She glanced back at the room where the argument was still raging. "Make it mid-size, a Taurus, something like that, nothing bigger."

"Okay. When's he getting in?"

"Who?"

"The writer."

"Oh, right. Tomorrow." She handed him a fax with the flight details, then leaned back against a desk and looked at Roger.

"Everything going okay?"

"Yeah, fine."

"I'm sorry I butted in with you and Ainsley. You're right, she's an adult."

"Yeah, but she is a movie star."

"She's doing great, though."

"Yeah?"

They stared at one another for a moment. It grew more awkward. Finally Judy said, "I might be coming back up in September with another production."

"Sounds good."

"If you're available."

"Yeah, sure."

A day ago Roger would have pursued this for professional and personal reasons, but now he just wanted to get out of there.

"Okay, well, I better find us a driver."

"Right."

"Right."

Judy continued to lean against the desk, holding a bunch of files in her arms. She watched as Roger went to the end of the hall and disappeared down the stairs towards the Transport office.

At the small desk he rarely used, Roger picked up the phone and took a long shot. He called Vicki, a real pro, who would never be available on such notice, and left a message. He made a few more calls, left a few more messages and was about to leave the office when the phone rang.

"It's your lucky day, pardner."

"Vicki?"

"I just became available."

"I figured you'd be on some huge fucking show."

"Yeah, I would have been driving J Lo by now, but I stayed in Cuba too long. Have you seen those beaches?"

"I've got this thing about tourist beaches with armed guards keeping the locals away."

"White sand, blue water, tequila. You should try it."

"Can you start tomorrow?"

"*Life and Death in Little Italy*... Which stud do I get?"

"The writer."

"Wow, is the show in that much trouble?"

"No, everything's fine."

"You're practically finished shooting and they called in the writer?"

"It's just script bullshit. The show's running fine."

"What did I ever do to you, Rog?"

"You came in late."

"The writer. Wow, a chauffeur-driven Escort."

"Mid-size. Pick it up at the Budget on King, across from the—"

"Business Depot, I know the drill. What flight is the writer on?" He gave her the details and hung up.

As Roger was walking down the hall he heard Myles yelling again. Something about the arc of the character. "My guy knows what he's doing at this point."

Charles was leaning on the wall outside the office, a cup of coffee in his hand and a tired expression on his face.

"Your guy doesn't know shit since Frankie started sleeping with Melodi."

Charles looked up at the ceiling and shook his head.

Roger nodded sympathetically as he passed.

LIFE AND DEATH IN LITTLE ITALY
2ND UNIT CALL SHEET

Italy Productions Inc.
Production Office:
345 Carlaw Ave.,
Suite 317, Toronto, Ont. M4M 2T1
Tel: 416.463-1266 Fax: 416.463-1950
Set Cell: 416.526-3516

Exec. Producer: Cathy Koyle
Producer: Renée Jato
Line Producer: Judith Nemeth
2nd Unit Director: Lenore Halmen
2nd Unit 1st A.D.: Amanda Vuldune

UNIT CALL: 2000
DATE: Tuesday April 30, 2002

(see early/special calls on reverse)

Location: Victoria/Richmond

2nd Unit Shoot Day: 4
Lunch: 0200 @ 7 Richmond
Weather: Cloudy
Hi: 7 Lo: 3

SCENE	SET DESCRIPTION	D/N	CAST	PAGES
61c	OUTSIDE APARTMENT Car goes boom	N5	A,B	1/8
				TOTAL PAGES: 1/8

BACKGROUND PERFORMERS		P/U	H/W/M	BLKG	SET
A	Melodi	OWN	2200	TBA	2300
B	Mario Photo Double	OWN	2200	TBA	2300

PRODUCTION NOTES

SPECIAL EFFECTS CREW:
On Set @ Call

LOCATIONS:
On Set @ 1730
PDO x 4 on set @ Call
ETF x 2 on set @ 2300

PRODUCTION:
Ambulance w/ paramedics x 2 on set @ Call

TRANSPORT:
Hot and Ready @ 1900
Water Trucks Standing by @ Call
Stunt Car x 3 @ Call

CRAFT SERVICE:
Hot and Ready   @ 1915
Early Breakfast x 15 @ 1945
Subs x 27   @ 2300

FIRST AID KIT / SAFETY GUIDELINE BOOK LOCATED AT CRAFT SERVICE
2nd Unit LOC Mgr: Lyle Peterson (H) 658-9849 2nd Unit Trans Cap' t: Wendy Rocks (C) 543-6532

THE SECOND UNIT DIRECTOR

It was already three hours after call, and the union-mandated substantial snack was going around. Lenore ran a loose set and it drove Judy and Amanda crazy. Lenore could never really get them to understand—it was only second unit. If the shot was all that important, they would have gotten the main unit on it. She slumped deeper into her chair and looked around at her crew. The electrics were still cabling up the three mighty Condor crane lights that would backlight the rain, if the effects guys ever got the rain towers rigged. Lenore had overheard they sent someone to open the shop and bring more hose. The stunts team was eating Pat's grilled cheese off the back of the Craft truck. "You need it on a cold night," Pat told her when he brought over the foil-wrapped tray of wilting fried sandwiches. She had peeked inside and shook her head. The blonde local talent playing Melodi and an ex-boxer stand-in for Myles were gulping down grilled cheese and gallons of coffee and complaining about night shoots, second unit, and film in general. Actors, Lenore sniffed her runny nose. Just another reason she would never direct main unit.

Amanda came over with her schedule. "We're going over tonight." Amanda had been in the business for a fair number of years. She could be First AD on more main units, she was good enough, but nobody liked her. That included Lenore.

"All we're here to do is get the shot," Lenore said. "And we'll get the shot and go home." Amanda looked at her watch. Lenore knew she'd be on the phone to Judy, even though Judy was on days with main unit, and needed her sleep. "Can I see tomorrow's call sheet, Amanda?" It was an official way of asking Amanda to fuck off and leave her alone. Amanda didn't miss it, but there wasn't much she could do about it either.

Amanda grumbled to Pat as she stalked back to the AD's trailer. Lenore's cellphone rang. Why couldn't she figure out how to reprogram the ring? Did Nokia really think she would want that ring? She flipped open her new phone, and poked at it until she found the right button. It was the overnight guy at The Lab. He was running her footage through the tank, and…

Lenore stopped breathing. "Is any of it usable?" Fuck, it was cold out. The wind off Shuter cut through the parking lot. The Effects guys swore as they got their hands wet hooking up the hoses. Lenore's mind closed off the set. A reshoot would mean digging up more film stock, getting her niece out of school again, driving to the cottage.

The overnight guy went on. He didn't panic. It wasn't his footage. "It's out of focus, grainy, the contrast's shot, the speed comes and goes."

Lenore released the air from her lungs with a whoop that stopped the work around her.

"Neil, you dope. That's how I shot the fucking thing! You scared the shit out of me." Neil laughed. The fucker was kidding. Lenore ground her teeth and Neil brought up the money. "I don't get the grant money for another couple of days," she said. Just like she had told Kodak. And the film co-op. And just about every other film shop around town. You weren't supposed to start shooting until you got the money, but those arts administrators and bureaucrats didn't know shit about what went into one of Lenore's films. Thank god she knew everyone on the peer evaluation committee. She exchanged goodbyes with the overnight guy and got Big Frank to show her how to hang up her phone.

John came trotting over. Lenore smiled at him. On the call sheet, he was listed as Second Unit Key Grip. But this second unit crew was relaxed enough that he was more of a swing—helping the electrics with their lighting.

"The Condors're almost rigged," he said. His dull brown dreads shifted around his head in a single mass, and Lenore had a magical moment where they seemed to be getting at his coffee. From under all the hair came the usual radio chatter that meant a film crew at work. John shrugged into his heavy blue film parka. A lot of the guys were wearing them. John had been Best Boy Grip on *Samurai, the Series*, a step below his position on Lenore's crew, but that had been main unit. *Samurai*'s producers had cursed Toronto's winters and sworn they would move to Vancouver next year. If they got their Telefilm money again.

"I got my boys helpin'." John laughed and did a little shuffle step. "You shoulda heard Philly." John mimicked the Best Boy Grip's whine. "If I had wanted to be an electric, I woulda dropped out of grade school and married my mother." Lenore laughed. That's why she liked John.

"I bet Omid's boys had something to say about that," Lenore said, and John nodded his head in absolute agreement, his dreads bobbing and weaving with their own laughter. "We're in no hurry tonight," she told him. "It's only second unit." She wasn't exactly sure how she meant it, but John took it in his usual good nature. He was about to go on when his hand went to his radio, and his gaze shifted to somewhere behind her. Lenore politely looked away.

"No," John said loudly into his radio. He had a different voice when he was talking to his boys. That was when they called him boss. He listened another second. "No," he said again sharply. "I said get the pee-wee off the fucking truck. Why would we send it back to White's when we fucking use it every goddamn night? Get it off the truck means have it standing by set, not to fucking send it packing!" He listened again. Lenore could hear the grip trying to explain.

She looked around the set. The crew was enjoying this, everyone with a walkie tuned to the grips' channel seven and chuckling at the poor daily grip at the other end. John stalked away. "You got shit for brains, Lester," he said as he went. People laughed, and went back to work.

Lenore sighed. "That's life in the big shitty," she said to herself. It was one of Rose's favourites. Thinking of Rose brought a smile to her face and made the cold April night a little less so—until Lenore began to miss her again.

The Condors were up and the HMI lights sparked, casting their triple blue-white glow across the parking lot. Lenore and Little Frank, the "A" camera operator, blocked out the shot, placed the three cameras, and walked through the safety with stunts and the talent. Little Frank had emerged from the camera truck when called, and his mouth was thick with beer. Lenore wondered if she'd have the energy to talk to him about it at the end of the day. Anne-Marie, the blonde local, looked very nervous and didn't say much in the safety. Lenore took her aside.

"Have you done a lot of stunt work?" Lenore watched Anne-Marie closely. Anne-Marie sipped her coffee and cupped her hands around its warmth.

"I'll be fine," Anne-Marie said—which answered Lenore's question without meaning to. "It's these shoes," Anne-Marie went on, showing Lenore the high heels that came with her terrible clichéd hooker wardrobe. "These damned shoes. How can I do a stunt in these fucking shoes? You people are trying to kill me!" Her voice was rising, and Lenore just wanted to slap her. Actors.

"Let's see what Wardrobe can do," Lenore soothed her. Lenore keyed her radio, and got Amanda to take Anne-Marie back to the Wardrobe truck. On main unit, Amanda would have got a trainee to do that. Lenore felt a bit of satisfaction that Amanda had to do it herself.

Stunts and effects worked on the car, the fresh paint dripping on them as they crawled under it. Lenore sank back into her chair and yawned as Big Frank came over, frowning at his continuity reports.

"I don't see this scene in the script," Big Frank told her in his slow voice. "What scene is it?" He flipped through, looking for it until Lenore stopped him.

"It's not in the script." Commercials are so much easier, she thought. Why didn't she take the commercial? Was the extra money for these second unit gigs worth it?

"What do you mean, it's not in the script?" Big Frank smiled and closed his clipboard. "How do I do the reports?"

"Why don't you give production a call?" Lenore said. Problem solved. Better—it was passed on. A slo-mo shot of laundry detergent bouncing on plump towels had to be better than this. With Big Frank looking for the set cell to call the office, Lenore closed her eyes and the crew let her nap.

Her cell rang. Why couldn't she reprogram that ring? The caller's voice was low, quiet, and not at all what Jason usually sounded like. He asked her if she'd checked her mail.

"I spent the day at LIFT again," Lenore told him. "Yeah, the film co-op. Step printing on the JK optical printer. I haven't been home for more than six hours a day in weeks." Jason breathed a cigarette loudly into the phone, and didn't answer.

"You'll get the grant," she said. "You know what, though? Even if you don't, you can use the same package for the Canada Council deadline in June…" She was being kind to him, of course. The Arts Councils generally didn't support short films about vampires, but Jason was a nice guy.

"I'm sure I'll get mine," she told him, trying not to sound arrogant, but knowing she was failing completely. "I've never missed an Ontario Arts Council application." Another pause, another burst of cigarette on the other end. Jason wanted to know what her film was about—listless, but not wanting to let the phone call go. She felt bad for him, but arts grants aren't for everyone. Make some money, shoot it yourself. But she had learned from past mistakes and lost friends, so she kept this advice to herself.

"My 16mm black-and-white five-minute experimental documentary uses visual metaphors to explore the emotions surrounding the artist's first sexual experience with a man, and contrasting that with the artist's first sexual experiences with a woman." She hadn't meant to quote verbatim from her proposal, but it came with practiced ease. Jason was quiet a second, and then quickly ended the phone call, leaving Lenore with the distinct impression he had been about to ask her out. Poor guy—he was almost as sweet as he was oblivious.

She found the end button, and when she looked up she saw Max and Jeremy waiting for her. They stepped forward when she was off the phone, and exchanged complaints about the weather, about second unit, and about film in general.

"I hear de main unit be days an' days behin'." Jeremy laughed. "Dey be callin' we up with dem long hands, askin' we t'bail dem out." Lenore had worked with him before. The short Jamaican was one of the best Special Effects guy in town, and he had the chip on his shoulder to prove it. Lenore had yet to figure out what his problem was.

"They let Myles Day have script approval," Lenore said, "and things went downhill from there."

"You read the script?" Max asked. He was the Stunt Key tonight, and by all accounts enjoying being boss. He sipped his coffee and watched her response carefully. Lenore had seen that look many times before—it was hard to miss in an industry where the ladies usually still worked in the "Pretty Departments," Hair, Make-up, and Wardrobe. Lenore ignored it. She was too tired to care. And at the end of the day, it wasn't her film. Thank god.

"There's not really a script these days," she said. "But you can check with Amanda. Maybe there's double yellow script pages."

Jeremy snorted. "Dey don' pay me ta seet around an' read. Dey say blow up de car, me blow up de car, mon." Lenore felt like she should say something, except she agreed with him.

"What do you guys need?" Lenore asked. She already knew—they hadn't really paid attention during the blocking. They all walked out to the car again. They wouldn't be pulling this shit with a man, she thought as they went through it. Once she got her grant, she wouldn't need another job for a while. No bigots for a few months.

A test spurt came from the rain towers. Lenore's screech was echoed and multiplied by the guys working on rigging the car. Jeremy stalked off, yelling at his boys for getting him wet. Lenore, knowing there was no way he'd be back to finish the blocking, retreated to "A" camera. Safe under a tarp. Max raised his arms, announced his defeat to his world, and headed for the music coming from the camera truck. Lenore had Locations bring her chair to her under the camera tarp and sat down beside the camera trainee, a thin Ryerson grad who knew how to giggle and smile and look cute when she made a mistake. Lenore wondered why there were so many groovy downtown camera trainee girls and so few camera women. But only to make herself laugh. The camera trainee sat on an empty lens case behind the Panaflex camera, smiled sweetly, and Lenore found her very easy to talk to.

"That's lunch!" Amanda's voice cut through the radio, and all over the set voices called out, "Lunch!" "Put that down, that's lunch." The camera crew spilled out of the camera truck, flopping across the parking lot's concrete surface, and rushing into the tent Locations had built over the caterers. The camera trainee looked after them wistfully, stuck behind on fire watch, the camera gear more important than she was. Lenore promised to make sure they would bring her something, and headed for the tent herself. Amanda caught up to her midway.

"So, my lunch report's going to say nothing shot," Amanda told her. "That's going to wind up on Judy's desk in the morning."

"We've only got the one shot," Lenore reminded her sharply. Sometimes, some rare times, Lenore enjoyed being the boss. Amanda pushed her thick glasses on more firmly.

"We should have done at least one take before lunch," Amanda kept on. "Every take is a half hour to rig." By this time they had reached the din of the lunch tent. Lenore was able to slip away. Movie lunch rooms always struck Lenore as feudal. There was a routine to the hierarchy, and the PA who got her lunch before the DP wouldn't be back on set the next day. Lenore fed her bad mood with politeness, and spent the next five minutes refusing to allow those in front of her to give up their place in line. Her game ended when she said, "I wonder what Karl Marx would have said about the film industry." A few people stiffened, fewer laughed politely, and all turned away from her, concentrating on the difference between the tofu and the chicken lasagna. Movie people, Lenore thought as she took her lunch back to her trailer.

After lunch, things didn't move any more quickly. Amanda paced and looked at her watch. "Four takes now, and we go over," Amanda told her. "Should we let production know? Hold the call sheet for a push?" Lenore rolled her eyes and just shook her head.

"We're almost there." There was no way Lenore was staying late. She had JK time booked at LIFT in the morning.

Another hour, and the Effects crew passed the word that the car was rigged. The camera crews were coaxed, then threatened out of the camera truck, Little Frank taking his beer with him to the camera. The camera trainee powered up Lenore's monitor, and smiled cutely at her before turning to flirt with the focus puller. Amanda got Locations to lock up the parking lot.

"This is a dangerous stunt," she yelled over the walkie. "Nobody comes closer than 50 feet to the car. Copy, Locations?" Lenore watched as Anne-Marie came out with her flatter shoes, and Max put her on her mark. The double for Myles Day, a local named Justin, stood by "B" camera and waited to run to her rescue. The focus pullers from all three camera positions ran around with measuring tapes.

"You shoulda been doing that during the blocking!" Amanda yelled at them.

"Nobody told us the fuckin' blocking was up!" some anonymous silhouette shot back. Little Frank looked up from the eyepiece.

"We gotta move," he said. Lenore gave him a hard look. Little Frank pointed at the camera. "Take a look. We gotta move five feet over." Lenore bent down and peered through the ground level camera. Little Frank was right, the balance in the composition was off. Anne-Marie was too close to the fence gate from this angle.

Lenore keyed her radio. "Stunts."

"Go for Stunts," Max answered her.

"What do you think about moving Anne-Marie 10 feet in?"

There was a moment of silence. "Move her closer to the car?"

"Yeah. Ten feet. That good?" Lenore listened carefully to the radio. It was Max's call, she told herself. It was all his call now.

"Yeah, let's move her in," Max said, and moved out to reblock Anne-Marie. Lenore smiled down at Little Frank, who checked the frame.

"That did it," he reported. The camera assistants went back out, got their focus measurements again, and scurried back under the tarps. They were professionals, and no one wanted to get wet.

Lenore nodded to Amanda and sipped her coffee in front of the one monitor. Why didn't they have a monitor for each camera? Second unit, that's why.

Amanda yelled into her radio, "All right, picture's up. Lock it up, and I mean lock it up." She paused, and turned to Little Frank, sitting with his eye at the camera. "We already slated?" she asked him. He looked up from the camera, and it took him a second to figure out who was talking.

"Sure," he slurred, and turned back to poke his eye on the camera's eyepiece.

"Fucking drunk camera crew," Amanda muttered to Lenore. She did one final visual check, and then went for it. "Action rain towers!" With a high-pitched spurting sound, it began to rain. Hard. The tarps drummed loudly overhead. The huge HMI lights shining down from the Condor cranes gave each drop a glowing vividness. Lenore leaned forward out of a leak. Anne-Marie got very wet. The fans along Shuter Street threw the rain around the parking lot, and generally made a hell of a lot of noise. Amanda, a good AD, could be heard above it all.

"Roll camera!" she screamed. To those gathered under the "A" camera tarp, the camera's high speed whirring added to the din, capturing the effect in slow motion. Lenore watched the monitor flicker and roll, and then stabilize as the camera found its speed. She waited a moment. Everyone waited on her. And she nodded. "Action."

"Action! Action! Action!" Amanda repeated.

Anne-Marie ran away from the car. Justin ran toward her. The rain pounded them. Lenore held her breath. Everyone held their breaths.

Anne-Marie and Justin met, stopped, and looked awkwardly from the car to where Lenore was sitting. Everyone in the tarp turned to look at her. The car, it was now clear, had no intention of blowing up. "Cut," Lenore muttered. "Cut!" Amanda screamed. "Cut!" echoed around the set. The fans shut off. The rain slowed to a stop. And Jeremy started screaming at his boys.

Amanda reported back to Lenore, "They didn't hook a wire up after lunch." And they set up for take two. Lenore moved her chair away from the leak.

Anne-Marie and Justin found their marks, Justin trying to strut in front of the "B" camera crew. Amanda started to yell again, "Lock it up!" It was locked up. "Action rain towers!" The parking-lot-sized storm returned to life. "Roll camera!" The three cameras whirred. Lenore leaned closer to the monitor, picked her moment, and called, "Action!"

"Action! Action! Action!" Anne-Marie started forward. Justin started forward. And the car whumped into a half-hearted flame that snuck out from under the car.

"Fucking cut!"

Lenore closed her eyes. "Cool blue ocean," she told her crew. "Cool blue ocean." She heard the camera trainee laugh. She heard the cameras shut down. She heard the water towers shut off. She heard Jeremy yelling at people to keep back from the car. And she heard the car blow up, an orgasmic outpouring of superheated air and noise.

Little Frank sat back from the camera, impressed. He nodded at Lenore. "That looked great," he said. "But we have to work on the timing." Lenore bit her lip against her reply, and sank back into her director's chair. The canvas seat was almost completely waterlogged, but it took her almost a minute to notice.

While they were setting up for the next take, John and Omid strolled up to Lenore, as she sipped her fourth coffee since lunch.

"We goin' over, sweetie, or not?" Omid asked, scratching his head.

"Not." Short and to the point, she thought with satisfaction. It was very late in the night, or very early in the morning, and time to be straight and to the point.

"'Cause I gotta sub off my guys up top," Omid reminded her in his singsong voice. "If we go over, I gotta sub them off."

"You can keep your boys in the cranes, Omid." Lenore's tone was low. Dangerous. "We won't go over."

Whatever John had to add, he didn't. He and Omid backed away from Lenore, slowly, nodding agreement, John's single mass of hair unnaturally still.

Lenore's phone beeped. Confused, she had to blink a few times to make out the green text, "One Missed Call." It was Rose, calling from home. It must have come during the last take, and she had missed it. Just like she had missed Rose's calls all day. Lenore got Big Frank to show her how to stop it from beeping.

"I've written those two takes up as no good," he said, showing her his reports. Lucky for him, Lenore caught the joke right away. What else could they have been?

The word came out that the next car was rigged and ready. The camera crews staggered out from the camera truck, and Lenore promised herself a cappuccino and a harsh talk with Little Frank. He sat heavily on the stool beside the camera and hunched over it.

"You sure you're about ready there, Frank?" Lenore asked him.

"Rock'n'roll, baby," he answered. He didn't look up, so Lenore wasn't sure if he had caught her sarcasm. But the camera trainee laughed. Amanda leaned in close to Lenore.

"We don't make this shot, we go into overtime," Amanda told her. "Should I get production to bring in second meal?"

"Call it," Lenore told Amanda. Short and to the point. No way was she going home late. Unless, of course, they didn't make this shot.

"First positions!" Amanda yelled into the radio, mostly at Anne-Marie, who continued to sip her coffee and flirt with Pat. "Anne-Marie! Let's go. First position." Anne-Marie made a big deal about handing her coffee to Pat, who promised to bring her a new one. A big part of the Craft Services' job was to make people, even people who really shouldn't matter, feel like they were being pampered. The people who did matter had their own staff for that. Anne-Marie walked off into the general direction of her mark. "I'm ready," she announced. Amanda ground her teeth.

"Okay! Lock it up!" Amanda yelled. "Action rain towers!" And the rain came down. "Roll camera!" And the cameras rolled. Everyone waited for Lenore. Waited for the director to feel right about the scene. Lenore, for her part, was wondering if her chair was wetter than her ass, or vice versa. Oh well, she thought, and called, "Action!"

"Action! Action! Action!" Amanda yelled and Anne-Marie and Justin took two steps toward each other when Anne-Marie's flatter shoes slipped out from under her in the wet pavement. She twisted her ankle, and went down.

The car exploded.

WHUMP! And the car rose six feet into the air, propelled on an expanding cloud of flame. The heat rolled over the set. Anne-Marie screamed, and the car held itself for moment in mid-air, indecisive, before it dropped back to the ground with a thud that shook up and down Lenore's spine. Anne-Marie cried out in sheer terror, covering her head. Little bits of liquid fire smacked down around her and flaming debris shot upward from the blast.

"Help me, goddamn you!" Anne-Marie shrieked as she crawled and rolled away from the flames.

Amanda, eyes wide, raised the radio to her mouth, but Lenore held up a hand. She watched the flickering monitor as Little Frank held the shot pure and steady, the camera's eye watching the flames roll out from under the car. Exactly how they were supposed to.

"And...cut!" Perfect.

"Cut!" Amanda yelled. The rain stopped dead. "Get the set nurse out here." But the set nurse was already helping Anne-Marie limp away. Anne-Marie's make-up was streaming down her face.

"I'll sue you," Anne-Marie yelled. "I'll fucking sue you." Amanda raced over. Little Frank leaned back from the camera, and met Lenore's eye. He was smiling. Lenore forgave him all past transgressions and turned to Big Frank and Tony, the clapper/loader.

"That's a good one," she said to them. "Print that." Tony stared at her, his eyes flicking from Lenore's triumphant face to Anne-Marie's torment. Big Frank simply nodded and noted it in his report. Tony did the same. Lenore and Little Frank cheered, and hugged each other close. Celebrations broke out from "B" camera and "C" camera.

"What are they so fucking happy about?" Anne-Marie wanted to know as she was lifted into the stand-by ambulance. Lenore picked her radio up from the back of her chair.

"That's a wrap!" she said into it. "Thanks for the excellent night, everybody." She looked at her watch. "No overtime tonight. Let's clean up and go home." The water trucks hosed down the flaming car, and Anne-Marie still screamed lawsuits from the ambulance. Little Frank cracked a beer. Lenore turned her back on the chaos and walked out from under the tarp, into the damp night air.

A red-faced Max steamed up to her, one angry fist clenched around the radio, and he shook it in her face like it was evidence.

"That's a wrap?" he yelled. "You almost killed that girl. You put her too fucking close. She almost fucking died, and you're calling wrap and walking away?" Lenore turned on him. She was done. Finished. Over with. Going home.

"You're forgetting three things, Max," she said. "And I'm going to tell them to you so you never forget again. One, she was nowhere near qualified to make that stunt. You brought her in. Two, I didn't tell you to move her; it was your call to move her close. You're the stunts guy. It was your call, and you blew it." Max went pale. She was right. Fuck, she thought, who hires these people?

"And three," she said. "Three, we got the shot."

"We got it?"

"We got it."

Max nodded and looked down at his feet. "Well," he tried, "see you tomorrow then?"

But Lenore was already headed off the set, looking for her driver. Around her, her crew was tearing out the location. Lenore knew they would still be at it in another two hours, after she got home. She remembered a time when she would have cared. Her driver found her.

"The name's Jerry," he said as he held her door open.

She tried to sleep on the ride home. She couldn't. She was too keyed up. But she knew that when Judy, Renée, and that New York idiot Nijar saw the rushes, they wouldn't give a shit about what went on tonight. They were second unit, and they got the shot. Jerry made the mistake of starting a conversation.

"So," he said, holding it, drawing the monosyllable out to announce the onset of small talk. "So," he said again. "Do you have another show after this?" Digging for work.

Lenore was fully reclined in the seat beside him. She stared at the dome light. "I'm making an Arts Council film."

"Great," he said, shoulder checking and merging left on Yonge. "Great," he said again. "What about after that?"

Lenore spoke slowly, choosing her words very carefully so as to leave no confusion to their meaning.

"I'm going to wait to get my cheque from the Arts Council, and then I am never going to do another patriarchial, machismo, alpha-male, phallic-symbol-driven, social-role-enabling, mass-culture placebo ever again."

Jerry was quiet while he eased up behind the three cabs sharing the quiet morning street with him. Lenore closed her eyes.

"I know what you mean," he suddenly announced when the light turned green. "I mean, I really liked *Magnolia*."

Lenore was silent for the rest of the trip, and watched the growing glow to the east.

Rose had left the porch light on. The sun was up. Jerry drove off. Lenore could hardly see straight. She dragged herself into the living room and flopped down on the couch. Rose didn't like her to flop on it. Different upbringings. Right there on the coffee table was a large envelope from the Ontario Arts Council. Lenore pulled out the letter from inside. And began to read.

"We would like to take this opportunity to thank you for your application to the Ontario Arts Council's Media Arts Program. We congratulate the following people who received funding:

Michael Brown	$5000.00
Doug Maddeaux	$5000.00
Raymond Huynh	$3500.00
Wayne Boland	$2200.00

Giovanni Camposano	$950.00
Owen Gotovsky	$650.00
Michael Peter Rodriguez	$500.00
Andrew MacRae	$500.00
Phillip Lau	$500.00

Please note that your name may not appear on this list…"

Lenore stopped reading.

She walked numbly to the bedroom, and stood for a moment watching Rose breathe and dream. One of Rose's slender arms covered her eyes, her moist lips and her waxy hair all that was visible. The duvet moved up and down, rhythmically, hypnotically, with her breathing. One leg shot out from under the covers, the foot dangling over the edge of the bed. Everything else was a suggestive lump. Lenore wanted to wake her up, hold her, make love to her.

Instead she gently slid under the covers, softly put her arms around Rose, and snuggled close. Despite her best intentions, Rose stirred.

"How was your night?" Rose asked, only half awake and forgetting about the envelope. Lenore kissed her softly.

"Fine." She shrugged into the pillow. "It's not my film."

THE TRANSPORT CAPTAIN

The water filtration plant on Queen Street East was a great art deco building from the 1930s, perched on a hill overlooking Lake Ontario. It had been used in dozens of movies, almost always as a prison.

The drive to the set was awkward, with neither Roger nor Ainsley wanting to start the conversation.

As soon as they pulled up, Tracy stepped out of Ainsley's Winnie and said, "Did you hear what happened last night?"

"What?"

"Shooting second unit, they were blowing up a car, there was some kind of accident."

Roger said, "Was anyone hurt?"

"A local actress."

"Why were they using an actress for a stunt?"

"I don't know."

Ainsley said, "There aren't any cars blowing up in this movie."

Tracy shrugged.

Ainsley turned to Roger. "I hope she's okay. Can you find out?"

"Yeah."

He started to walk away but Ainsley grabbed him by the arm and pulled him close. She kissed hard him on the lips. "See you soon."

He said, "For sure," and then walked away.

Roger heard about a dozen rumours before he got hold of Jerry, waking him up. Jerry told him what had happened on Second Unit the night before. They had been pushing and pushing to get the shots in. Lenore kept everybody working steady, but the actress had very little experience and none with stunts.

"This is just so fucked up," Jerry said. "This whole fucking shoot. If something doesn't happen to snap this tension, something really bad is going to happen."

"How bad was she hurt?"

"I don't know. The set nurse was with her. They took her to the hospital. She wasn't burnt, I don't think. She might have broken her leg. It's probably mostly shock. She said she was going to sue. I tell you, these fucking stunt guys. Max said she'd be able to do it, but she didn't know what she was doing and she was too scared to say anything. You know, she's got lines in other scenes with the high and mighty Ainsley Riordan and she was scared they'd get cut, so—"

Roger cut him off and closed his cellphone.

It was all anyone was talking about on set. Roger couldn't take it and headed back to Ainsley's Winnie.

Ainsley was still pretty shaken up. She'd found out a few things herself.

"It was Anne-Marie. We had a couple of scenes together and she's pretty good. She's got great instincts. She's from Toronto."

"Well, she's not hurt too bad. Maybe a broken ankle."

"These assholes are more worried about a lawsuit than about her."

"This show really is cursed."

Ainsley shook her head. "No, I've been on cursed shows. This one is totally fucked up."

Roger had no idea what to say. He didn't say anything.

After a minute, Ainsley said, "I'm glad you're not trying to reassure me or anything."

"I have to admit, tension like this, normally I would have quit by now."

"No, you wouldn't have," she said. "You finish what you start, you gave your word, and you've never quit a show in the middle."

"How do you know that?"

"I've got, like, four assistants. I had you checked out."

"Glad to see I did okay."

"Well, I'm never lending you any money."

He didn't know what to say again, so this time Roger kissed her. She locked the Winnie's door.

Later, when Ainsley had been called away to Wardrobe, Roger walked around the set. The big old building was a great location, right on the lake. It was peaceful. Or it would have been if it weren't for the 25 trucks and Winnies and huge crew.

Roger watched a short grip walking along beside the row of trucks. The guy was wearing his *Samurai: The Series* parka, even though it was hot in the afternoon sun. He had the hood up and his head down and his untied Kodiaks were too big.

As the grip got closer, Roger stepped right in front of him, grabbed him by the waist, lifted him off the ground and kissed him full on the lips.

Ainsley pulled back the parka's hood and said, "You're lucky it's me. Or is there something I should know about you and the grips?"

"Like I don't know you?" Roger said.

Ainsley looked at him and said, "Yeah, I guess you do."

A dozen crew members stopped what they were doing and stared at them. Roger looked at Ainsley. She had her hooker make-up on and under the parka she wore the miniskirt and fishnet stockings.

Roger said, "But I have seen grips in those stockings."

Ainlsey held the parka open and pointed a foot forward. "Not with legs like these."

He had to admit, no, not with legs like those.

She put her arm around him and they started walking back towards her Winnie.

"So, you still owe me dinner on top of that tower."

"Next day off."

"We sure started a lot of gossip."

"Yup."

"Do you care?"

"Nope."

"It's not too awkward, us on the same set?"

"I dated a Craft Services woman once. When we broke up it was awful."

"She broke your heart?"

"I couldn't get a cup of coffee for a month."

"Well, if I break up with you, you won't even notice."

"You planning something?"

She stopped and looked at him. "I should tell you before we go much further, I haven't actually, been with anyone, seriously, for a while. Quite a while."

Roger kept looking at her. She still had her arm around him and she turned to face him straight on. She put her other arm around him. "I like you, a lot, you know, and I'd like to give this a shot."

"Me too."

"It's going to be weird, you know. People are going to talk all the time."

"I saw *Notting Hill*."

She smiled and stood on tiptoes to kiss him. "They didn't work on the same movie set."

Someone off by the trucks wolf whistled, loudly.

Roger and Ainsley kissed and heard a howl. She laughed. "You see what I mean."

"Is this going to be a real problem for you?"

"Well, there's nothing we can do about it. I just wanted to warn you."

They continued walking back around the huge brick building. Roger said, "I was in Nicaragua once, well a few times, but this one time I was with some people in a boat."

"What were you, a Sandinista revolutionary?"

He glanced at her sideways and her eyes widened, questioning. He just went on, "Anyway, one of the guys in the boat, an American, took off his boots and put his feet in the water. One of the Nicaraguan guys warned him, told him it was a bad idea, but the American, he didn't want to hear anything about it, he wanted to cool off his feet."

"So?"

"So, an alligator bit them both off."

"I see." She thought about it for a moment. "So, am I the alligator in this little story?"

"No."

"Oh, okay, so I'm a revolutionary? Wouldn't I be like the American journalist, or, or maybe someone looking for her brother? Maybe a nun. Latin America's Catholic, right? There's no way I'm a Contra."

"No," Roger said, starting to get annoyed, "I'm just trying to say that I understand warnings, I take them seriously, I—"

"Gotcha!"

She was smiling that movie star smile. A real honest-to-goodness movie star smile. He growled at her.

THE WRITER

TITLES:
   IT'S A LONG WAY DOWN

FADE IN:

"The airplane swooped down out of the sky with its human cargo and settled on the runway to tease with the terminal's proximity. The proximity of the…the terminal's… Wait. The airplane was swooping down…swooping out… The airplane didn't… Damn."

Ricky shut off his mini-recorder in frustration.

The obese man in the seat beside him leaned his weight against Ricky to gaze out the window. "It's the new terminal construction." The man's moustache jerked around his face. "Slows everything down."

Ricky nodded absently and looked out the narrow oval. The city of Toronto was out there. And somewhere in that city was his movie.

Ricky sighed and pulled out his old copy of Syd Field's *Screenplay*. The one with the torn cover.

DISSOLVE TO:

Ricky walked out from the baggage claim with Syd Field in his pocket and his luggage in his hands. He was now officially a guest of the Dominion of Canada. One hand pulled his suitcase by its leash, the other fumbled with his carry-on and his mini-recorder.

"Movie about an elite team of international baggage handlers called together to fight terrorism in the world's airports."

He waded out into the chaos. Ricky found himself surrounded by reunions—young couples with mountain sherpa backpacks very much in love; old friends remembering how long it's been; parents greeting children and children yelling "Daddy! Mommy!" and knocking Ricky in the knee. Airports are happy places, Ricky thought. Symbolic. He turned on his recorder again.

"Airports are symbols of travel."

And amongst the waving, rippling, breathing mass of greetings he saw his name. "Mr. Spellman" the sign said. He waved at the sign, and the stocky woman holding it made eye contact and tightened her lips.

"Mr. Spellman?" Her voice had an odd cadence, a pleasant 1950s sound. Her skin had a slight tan, the kind Ricky's mother used to call healthy.

"Yes!" Ricky offered her his hand. She took the carry-on from him, and grabbed the leash to the suitcase.

"I'm Vicki," she said patiently. She heaved his carry-on over her shoulder and started for the exit. "I'm your driver," she said over her shoulder.

Ricky hurried after her. "I was hoping I could see some sights."

She shook her head. "I'm sorry, Mr. Spellman." She didn't sound sorry. "They need you to come to set."

Ricky straightened. "Of course. I'm needed on set." Vicki tightened her lips again. Had he upset her? The first person Ricky had met on his movie and he'd upset her. They walked through the automatic doors, and out into the sunny cab lanes. Ricky waited on the corner for the rather large tour bus to come to a stop. Vicki and his luggage did not.

"You picked a good time to visit." She had to raise her voice over the squeal of the bus's brakes. Ricky made sure it had stopped and hurried after her. "It got really cold there for a couple of weeks." The parking garage was through another couple of automatic doors. They joined a group of turbaned men at the elevator. Seizing this lack of forward momentum, Ricky turned to his escort.

"I'm sorry, what's your name?"

"Vicki," she said patiently.

"Ah, thanks. Vicki. Vicki, did you get a chance to read Edward's draft?" She stared at him for six seconds without answering. The elevator arrived, and she pushed through the turbaned men. Ricky let them board, and followed them in.

"Three, please," Vicki called out.

"The director's rewrite of the script?" he tried. She blinked at him.

"Did I read it?" She seemed suspicious of the question. "No, I'm sorry. I didn't."

The turbaned men got out on the second floor with reproachful looks at Vicki. She stabbed the three button until the doors rumbled closed.

"So, did you find the original draft confusing?" He pressed on.

"Of the script?" She tightened her grip on his bags as the elevator slowed.

"Uh, yes. Was it confusing? Did you understand the story?"

"I just told you, I didn't read it," The doors opened and Vicki plunged out. The doors had almost closed again before Ricky followed her.

Vicky tossed Ricky's bags in the trunk of the Ford Taurus and pretty soon they were merging with traffic on the freeway. Ricky tried to avoid staring at the speedometer. He kept telling himself 100 kilometres was really only 60 miles.

"How's the filming going?"

"Fine," she said, keeping her eyes on the mirror. "We're keeping a schedule."

Ricky waited until she had deftly merged between two eighteen wheelers, and out into the open lane beyond. "But how does it look?"

"Oh, I bet it looks great," Vicki turned on the radio, and The Talking Heads sang about middle-class America. "Franz Woceski is a great DP. Did you see *The Ways of Man*?"

"Uh, no, I rented it once but…"

"It's beautiful. It gave me a lot to think about." Vicki hummed along with the radio. "Same as it ever was," she sang. "Same as it ever was."

Vicki guided the car along a raised, high-banked off-ramp onto another freeway. Through the haze Ricky gazed up at Toronto's Space Needle. How tall was it?

"Mr. Spellman," Vicki turned down the traffic report on the radio. "You're the writer, right?"

"Are you asking me or my accountant?" Ricky laughed. Vicki didn't.

"Right. I was wondering. What's this movie about?"

Ricky sucked his bottom lip, and nodded. "Okay. I'll pitch it to you." It was the pitch that had impressed Renée, all those years ago at the pitch workshop. To Ricky the script was never more alive than when he pitched it. He picked pitch three, the short paragraph, and rubbed his old copy of Syd Field for luck. "It's about how we are all witnesses," he said. "It's about how we are all called upon, at some point in our lives, to stand up for our own personal take on the world, declare what we feel is right, and fight what we feel is wrong."

There was a pause. Ricky felt breathless. Vicki found Bruce Springsteen on the radio. "And the witness in this one is the prostitute?"

Ricky looked out the window, and gathered his temper. She's only a driver, he thought, don't expect too much from her. "It's a cops and gangsters… uh, it's a thriller, basically."

Vicki tightened her lips, and drummed on the steering wheel. "Glory days," she sang softly.

DISSOLVE TO:

Vicki said the big beautiful building was just a water filtration plant. It was tucked away by the shore of the biggest lake Ricky had ever seen. "A lot of films shoot prison scenes here." Vicki smoothly guided the car through the gates.

"Movies have shot here before?" Ricky asked, his face pressed up against the window. "Won't people recognize it?" The plant grew larger, the dull brown building squatting windowless in the shoreline's sludge.

"No way." She dismissed the location with a wave of her hand and switched subjects. "We've parked so many units here we can do it in about half an hour."

"That's a lot of, uh…parking." He wondered what she was talking about until they turned a corner in the compound. Spread out in the parking lot below was a carpet of trailers and RV's. Vicki drove down the sloping driveway and pulled up to where the trailers met the plant's loading dock. She used her walkie-talkie to let someone know they had arrived.

"She'll be here soon," Vicki said, and waved goodbye.

A not-quite-sweet odour of decay blew in from the lake. The sun hung low in the cloudless sky. Ricky pulled his sweater off, and shoved it into his briefcase. Then he wished he hadn't. But, too embarrassed to put it back on, he stood and shivered and waited. A rumbling came from deep in the trailers until an oversized laundry cart burst from the trucks—headed right for Ricky.

"Heads!" the thin guy in the muscle shirt, the guy skipping in front of the cart and steering, screamed at Ricky as it roared past. The cart went down the slope to the loading doors and picked up speed. The thin guy with the winter vest, the guy in back, rode it down dogsled style. The lead guy lunged forward, jerked open the door, and the cart slipped through and inside with one last echoing "Yee-haw!"

"Mr. Spellman?"

Ricky whirled, ready to jump. She was the skinniest girl he had ever met—and he was from LA. All except for her head—her thick black hair was tied back using a kerchief and her walkie headset, and the features of her face were of a few magnitudes larger than her rapier body might have needed. Her smile might have been grotesque if it had not been for the dancing light of her eyes. All Ricky saw were her eyes, and he was in love.

"Call me Ricky," he breathed.

She laughed, a deep throaty cigarette-and-booze sailor laugh.

"I'm Debs." She stuck out a knobby arm, all bone and tattoo. "I'm the trailer TAD." His face asked the question, and she told him, "Trainee Assistant Director."

"Great!" Ricky said, for no good reason he could think of. They nodded at each other a few times, and then she pointed her clipboard at the loading dock.

"Okay. I'll take you inside." She led him inside and through the narrow concrete tunnels.

Their way through the building was guided by clumps of cables hanging like spider webs and slumped piles of sandbags huddling like gnomes. They came out into the centre of the plant. A six-story inner courtyard loomed dizzyingly overhead. Four cranes in the corners cast an oppressive glow on the suspended catwalks; heavy shadows lurked over them. Set dressers were stenciling "CELLBLOCK 24" along the walls. The whole thing looked like the kind of place violent people were dumped in and forgotten about, a purgatory where Death walked among the hopeless. In short, it looked nothing like Ricky's script:

```
INT. CITY LOCK UP C-NIGHT

The CAMERA MOVES THROUGH a modern
downtown overnight holding facility, PAST
a bored guard leading a skinny teen
wearing a bright orange jumpsuit, PAST a
holding cell with a few sleeping
prisoners also in orange, until WE SEE
FRANKIE, a twenty-something hooker who
would have been pretty if she wasn't so
dirty.
```

Debs led him through a clutch of extras lounging in the corner, drinking from boxes of orange juice. They all looked identical—shaved heads and dirty grey overalls. Ricky shook his head. Debs held open a door for him. On the door was a ripped piece of paper with block letters reading "Video Village."

"Welcome to the Village," she said.

Ricky crept into an unlit concrete room, crowded with people eating soup from take-out bowls. Some of them—the important ones—sat on tall chairs staring intently at small TVs. Ricky snuck a peek at one. It was blank.

"Richard, darling!" There was no mistaking that voice. Renée Jato jumped up, her soup bowl held triumphantly, and shuffled rapidly over to give Ricky a soft hug. "Boy, am I glad to see you." She took a sip of soup over his shoulder. "You have no idea." She broke off the hug, and held him at arm's length—like Ricky's mother inspecting a sweater.

Renée Jato's bio listed her in her mid-thirties. Most people would add a polite 10 years to that. Her dirty blonde hair was short and wild, her face flushed under a thick layer of make-up and her clothes flowed voluminously around her. But the thing most people remembered about her was her oversize shaded glasses. Her eyes were wolves lurking in the night, peering at you.

She turned to her fellow soup eaters. "Judy, honey? This is Richard Spellman—our writer." Judy was the Line Producer. Ricky had spoken to her on the phone. In fact, she was on the phone now. She was all business, and Ricky was glad he wasn't working for her. She leaned over and lightly touched

Ricky's hand with the shortest hello she could get away with. Renée was already out of the room. "If anyone needs me, Judy honey, I'll be in my trailer. And can you get what's-her-name at the trailers to bring us some coffee? She knows how I like it." It took Ricky a second to realize he was supposed to go with her.

CUT TO:

Ricky dropped hard on the thick couch in Renée's Winnie. There had been paperwork waiting for Renée, and she was deep inside the first purple folder, signing and talking. "It has been a hell, Richard. A living, breathing, lying-awake-at-night-wishing-you-were-dead hell. And where's yesterday's DPR?"

"I don't know," Ricky said.

Renée dialed her cellphone. "Of course you don't, Richard honey. Yes, Anne, please." She was talking on the phone. Ricky wondered if he needed to make any urgent phone calls.

There was a rap at the door, and Ricky opened it. Debs smiled up at him, and he smiled right back. She leaned in and offered Ricky two coffees. "Edward's looking for you, Renée."

Renée shouldered her phone so she could peel open her coffee. "Tell him to come see me."

"Hi, Debs." Ricky kept smiling. Debs smiled somewhere over his head, and skipped away.

"Oh, for godsakes, Richard, she's 16." Renée took out a cigarette. "Or 25. Too young. Yes, hello, Anne? Renée. I am looking at a cost report for yesterday, and I am not looking at a DPR for yesterday." She lit her cigarette with an unconscious precision, and mumbled around it. "I know you will, Anne honey. Okay, goodbye."

She turned off her phone and turned on the CD player. Willie Nelson sang about the folksy beauty of rural America. "What would I do without Willie?" Renée asked over her coffee. "God knows, I've needed him on this show."

There was a pause that Ricky felt he was expected to fill. "Things been that hard?"

"Oh!" Renée put her hand over her heart dramatically. "You have no idea, you have no idea, you have no idea." She looked down at herself. "I got cigarette ash all over me." She wiped at her dress with her smoking hand, which only left new ash in place of the old. "First it snows. Lucky we had rain cover—snow cover. Ainsley starts fucking the Transport captain, and they don't even have the decency to keep it to themselves. How do we find out? On TV. On TV! You can imagine how pissed off people were over that. A camera assistant screws up, and exposes a whole day's film. We have to reshoot four scenes. You did not want to be around me that day, believe you me. We fired him on the spot. Not that the girl who replaced him is any better. Then, some local almost died on second unit. Now she's suing everyone and their uncles."

"Almost died? Really?"

"Between you and me, it's the best footage we have. If you tell Edward that, I'll deny it." Renée sucked at her cigarette. "And then Linda Grigette refused to wear her wardrobe. We had to have her own clothes flown in. You know about the whole script thing with Myles. That man's a nightmare—I love him dearly—but an honest nightmare. We lost half of our locations, and fired half the crew and I tell you, Richard, I have been out of my mind." She took a long drag on her cigarette. "And that was the big stuff."

"Wow," Ricky said.

"Wow," Renée echoed. "That's what I say on the phone to Cathy and Michael in LA. Wow." She cackled again.

The door was flung open. A short man bounded up the steps, rocking the Winnie and spilling Renée's coffee. He was wearing an oversize LA Kings jacket and a LA Kings ball cap. Behind him came a shaved head and a set of shoulders wearing an oversize LA Kings jacket. The big guy was more careful, but rocked the trailer considerably more.

"So now," the first guy was saying, "they're telling me that second unit stuff is going in the trailer? Second unit?"

"Cathy and David made that call," Renée said. "My hands are tied. Edward honey, this is Richard. Richard, this is Edward, and Charles, our technical adviser."

Ricky stuck out his hand.

"You're the one who wrote this shit," Edward said, sprawling across from Renée.

Charles quietly shook Ricky's hand.

"Well, uh, I don't think it…"

"Richard honey, I love you. I adore you," Renée took a loud sip of her coffee. "Mn! It's cold. Where's what's-her-name? Never mind. This is important. I'll go without. Richard, you are the best writer in Los Angeles, and I don't pay you half of what you are worth…"

"You haven't paid me at all yet."

"…but no one could make heads or tails of your script. That's when I sat down one night and read through it. You know, actually like it was a story? It needed more work. And that's why you're here."

"The reason Richard is here," Edward clarified, "is because Myles called up Cathy and David and threatened to quit in the middle of my movie." He turned to Ricky. "Let's just start over. Give me the story."

Ricky sipped his quite warm coffee. "You mean, like, pitch it to you."

"That's right, honey." Renée settled back with her cigarette. "Pitch it to us."

Ricky smiled. Now he had them. He swallowed his excitement and closed his eyes. His fingers rubbed his old copy of Syd Field. He selected pitch number one, the long form, and began. "Uh, really it's all about how we as humans are all witnesses called upon to…"

He stopped. Edward was waving his hands madly in his face. "Sometimes I wish I could just say cut in real life." He winked at Charles. "I guess that's what makes me such a good director."

The air directly surrounding Ricky dropped by at least 23 degrees. He wasn't sure if he was more worried about himself or his movie, but he was sweating.

Edward turned back to him. "Did you go to film school?"

"I took a workshop."

"Did you go to film school, Charles?"

"Nope." Charles chuckled.

"I sure as fuck didn't go to film school," Edward said, his attention once again focused on Ricky. "If none of us went to film school, why are we talking this film school film-about-humanity crap?"

"We need a constructive approach, Richard honey." Renée moved her hands in a great arc, complete with cigarette ash trail.

They were interrupted by a soft knock followed by a woman's tentative, "Edward?"

Edward let his head fall back wearily. "I'm in a fucking STORY CONFERENCE!"

With the only voice in the trailer Willie Nelson's, they heard rapid footsteps retreat from Renée's trailer. Charles covered his face with both hands and shuddered with laughter. "No more double cappuccinos for you," he muttered.

"These people won't let me focus," Edward told the cupboards. He looked around the room. We're all from LA, right?"

"Orange County," Ricky said. "Originally."

"Orange County?" Edward stared blankly at Ricky, his look of total indifference a bullet to the head. With a show of effort, he continued. "I gotta say, the type of shit on this shoot would never happen with an LA crew. I got buddies back home selling their homes to buy groceries, and we're paying these people to wander around with their dicks in each other's asses."

"If I didn't come north," Renée said quietly, "I would not have been able to make this picture. You have no idea, honey. No idea."

"That's what I mean." Edward leapt to his feet, hands wild above his head. "The fucking government…"

"Government." Charles laughed behind his fingers again.

"Fucking government should have the same tax incentives that…"

Renée broke in. "Can we PLEASE talk about the script?" Edward slumped back onto his bench at the table. Willie Nelson took the opportunity to reminisce musically about the various loves of his life. Ricky sipped his coffee.

"Okay, Mr. Writer." Edward pinched his fingers together and milked the air. "This isn't a movie about humanity. This isn't a movie about all of us. This is a movie about a crack whore on the run from the cops."

Ricky choked on his coffee. "Crack whore?"

"We can't show crack use in a PG13, Eddie honey."

"She's not a crack whore!"

"Haven't any of you heard of subtext?" Edward rubbed his temples and glared at them through his fingers, hurt. Renée puffed loudly for attention.

"You know, Richard honey, really there are a few key problems we need to address."

"Such as?" Ricky was wary.

"In the script, as it is written, we never do find out who is behind it all. Who is Mr. Big?"

Ricky was confused. "Mikey ties it all up in his death speech." He flipped through his script and pointed it out to them.

"No, he doesn't." Edward was getting angry.

That set Ricky off.

"Yes, he does." Ricky stabbed his finger at the script.

"Not in the script that I read, Richard honey," Renée mumbled around her newest cigarette. "She asked him and he never answers."

"He answers." Ricky was completely bewildered. "He answers her off-camera."

"Off-camera?" Renée and Edward were united by their shock. "Well, who is it?" Renée managed.

"You don't know who it is?" Ricky yelled at them. They looked blankly back at him. "You've been shooting for three weeks and you don't know what the ending is?" Ricky's heart stopped. "It's her father!" He threw the script across the room. "Frankie's father is the one connection that ties everything together! He ran the dope dealer that killed the kid. He hired the crooked cops that are after Frankie. He ran the brothel that his daughter worked in. He's the reason her ex-husband and all the cops went bad. That's why he gets killed in that last scene."

Everyone looked away from Ricky. There was a something's-wrong feeling that made his gut go weak. The moment was quite anti-climatic.

"And, uh," he said.

Renée let out a lungful of smoke very slowly. "Richard," she said carefully. "Honey. Frankie's father doesn't get killed at the end."

"Wh…?" Ricky's knees felt like water, and he sank to his seat.

"We already shot that last scene. They go for a picnic." And that was the most terrible word Ricky had ever heard. Picnic. He tried, but he couldn't bring himself to say it.

"And then there's the other problems," Edward said. "What about the car bomb?"

"Richard honey, we shot a car explosion we have to work into the story." Renée nodded. "Because it's going to be in the trailers."

"We needed more week two," Edward explained.

"More week two," Ricky repeated dully.

"It's a theory I have." Edward got excited now that they were talking about him again. "I know my cast will give us a strong opening weekend. Week two depends on the stunts. It's week three that you're going to give us. On week three people come because they like the story. Think week three." He leaned forward, staring Ricky down. "You give me week three, and we'll finally have a movie. Something I'll watch thirty years from now."

Ricky felt the trailer start up and drive off a cliff and sink under the ocean and rest there under the silt for a long, long time. He was completely at a loss for a response, and more than that, he was terrified. Edward had just proven to him that he had absolutely no idea what he was doing with Ricky's movie.

FADE TO BLACK

TITLES

    THE VAST DESERT OF ACT TWO

FADE IN

Ricky was painfully lost. He had staggered, shell-shocked, from Renée's trailer into the dark of night. Now, struggling with 15 days' worth of raw footage on 15 video tapes and the binders of continuity dialogue, he was headed in a vague idea of the direction of a trailer of his very own. His own trailer. If he could only find it. He squeezed the mini-recorder from his pocket and snapped it on.

"He came to the hard, halting realization that he had been walking in circles for some time now. He began to wonder if he should be marking his path by dropping breadcrumbs. But where would he get breadcrumbs?"

He snapped off the recorder, reminded that he hadn't eaten since leaving LA.

"Spellman!" The voice shot through the parking lot like a CIA sniper's bullet. Ricky jumped. Through the collapse of his stack of video tapes, Ricky saw a man sprinting down the alleyway between the trailers, right at him, a flash of yellow worklight reflecting off something in his clenched fist. Ricky's Orange County street instincts failed him completely. "Knife!" he thought. His knees buckled and the video tapes cushioned his fall. From a few yards back, the man slowed to a stop, his muscular arms braced tightly on his hips. The breeze off the lake caught the make-up towel billowing around the man's shirt collar. The stars twinkled in the man's gel-locked hair. Ricky's eyes went wide. It was Myles Day.

"I'm Myles Day," Myles Day said. "Sorry about your tapes. I play Mario."

"I know," Ricky said. "I wrote the script."

"I know. I've been waiting to meet you for three weeks," Myles Day said.

"Me too." A moment of understanding passed between them, but Ricky had no idea what it was. "I was a big fan when you were on *Downtown Heat*."

"We had a good run," Myles Day allowed. He slipped his glasses, glinting in the yellow worklights, over his ears dismissively. Which only reminded Ricky how good an actor he was. "That was TV," he said. "This…" He was the master of the pregnant pause. "…is cinema."

"Yeah, well, you were good in that, and I'm glad to have you here." Ricky scraped his tapes off the concrete. "I guess I have you to thank for any of this. You convinced Cathy and David."

Myles knelt down beside Ricky, and fished under the truck. "When my agent sent me your script, I knew it was right for me. The life, the drama, the verve! Anyway," he grunted, and flattened out to grab the last tape. His voice drifted out from under the truck. "We artists must band together." He handed Ricky the tape and rolled out. "We must ward off those who would reduce our chosen realms of expression to mere entertainment."

Ricky's instinct was to agree but wasn't sure if he should. A flurry of footsteps and Debs was helping Myles Day to his feet. Anxious. "Myles, your wardrobe!" She keyed her walkie. "Debs for Wardrobe. Can someone meet Myles in Make-up?"

Myles brushed at the stain on his trousers, which continued to spread up his leg. "Must've knelt in an oil puddle."

"Hi, Debs." Ricky smiled up at her. The tips of her mouth stretched across her cheeks.

"I have to get him back in Make-up." She took Myles' arm and led him away.

"Um, wait." Ricky hugged the tapes close and hopped to his feet. "I don't know my way around. Can you help me find my trailer?"

Myles leaned on her, swatting the stain on his pant leg. Debs shook her head. "I have to stay with the talent."

Myles straightened. "I am merely one who speaks when his cue line comes up," he declared. "This man is the real talent. You will show him to his trailer. I will make my own way to the make-up chair." And he strode off, shaking his stained leg.

Debs watched him go, her teeth tugging at her lip. "Well," she said finally, "he'll be fine for five minutes."

Myles turned, and cupped his hands to his mouth. "Spellman! We'll talk soon. I have some notes to work into my character." A tall, thin black man rushed up to Myles with a shrill "Oh my God!" He examined the ruin that had been Myles' wardrobe, his voice shaky. "Don't fuss with me so much," Myles said good-naturedly.

DISSOLVE TO:

An old call sheet with "WRITER" scribbled on it was taped to the door of what turned out to be Ricky's Winnie. Ricky had eased their pace down to a slow crawl. Even in ideal circumstances his skills at chit chat would have been on par with "the cigarette-smoking-man" from *The X-Files*. Ricky's walk with Debs had been less than ideal, from his point of view. He tried again.

"So, is Debs short for something?"

She opened her mouth, thinking the question over. "Debbie."

Ricky paused, his hand on the door. "I had a good time."

"On the walk here?"

"The walk here was good." Ricky smiled. He'd been doing that a lot. "We had some good times."

She rolled her eyes, but she was smiling too. "Memories for a lifetime," she said in her best Ainsley Riordan. She hurried away, but as she ducked around a trailer and out of sight, she might have looked back to see him looking after her. Ricky thought she did.

CUT TO:

The 15 days on 15 video tapes and the binders of continuity dialogue were less than useless. By the time he was finished writing the script pages for tomorrow, even he wasn't sure what they were about. He checked his watch. Four in the morning? He stepped out into the cold night air, scripts in hand, and checked for directions with the sleepy seamstress in the Wardrobe truck.

"It was that time of the morning when even the night has gone to bed," he said into his mini-recorder. "When you think maybe the day has given up the fight, and the sun won't ever rise again. When the dark seems like a living thing all around you, clutching at you with cold tentacles of death and forgetfulness." Pleased, he shut off the recorder and found his destination on his second try.

The old call sheet said AD OFFICE. Light spilled out from a door in the side of a truck, above a set of stairs that were almost a ladder.

"Hello?" Ricky called. There was a loud bang from inside and a head poked out sideways.

"Can I help you?" The face was Asian, the accent wasn't. Ricky felt guilty that he was surprised.

"I'm the writer," Ricky told him. "I've got the pages for tomorrow."

"I'm Walt. Walter. The Second AD." He took the pages Ricky held up to him. "Thanks." And shut the door.

A bunch of thin guys in baseball caps with somewhere to go pushed by him. Ricky headed back toward his trailer—he hoped. He got stopped near one of the equipment trucks. The man's beard was stained yellow. His parka was strained across his beer gut. "Gotta light?"

"I don't smoke," Ricky said. The man pointed his hairy face at the night, laughed, and spit.

"You don't smoke?" He looked Ricky up and down. "How long you been in film?"

"I'm the writer."

The man's impressive nostrils flared. "I work for a living." He spat again and moved on to a group sitting on the trailer's ramp, who promptly lit his cigarette.

Ricky found his trailer and dropped onto the bed, exhausted. He was dreaming about sailing when Barry shut down the generator and everyone went home.

DISSOLVE TO:

Ricky's arrival at the Lunch Room did not go the way he expected it to. Someone choked out, "Oh my God!" and the room went silent. Everyone turned in their plastic chairs to stare at him. Ricky ran his fingers through his greasy hair, and straightened his clothes. "Is it him?" someone whispered.

"Sorry," he said. "I didn't get a chance to shower."

Renée jumped up from her lunch. She advanced on him, cigarette held high. "Richard honey, where the hell have you been?"

Myles leapt to his feet, spilling his diet cola. "Spellman, I've got notes! Character notes!" But Renée had already pushed Ricky out of the Lunch Room. Conversations started again in anxious whispers.

Renée held Ricky against the wall with the threat of her cigarette. She lifted her tinted glasses and searched his eyes. "What are you on? Pills? Booze? Powder? Grass? And don't lie to me, your eyes are bloodshot."

"Because your cigarette smoke is pouring into them." He tried to shake her off.

"This entire production crew has been looking for you all day!"

"What? Why?"

"Why?" She repeated. "Why? He goes missing from the hotel on his first day in town, and he asks me why we were looking for him." She pressed even closer, and he eyed the cigarette nervously. "Now you better tell me where you were."

It hit Ricky that she was serious. He meekly held up the next day's script pages. "Here."

She stepped back and folded her arms. "Tell."

He swallowed and rubbed his eyes. "I woke up in the afternoon. Everyone was gone. I went for a walk. Ate some fish and chips. Read the paper. Came back. Wrote your script pages. If you want to know, I watched TV in my trailer. Came to lunch. All in all, I was thinking, a very quiet, peaceful, relaxing, easygoing day."

"I'm glad for you." Renée was nodding dangerously. "I'm really glad that you had such a nice day. Let me tell you something. If you're working on a movie and having a relaxing day? Something's wrong, every time. We have been in a constant state of panic over your wellbeing. I've smoked so many cigarettes today, you have no idea. Your driver waited an hour in the hotel lobby before she called us. We sent a girl over to your hotel. It hadn't even been slept in. I thought maybe you had flown back to LA. Edward didn't help. He insisted you were lying half-dead after picking the wrong cheap hooker. He tells me it happens all the time in Toronto and Amsterdam. Myles! Poor Myles! He insisted that we call the harbour patrol in case you had flung yourself into the lake—of course, he's not the most stable of people. And now you show up—for lunch I should have known!—wondering why we were looking for you? You have a lot of nerve, Richard Spellman. A lot of nerve."

Ricky recognized that last bit. It was in yesterday's dialogue.

WEEK 5

THE TRANSPORT CAPTAIN

A couple of days later, when the filming was stalled and the rewrites were coming in slowly, the mood on set went from the usual cranky to openly hostile. Everyone complained about the lost days, worried that the shoot would extend so long they'd miss out on the next big show and end up with nothing over the summer, the busiest time.

Nijar was storming around yelling at everyone for no reason. Even Judy Nemeth hid out at the production office as much as she could.

Ainsley had started hanging out with Roger during breaks. She'd sit with him in the Crown Vic and take off her spike-heeled boots and they'd both read. She bought him *How the Irish Saved Civilization* and he gave her Elmore Leonard novels. She laughed pretty hard as she read *Get Shorty,* saying she knew movie guys just like that. She even started on the westerns.

She looked up from a paperback of *The Tonto Woman* and said, "Have you ever been to the Grand Canyon?"

"Nope."

"Have you ever slept under the stars in the desert?"

"In the Canadian badlands. It's a kind of desert."

"Do you want to?"

"What, go to the Grand Canyon? Sure."

"No, I'm serious. When this is over why don't we drive back to California through the desert? See the Grand Canyon and Mount Rushmore and the Rocky Mountains."

"What do we do when we get there?"

"Well, I have to work on *Steel Shroud Two.*"

"They must have changed that story an awful lot if there's a sequel."

"Hey, I died in the first one. If it cracks 200 million, there's a sequel. But it's almost all in the studio. You can do whatever you want." It was the first time they'd talked about any kind of future, a subject they had managed to avoid effortlessly.

"You mean, be like a kept man?"

"No, not like that all, there are lots of jobs, I mean—"

"No, no, wait a minute, I like this idea. Could I stay at your place?"

"Well, you're not just going to do nothing."

"I don't have a green card."

"So you'd come to California and just lie around the house all day while I work?"

"I wouldn't be in the house all day. You must have a pool."

"You'd do that?"

He smiled. "Gotcha."

She punched his arm. "But you'll come?"

"Okay."

She wrapped her arms around him and hugged hard. He'd surprised even himself but he couldn't think of a good reason to say no. Why not, he figured, at this point in his life, take a chance. It wasn't like he hadn't just taken off in the past.

A loud knocking on the window startled them both. It was Ainsley's assistant Tracy. She looked very upset. "Edward needs to see you right away."

Ainsley sighed and reluctantly let go of Roger. "I just hope I don't get fired. I'm screwing up so badly. My head's really not in this one."

"It's been a tough shoot. Everyone's pissed."

"There's like one week to go. You think we can hang on that long?"

Roger said, "Sure."

"Unless we go over. God, I'd be so screwed if this thing went long."

Roger said, "The whole crew would be. People would lose their whole summer. It can't go long, can it?"

"Everybody's so tense right now, we're not getting anywhere near our days. We've got to do something."

Tracy knocked on the window again.

Ainsley ignored her. "It'll be fun to drive across America, though." She suddenly smiled. "We could take Route 66!"

"We could."

"Okay."

When they walked back to the set along the big lawn by the lake—they were still shooting at the water plant, still shooting the same scenes over and over—they could feel it. Wound up so tight. Ainsley held on to Roger's arm and spoke quietly. "I wish something would break this tension and the rest of the shoot would just fly by."

Before Roger could say anything the director, Edward J. Nijar, all five foot eight of him, came rushing towards them. His hair flew in all directions and his eyes bugged out of his head. "Where the fuck have you been? We're trying to get this fucking thing done today, you know!"

"I'm here."

"Go and change. Now you're just coming back from school, different wardrobe entirely. That is, if these fucking morons can get it together."

The crew grumbled loudly.

"Take it easy, Eddie," Ainsley said.

Steven had stepped up beside her with the new wardrobe slung over his arm.

"Do not fucking tell me what to do, I have been exiled to fucking Siberia long enough. Every simple fucking thing we try to do, these idiots screw up." He glared at Steven. "Are those even the right fucking clothes?"

"Eddie."

"No, I've had it with these goddamned Canadian crews, these fucking Mexicans in tuques."

Someone said, "Fuck you."

Nijar turned. "Who said that? Who the fuck said that?"

Everyone, 25, 30 people all stared silently at their feet.

Garry stepped up beside Steven.

"Yeah, right. Gutless fucking morons, useless fucking idiots. You assholes are nothing but fucking snow niggers! No one would ever shoot in fucking Canada if you weren't so cheap, you fucking useless—"

Roger's fist slammed into Nijar's face and shut him up in a hurry. The second punch landed him on his ass, a real movie fall, with his legs flying out from under him.

The whole set was silent. No one moved. Roger stood over Nijar and stared at him. He was curled into a ball and whimpering.

Ainsley laughed.

Roger looked at her and said, "That should do it."

Charles, the ex-cop technical advisor and closest thing to a security guard on set stood in front of Roger. He said, "Come on, let's go."

Roger nodded and took a step towards Ainsley. "I'll see you later."

"You sure will."

Every one stared as Charles walked Roger off the set.

They walked around the water plant building, past the temporary barbed wire fence. They didn't say a word to each other.

As they passed the Craft Services truck, Charles said, "You want a coffee or something?"

Roger said, "No thanks."

They got to Queen Street and looked around. There was no traffic. A few apartment buildings and a convenience store.

Roger said, "I guess I can catch a streetcar there."

But Charles began to chuckle and then the chuckle became a big laugh. "Did you see that pussy on the ground?"

Roger started to smile. "I've never seen a guy crumple like that."

Charles laughed and laughed. After a minute he got it together again and looked at Roger. "Thanks, man. I needed that."

"You're going to catch shit for it."

"It's worth it. I'll tell him I kicked your ass when we got out of sight."

"He really is an asshole."

"Hey, I wouldn't be here if it didn't pay so well."

Roger unclipped his walkie and handed it to Charles.

Charles pressed the button on the walkie and said, "Transport, I need a driver, corner of Queen and Neville Park." He looked at Roger. "Might as well get one of your guys to drive you home."

Roger said, "Thanks."

"Don't mention it. Shit, that was funny. Say, if you're ever in LA, look me up."

Roger said he just might.

THE PRODUCTION ASSISTANT

It was a Saturday. Greg had nothing to do but sit around and watch the tube, vegging, not thinking about any of it. He hopped on the streetcar and cruised down to HMV and Sam's on Yonge. He joined the rest of the media zombies who roamed the aisles, looking for a new fix, some way to find the high in their jaded, overproduced, re-mixed, accelerating culture. Greg spent too much money on CDs he didn't really want, but the purchase made him feel better. As an added escape, on his way home he stopped in at Blockbuster Video and rented the only three videos he hadn't seen on the new releases wall.

Around 8:00 the phone rang.

"Hey, PA!"

Holy fuck. "Carmen?" He already knew the answer.

"Saddle 'er up, cowboy," Carmen yelled into the phone. "I'm not spending another night rotting in this hourly rate motel." He was staying in a suite at the King Edward. "Come on, put down the hand lube and the naked picture of your sister and let's go get some real Betties."

"What?" Greg said that a lot, talking to Carmen, but this time he meant it.

"There's gotta be some hot spot where the dirty girls dress all slutty and are looking to find love or a reasonable hand-job facsimile. Let's go. I'm buying."

"Look." Greg laid it out. "I'm not your friend. We're not working right now. So fuck off."

But Carmen was not listening. "Let's go," he chanted. "Let's go. Get some booze. Let's go. Let's go."

"No. I got plans."

"What plans?" he yelled. "What plans can you have that are better than a free night of booze and women?"

So inside of an hour Greg found himself in a cab with the most obnoxious person he had ever met, being dragged along while he blew off some steam.

"What clubs can you get us into?" Carmen asked Greg, staring out the window as the cab inched along Richmond Street. The club district was overflowing with the weekend crowd.

"None," Greg told him sullenly. He sat back and tried to remember what movies he had rented. He couldn't.

"I gotta do everything for you?" In mid-sentence, Carmen threw his torso out the cab window. "Hello," he called at some chick in tight pants.

"Git yourself inside, please," the cabby said, angrier than his polite words might have otherwise indicated. "Git inside, or git out now, please."

Greg grabbed Carmen's shirt. "He's not my friend," he felt the need to inform the cabby.

Carmen slapped at Greg with one hand, and cupped the other around his mouth. "Hey! What club are you going to?"

"Get the fuck in the cab," Greg ordered his handful of Carmen's shirt.

The cabby slammed on the brakes, halting the cab, the crowd, and the traffic. "You are gitting the fuck out of my cab now, please," he informed them. "Now, please." Carmen, as usual, noticed nothing.

"Hey, gorgeous!" By now Greg wasn't pulling Carmen's shirt, but pushing him forward. "What club are you going to?"

"Fuck off," the tight pants chick said. But her friend was a little drunker. "The Joker!" she told Carmen.

"We'll see you there," Carmen promised them, and came back into the cab. By now the traffic was jammed behind them, and Greg envisioned city-wide gridlock caused by Carmen's libido. "We're going to the Joker," Carmen calmly related.

"Well, we can walk from here," Greg said, hoping he was right.

"You can walk to hell!" the cabby screamed as Carmen tossed some money over the seat and they got out. The cab peeled off, avoiding the frat boy racing across the street with a stolen banana held high. Greg thought to himself, the cabby's very angry, he's got issues. They hadn't damaged his cab or anything. Why did they get the angriest cab driver in all Toronto? But Greg knew the answer.

"You should be a superhero," he said to Carmen when he caught up to him. Carmen was swaggering down the street, in the direction the tight pants went when he lost sight of her. For the first time, Greg got him.

"What?" he said. Greg felt good.

"You have a superhuman ability to piss people off by your very presence," Greg told him, scholarly. "The government should capture you and study how this mysterious power works."

"You fuckin' tight-assed no-fun Canadians need to be weaned earlier," Carmen said as he stepped up to a group of party girls and slipped his arms around them. "Hey, ladies…" His voice dropped to the smooth and artificial tone of a late night FM DJ. "…can you lead us to the Joker?"

Somehow he didn't get beat up in the street by some hair-trigger boyfriend. Somehow he talked their way past the line-up and straight into the club. Somehow he got them drinks from the bar within seconds of joining the throng of jittery young functional alcoholics. He was clearly in his element, a shark among the chum. The pounding, palpitating music swirled around them. Laser lights played on body parts, and sweat refracted tiny rainbows in the regulated twilight. A disco ball reflected a thousand individual beams, so each person could have their own spotlight, just for that instant. Chicks moved trance-like, arms held above their heads, the long slit of their flowing skirts showing off their perfectly toned legs. Backless dresses made Greg's fingers itch, and his crotch throb. It had been a long time.

Carmen moved out on the dance floor. He would ease up behind a chick and then suddenly he was dancing with her, but only for a moment before moving on. He made it seem effortless, and Greg could only sip his beer and watch him. Carmen didn't care, and chicks dug it. He didn't care whether they would like him or not. And not just chicks either. Greg saw guys stand back to let their girls grind against Carmen for a while. A perfect specimen of a guy who was so cut off from those around him that everyone tried to break in, wondering what he had in there. What was he hiding? What made him so confident, so sure? The answer was, he had nothing in there. He was hiding nothing. He held nothing back, kept nothing secret. And that made him strong. And the rest of them weak.

Greg was reminded of a short but profound conversation he once had with a used-car salesman. He didn't strike Greg as a particularly successful salesman, but he must've heard this from someone who knew.

"The key to getting what you want," the salesman told Greg between swigs of beer, "is to not want it. The guy who is ready to walk away first will always come out ahead." He swallowed another mouthful of beer. "Oh, and once you have made your offer, don't say anything. Whoever talks first is the one who can't walk away." It made perfect sense at the time—Greg was young and had had a few beers himself.

But Carmen was like that now. He was casual—no, indifferent. And he always broke off first. He worked his way around the room, and Greg watched him until he finished his beer. Digging in his pocket, he found the seven bucks change he had got at Blockbuster and waited fifteen minutes for a Rickard's Red. He dropped the money on the bar, which turned out to leave an embarrassingly small tip, and pushed his way out from the mob and into the relative openness of the dance floor.

Carmen was by Greg's side again. "Honeys," he said. "Honeys! Fuck. I wanna make babies." Greg made a sour face at him, and sipped his beer.

"Come on," Carmen said. "Let's do some shots."

He pulled Greg through the crowd to the bar, and the world closed over them.

Greg woke up on his bathroom floor, cold. No. It wasn't his bathroom, and he focused just enough to figure out it was a hotel bathroom. Carmen's hotel bathroom. Greg's skull was squeezing in on his brain, he was completely dehydrated, and his cheek was encrusted. His stomach punched him every time he swung his head but he managed to sit up, with a vague idea of going home. He tried to imagine riding the subway in his present condition. The effort made him lean over the toilet bowl. The water was murky, and smelled sharp. He flushed. The swirling water threatened to carry him down with it, and he turned away. What the hell was going on? What time was it? He looked for his watch, but it was gone.

It took a while, but Greg drank some water, stripped out of his soiled clothes, and stepped in the shower. The heavy hotel water pressure pounding on his scalp almost murdered him, but it revived the rest of his body and after about 20 minutes he felt like he could deal with the unknown morning. He cringed as he put on the clothes from the night before, but they were all he had. He prepared himself to leave his womb of a bathroom. Outside a TV was playing. He opened the door.

Carmen was sprawled on the couch, arms around some chick. Greg leaned against the corner of the room, swaying uncertainly.

"Well, good morning," she said, and they burst out laughing at him. All this standing was making Greg's head hurt, and he sank gratefully into the wing chair nearest him. He closed his eyes. The sounds of the 'toons on the TV soothed him. Carmen's voice did not.

"You remember Diane, don't you?" Carmen nodded at her. She was gorgeous, blonde hair, tattoos that curled under the hotel bathrobe she was wearing. She smiled at Greg.

"No," Greg answered feebly. "I absolutely don't." Carmen made a show of stretching out his right arm and held it up, hand flared back.

"Then you don't remember this?" His grin was too predatory, and Greg didn't like it. He squinted to focus his bloodshot eyes.

"That's my fuckin' watch." Greg tried to sound something other than defeated, but he didn't even fool himself. "Why do you have my watch?"

"You bet me that I couldn't fuck Diane here." Carmen sounded almost hurt that Greg didn't remember his victory. Diane slapped Carmen on the chest.

"You shit." She didn't sound angry. Her voice rose subtly in volume and confidence. "I'm not some bauble to be won in a gentlemen's wager." Greg blinked at her. Who was this girl? She leaned forward and snatched up a pack of cigarettes. "English major," she explained, and lit a cigarette. Greg's eyes flickered over to the "Thank You For Not Smoking" sign on the wall. She pointed her cigarette at Carmen, and squinted over it like she was sighting down a gun barrel. "You said we would go for breakfast when he got out of the shower."

"Get your ass dressed, girl, and maybe we will."

She blew smoke in his face, then disappeared into the bedroom. Greg tried to pull himself up from the deep cushion, but couldn't.

"Listen," he croaked, "maybe you can spot me cab fare, and I could just…go home." He waved his hands in a gesture of complete hopeless resignation.

"Nope." Carmen didn't look away from the TV. Greg realized how trapped he was. Even when he was not hosting The Highland Games Caber Toss in his head, he could barely have a simple exchange of dialogue with Carmen, let alone win an argument. They watched 'toons in blessed silence until Diane came back out dressed in Carmen's jeans and sweater.

"I've left you a little something," she said, and hung her gitch on the bedroom door. Carmen winked at Greg and fingered his watch.

They headed down to the hotel restaurant, and allowed themselves to be seated. The hostess took one look at Greg, and placed them in the far back corner. But she brought coffee right away, and she smiled at Greg—pity is such an odd emotion, but he appreciated it now, feeling lower than he had previously thought possible.

They sipped their coffee, and Greg tried to decide what he could keep down. In the end he ordered what he almost always had for brunch; eggs bene with a side of bacon and OJ. Carmen ordered a three-cheese omelette, two sides of toast, and stuck with the coffee. Diane ordered crêpes with strawberries and chocolate.

The silence congealed around the table. Greg stared at his knife, finding the fulcrum of the universe in its tiny quillons. Carmen, for once, was lost in thought. Diane looked from Greg to Carmen, and raised her eyebrows.

"So." She broke into the dead air. "What is it you guys do, exactly?"

Carmen's head shot up. "Greg here is a production assistant on a movie shooting in Toronto."

"Oh yeah?" she asked politely. "Do you like that, Greg?"

"No," Greg answered without thinking. "I don't like it. I don't like a single moment of it. I don't like the driving. I don't like the office work. I don't like the hours. I don't like the people. I don't like the environment." He stopped himself, his voice thick. How long had he felt like this? He dropped his head into his hands. He told himself that it was just the hangover, that's why he felt like he was about to cry. On Monday he would feel better, he told himself.

He raised his head. Carmen was calmly sipping his coffee, with a smirk on his face. Diane was staring at Greg, her face a mixture of concern and acute embarrassment.

"It's not that bad," Greg reassured her. "I get a free car, gas paid for, the work isn't…hard, I guess. It's not hard."

The food arrived, and for a moment the attention shifted off Greg. He hadn't been sure if he could eat, but now that the food was front of him he was starving, and he shoved a slice of crispy, salty bacon into his mouth. He sliced off a large piece of poached egg and English muffin.

"What do you want to do?" Carmen asked. Greg didn't answer. He chewed his food and stared off into space in a way he hoped was thoughtful. Carmen went on.

"Me," he said, waving a piece of omelet on the end of his fork, "I'm gonna get a studio gig. Vice President, for starters. And do you know why?"

"Money?" Diane asked.

"Ego," Greg offered. Carmen shook his head violently, then seemed to reconsider.

"Okay, yes," he admitted. "But those aren't the real reasons. The real reason is because people, all people, everywhere, are assholes. Everyone is out for themselves, I don't care what they say. Even when they want to help other people. Even Mother Teresa, she did it because it made her feel good. If it hadn't, she wouldn't have done it."

He paused and looked at Greg and Diane in triumph.

"Are you saying Mother Teresa was an asshole?" Diane asked him.

"Yes," he barked. "Or a bitch, if you want to be gender specific." He bit into some toast and chewed vigorously.

"That's a…" Diane searched for the right word. "…unique point of view."

"I don't get it," Greg admitted.

"I'm not surprised," Carmen assured him. "It's very simple. All people are assholes and self-interested, and nowhere is this basic human condition more of a factor than in the politics of the Hollywood studio system."

"You're cracked," Greg mumbled around a stick of bacon. He found it odd to hear the admiration in his voice. "Absolutely cracked."

"And where did you get this insight into human behaviour?" Diane pressed him. She hardly seemed convinced. Carmen set down his fork, took a loud swallow of his coffee, and leaned forward, whispering excitedly like a nouveau Guy Fawkes.

"When my mom left my dad, I was ten. My dad had nothing to do with me in the summer except take me to work. I was on a film set for most of my teenage years. And because I was young, people didn't pretend around me. I would sit around with producers as they talked about directors and actors, and sit around with actors as they bitched about producers. But when they were face to face, it was love and kisses on the cheeks. That's what people are like, really, when they let themselves be honest."

"Dishonest," Greg attempted to clarify.

"Exactly," he said, and leaned back with a decisive bite of his toast. Diane and Greg exchanged a look. But Carmen wasn't finished yet.

"Now," he said, pointing to himself, "I want to be a studio guy." He aimed his toast at Greg. "And you want to be… "

Greg felt queasy again. And the answer spewed out past all his defenses. "Nothing. Absolutely fucking nothing. The only thing I have ever been any good at is being a PA. That's it. I'll never be anything more than that. I won't be a studio guy. I won't be a producer." And he was crying. He was fucking crying—he saw the waitress across the room glance away. He was telling himself that it was just the hangover, that he would be all right on Monday, that he would take a break after this show, but he was still crying, and he was still talking. "I hate having my life revolve around everyone else. What everyone else wants is always more important than what I want." He had to stop here, to get some control. "For fuck's sake," he thought. "Get some control, Greg. No one wants to see you break down like this."

Carmen poured some more water from the pitcher. He pushed it over to Greg, and Greg took it and slurped at it.

Diane tried to be gentle. "Maybe you should find another job?"

"I can't do another job!" he yelled at her. Someone at another table dropped a fork. The hostess whispered to the waitress. "I'm no fucking good at anything. What can I do?" How long had he felt like this?

"I think he's having a severe emotional crisis," Carmen said.

"I'll be okay," he told them. "I'll be fine. I just need some rest."

Carmen slipped some cash over to Greg. He grabbed it, and stood up, unsteady.

"Greg," Diane said, and was going to say something else, but Carmen stopped her.

Greg puked once on the way home, but he was able to get the cab to pull over in time.

Monday he showed up for work. He was on the late shift, and started at 11:00 a.m. He stood outside and smoked until 20 after. Anne looked up at the clock as he came in.

"Go see Accounting," she told him. "You're going to the bank for them." Greg stared at her. The world around him went soft. "Did you hear me?" she asked. He nodded mutely, and headed into the accounting office. The accountant made out a cheque in his name, to pick up the cash that kept the production flowing. He evaded small talk and questions about his evasiveness, and headed out to his car.

It was hot, and he had the windows down and the air on max. It was Monday, and he didn't feel any different. He was driving a rented car with a full tank of gas, he had a cheque in his name for 50,000 dollars cash, and he was only a few hours from the US border. He smiled. It would be days before they started to look for him in the States, and by then he might even know where he was going.

THE WRITER

Ricky's hotel phone rang at 12:13 p.m. By the sixth ring there was nothing left to do but answer it.

"Odsbodkins!" the phone said. "I thought perhaps we had lost you again. Do you mind if I stop by?"

Ricky tried to calculate how long he had slept after shooting all night, but the only answer he could come up with was not enough. "Who the hell is this?" he mumbled.

"Is this room 1421?"

Ricky tried to squint at the faded sticker on the phone. "I have no idea."

"Spellman?"

"Yes."

"This is Myles Day," Myles Day said.

CUT TO:

Ricky rubbed his damp hair and tried not to watch the girl wrapping her legs around the golden pole onstage.

"You come here for breakfast?"

"It's so close to the hotel. And only for character study, of course." Myles tore into his eggs and steak. "I'm so glad to be working with you," he said. He pointed at Ricky with his glasses. "I'm ecstatic to have an opportunity shape my character's arc." Ricky nodded and wiped the water from his ears.

"Do you have, uh, any written notes?" Ricky asked. "I could work on them, uh, maybe someplace less noisy."

"My art is feeling." Myles straightened in his chair, and spoke over the music. "Your art is words, the aesthetic arrangement of the English language. I *feel* my character. That is what I humbly offer to you." He placed his glasses on his nose. Ricky tried to figure out if the glasses were cosmetic or just a very light prescription. But the lighting in the strip club was on the dim side.

Myles leaned forward. "I'm thinking of a scene in which I use a fish," he said. Ricky blinked. Myles shifted his gaze over Ricky's shoulder. "A fish that I keep in my pocket, that I call Esau. You know of course that Esau was the Greek god of love?"

"I think that was Eros. Esau was Jacob's—"

"Roman, then." Myles waved off Ricky's theogonic doubts. Ricky shook his head at the tall woman, who seemed to be wearing mostly boots, when she came around with her tray of shooters. Myles went on. "The point is that the fish, Esau, is a symbol of my character's love for Margaret. The love I have had since we were innocent children. I could have a speech."

"I, uh, I don't know, Myles." Ricky said. "Why don't we ask Edward?"

"A speech!" Myles pushed on. He swung his glasses off his nose, and pointed them grandly into the air, directly at the DJ booth, where he appeared to be reading from a divine teleprompter. "When I was young I used to take my fish out to the backyard to enjoy the sun with me. That fish was my friend, my guide, my confidant, my shelter from the coarse unfolding of life."

Myles' face went dark. Dim. Like a cloud over the sun. Even while a blonde was stripping to her poppy dance music. Ricky wondered how long he had been rehearsing this. "When that damned yellow cat would prowl around, sulking by the fence, I would get my mother to chase the cat away. I hated that cat. I hated it most the day that cat ate my fish. I learned to kill that day."

Myles' eyes flicked to Ricky, to see if he got the whole hitman chrysalis thing. He did. Myles' face went bright again. Myles' glasses slowly swept upwards, until they shook with barely restrained emotion at the end of Myles' outstretched arm. "I met Margaret the next day at the pet store, my heart still a dull stump. We held hands and searched the tanks, watching the fish and counting my pocketful of coins, until we found the perfect fish. We called him Esau." Myles reached into his breast pocket and, with great reverence, pulled out a ziplock bag of water. Inside was a platinum gold fish. He unsealed the bag and scooped out the fish. He extended it toward Ricky, the living fish vibrating feebly. Ricky felt cold and sick.

"Then after the scene when she dies—" Myles said in a quiet tone, careful not to break the spell. The redhead did a handstand and spread her legs. "—I could be at a fountain, one of those ornate fountain gardens with great arcs of water." Myles used the fish to illustrate the flowing water. Its struggling grew weaker. "I take Esau out of my pocket, and let it free in the water." Myles held the fish carefully in two cupped hands, and let it slip out. "Where it swims away forever." The fish flopped twice on the booze stained floor, picking up dust and a cigarette butt. Then it was still.

"Quite a moment, huh?" Myles said around a mouthful of steak.

"You, uh, I think you killed the fish."

Myles shrugged. "I got a bunch of them when the idea pressed itself on me. I'll invoice the accountants." He leaned back and put his glasses on. "So," he announced, "do you want to hear it again?"

"No!"

"Or will once be enough? And remember, I want you to feel free to improve on the basic concept." He held out his left hand. "My feelings." He held up his right hand. "Your words." His hands crashed together. "Cinema."

The redhead looked at Ricky from between her legs as Ricky did the strangest thing he had ever done to this point in his life. Stranger than spending a drunken night writing "FUCK YOU" in ketchup and mustards on the roof of his high school. Stranger than driving a hearse of dead pets from LA to Miami. Stranger than canceling a day's worth of appointments to see the Mexican Day of the Dead festival in Ensenada. Something that, in retrospect, would rank up with his first meeting with Renée as a career-defining moment.

Ricky nodded. "Let's do it."

LIFE AND DEATH IN LITTLE ITALY
CALL SHEET

Italy Productions Inc.
Production Office:
345 Carlaw Avenue
Suite 317, Toronto, Ont. M4M 2T1
Tel: 416.463-1266 Fax: 416.463-1950
Set Cell: 416.526-3516

Exec. Producer: Cathy Koyle
Producer: Renée Jato
Line Producer: Judy Nemeth
Director: Edward J. Nijar
1st AD: Walter Ho

UNIT CALL: 0900
DATE: Monday May 13, 2002

(see early/special calls on reverse)

Location: R.C. Harris Filtration Plant

Shoot Day: 26
Lunch: 1500 @ on site
Weather: Sunny. Hot! Hot! Hot!
Hi 28 Lo: 20

SCENE	SET DESCRIPTION	D/N	CAST	PAGES
74	SCHOOL GROUNDS Frankie and Melodi	D	2,24	3 5/8
88	FRONT GATE Frankie, Dad and Mario	N	1,2,16	2 4/8

CHARACTER	ARTIST	P/U	H/W/M	BLKG	SET
2. Frankie	Ainsley Riordan	0730	0830	0900	1000
24. Melodi	Anne-Marie Robinson	0730	0830	0900	1000
16. Dad	Glenn Cockburn	1400	1430	1600	1700
1. Mario	Myles Day	1400	1430	1600	1700

PRODUCTION NOTES

TRANSPORT:
Hot and Ready @ 0730

CRAFT SERVICE:
Hot and Ready @ 0745
Early Breakfast X 10 @ 0830
Subs X 28 @ 1200

SPECIAL CALLS:
1st AD: 0830
2nd AD: 0800
3rd AD: 0745

HAIR/MU: 0900
WRDB: 0900
LOCATIONS: 0730

FIRST AID KIT / SAFETY GUIDELINE BOOK LOCATED AT CRAFT SERVICE

2nd AD: James Watts (H) 416.534-3865
LOC. MGR: Morton Gibson (H) 416.699-2270
TRANS CAP'T: Rahim Singh (C) 416.689.3385

THE SECOND ASSISTANT DIRECTOR

"The show was going to go down."

Hillary turned from the cappuccino machine and gave Walt a skeptical glance. "No shit?"

"I spent all day booking the talent for the revised schedule. We just got today together at 10:00 last night. And then they walk in with another revised schedule. For today. All of a sudden, we had no cast. No background extras. Nothing. All because Spellman, he writes up a brand new speech for Myles."

"Never should have let the damned writer come on set," Susan said.

"Hey," Walt came back quickly. "Far as I'm concerned they should never have let the director in the country."

Hillary burned herself on the cappuccino machine and sucked at her thumb. "Edward's music videos are really fucking cool. Have you seen them? The guy's a real artist."

"So the First AD quit?" Susan asked. "Allen quit?"

"I'm telling you the story." Walt leaned back against the counter in the Craft truck, and turned to make sure Hillary and Susan, Myles' driver, were listening. Outside, the set was just coming to life as the sun peeked over the horizon.

"So right away I'm on the phone. I'm waking up background casting. I'm waking up agents to get people in. I'm waking up the union people to get the extra crew in. I'm doing all this, and Allen? Man, Allen is fuming. I'm on the set cellphone, I'm on the fax phone…"

"You got a fax in there?" Hillary put a lid on the coffee and turned to scramble the eggs for Myles' breakfast.

"Yeah. You didn't know that?"

"No. In your AD office? On set?"

"Yeah. We got the set cell and a cellular fax machine."

"No shit," she said.

"Can I tell my story? So I'm talking to two people at once. I got the office trying to get through with the call sheet. And Allen's screaming at anybody who walks by. Barry's waiting around, you know, and he's trying to talk Allen down."

"Barry, the genny op?" Susan asked.

"Yeah, he's waiting 'cause he's got to turn off the generator truck, right?" Hillary and Susan nodded. They knew how it was done. "So I'm keeping all my balls in the air, and Allen's screaming, 'We're the one's get all the shit. We're doing our job and they fuck around on us. We're the first ones in in the morning, we're the last ones out at night,' right? So Barry, he says, 'Hey man, there's some Transport guys here later than you,' right? And so Allen says, 'Fuck Transport!'"

"Easy, buddy, easy," Susan said.

Walt laughed so hard he kicked at the floor of the Craft truck. Hillary wrapped the plate of eggs in foil and handed it to Susan, who already had Myles' cappuccino.

"That's exactly what Barry said," Walt told them. Susan shook her head and left to bring Myles his breakfast. Hillary pushed her hair back and sipped her own coffee.

"And then what happened?"

"Right. So I have to get off the phone. Clock is ticking. I'm in overtime. Allen's in overtime, although he could go home. Barry's in triple time, or something. I have to break them up."

"So Allen was looking for a fight?"

"Hey, I've worked with Allen on something like ten shows in two years. I can see how he thinks, right? So I sent Barry back to his truck, and I got Allen to calm down. 'Cause I can see he's coming off as angry, but really he's upset 'cause it looked like he couldn't keep the show on schedule. And we might not be shooting in the morning. And it all looks like his fault. Like he can't do his job.

"So I got back on the phone, so that any of us still have a job. And I'm sitting there, wondering if Allen's going to break into tears, he's that far gone. You know, the guy hasn't been sleeping since things went bad. Then who shows up?"

"Who?"

"Guess."

"I don't know. Who?"

"Judy."

"Judy Nemeth?"

"Right! So I think, oh no, Allen's going to flip out on her, right? But I can't get off the phone. Judy, she says, 'Hey, Allen.' He says, 'Hey, Judy.' She says, 'Heard you're quitting because we changed the schedule again.' And I'm thinking, oh no, here it comes, right? He says, 'You got that right.'"

"Here it comes." Hillary leaned forward.

"Right! That's what I think! Here it comes, right? She's going to give it to him about leaving her stuck, and about loyalty and all that, right?"

"But she doesn't?"

"I'm telling you the story. What she said is, 'Good for you.'"

"She didn't!"

"Yep. He tells her he quit and she says good for you, and walks away."

"What did he do?"

"Allen? Well…" Walt thought about it for a second. "You know *Jerry Maguire*?"

"The movie."

"Yeah. You know the bit where he comes in and says this whole thing, and she just says 'You had me at hello'?"

"Love that bit."

"Yeah, well, that was Allen last night. I think that was the nicest thing anyone has ever said to him."

"Wow. Then what?"

"Then what? You're working today, aren't you? I saved the show. I woke up the people I had to wake up and I booked us the show today. I was here until two in the morning. And do I get one word from Judy Nemeth?"

"Nothing," Hillary said.

"Nothing," Walt said.

THE WRITER

Ricky wandered through the trailers until he found Debs standing outside the Wardrobe truck. He waved, but she looked away and pretended she didn't see him.

"Hey," he said.

"Oh, hi," she said back, and busied herself with her clipboard.

"I heard your boss quit."

"Allen? Yeah."

"Because of me."

Debs shuffled a little, and then spun slowly around to face him again. "His schedule kept changing on him. His job is to keep the shoot organized. He couldn't do that. So he quit."

"Because of me."

Debs looked up into his eyes. "Yeah."

"I'm sorry."

"Oh." She looked down at her clipboard and smiled. "It's not your fault." She filled the moment by fussing with her kerchief. "But very sweet of you to say." And she leaned forward and kissed him, quickly, on his cheek.

"I thought maybe you'd go too. You know, solidarity and everything."

"Nah. I need the money too much. I'm sticking around."

"I'm glad."

"I'm glad you weren't at the bottom of Lake Ontario."

Ricky took that as a good sign. When he got to set, Renée had a different take on losing her First AD. "He's left me stuck with another five days to shoot. Is that loyalty?"

At first, Myles had insisted that his speech be shot at a fountain garden, but Renée had intervened, and the speech was shot at the plant's filtration pool. Only Franz Woceski could have made it look so good, the crew said—at least those who could talk in the pool's stench. By the time they shot, word had gotten out that it was Myles' speech, and after the master take Video Village erupted into not so spontaneous applause that Myles accepted with due humility. Edward clapped Myles on the back, "Week three, here we come."

Ricky sipped his soup, watched the scene, and then locked himself in his trailer, complaining that he wasn't feeling well. Which—in a sense—was very true.

DISSOLVE TO:

Ricky was stretched out on the couch in his trailer, sipping at his whiskey, and flipping through the channels on the TV. He had told himself an hour ago that he was watching the news for inspiration, but as a writer he was pretty sure he could tell self-justification when he saw it.

There was a knock at the door. Ricky got up and unlocked it.

"Am I disturbing you?" Charles asked. Ricky glanced at the TV and the whiskey glass, and the inactive computer and his old copy of Syd Field beside it.

"No." He turned off the TV, and pointed Charles to a chair. Charles sat down gingerly, testing his weight in the chair. Ricky wondered if he was nervous about something.

"What scenes are you working on?" Charles asked.

"There's just tomorrow left," Ricky said, digging out the schedule from under his butt. "Last day. Scene 101c. Mikey confesses with his dying breath." Ricky read that off the call sheet, and added, "Then they go to a picnic."

"I tried to tell Edward about your ending."

"You did? About her father?"

Charles nodded. He was quiet for so long Ricky considered how impolite it would be to turn the TV back on.

"I've been thinking about the script," Charles said suddenly. "I don't wanna piss you off, you know, yank your dick."

"Hey, no," Ricky soothed him. "You're the technical advisor. My dick is fine." Silence again. "What exactly do you do, anyway?"

Charles cracked his knuckles. "They pay me to let Edward feel cool. Sometimes I pop some caps with the Effects guys at lunch." He raised his eyebrows in a way that Ricky felt was a what're-ya-gonna-do gesture. "What did the guy witness?"

"What guy?"

"At the start of the movie." Charles kept his eyes on the floor. "The guy they bust out of jail. Burt."

"Well, uh," Ricky paused for a second. "A crime involving the cops."

"Yeah, but, what crime?"

"I don't know," Ricky confessed.

"And when Frankie and Mario are in trouble," Charles said quickly, while Ricky sank deeper into the couch's foam, "why do they go to her old man's house, instead of calling Mario's boys? If my man was in trouble, I'd help him out."

"Uh, because…" Ricky trailed off. He tried to hold onto his story pitch, but it was cheap candy in a kid's sweaty palm. "I don't know."

"And why don't Eddie and Mikey just pop Frankie when she sees them at the start?"

"I don't know." The hum from the refrigerator grew loud in the tight space between them.

"Why don't they pop her at her old man's house?"

"I don't know."

"Hey, you okay?"

"I don't know."

Charles sat back in the chair. "Ah, man. See? I didn't want to get in your face." He stood up and faced the door. But he didn't go out. Instead he said, "That's why you're the writer, right?" It took a moment for Ricky to understand what Charles was feeling. It was fear. Evidently he wasn't very good at it. "There's a lot of time sitting around, you know? Doin' jack all. I scribbled some things down and—" He pulled a crumpled piece of paper from his back pocket.

"And you didn't bring it to Edward?"

"Not these days. He's pissed since I didn't get his back when Roger punched him."

"Someone punched him?"

"Jesus." Charles laughed. "Where have you been?"

"It's hard to watch your movie go down the crapper." Ricky scratched at his chin, surprised to find a week's growth there.

"Besides." Charles looked at the paper in his hand. "I don't think I could have shown this to fuckin' Eddie anyways."

"I'll take a look at it."

"I know it's not great or anything." He held it out to Ricky.

Ricky started to read.

It was the confession speech. The dying confession. The one that Ricky had been avoiding all night. It wrapped up all the loose ends, tied everything up, cleaned up all the details. It was everything that needed to be said but Ricky had been unable to write. Ricky recognized something else. It was Edward's week three.

When he finished, he got up. Ricky slowly put his arms around Charles and hugged the big man close. He held him for a very long time. Just held him. Until Charles said, "Um. Hey, man?" And Ricky let him go.

"My dad used to hit me," Charles said.

"Mine too."

"He died last year."

"We'll use this scene tomorrow." Ricky moved to hug Charles again, but Charles stepped back. "Do you know what this means?" Ricky asked, and his voice was thick and his eyes were heavy. Charles shook his head.

"It means I'm going back to dentistry."

FADE TO BLACK

TITLES

    OF WISDOM AND TEETH

FADE IN:

The sun was already behind the hotel when Vicki collected him for the final night's shooting, but Ricky was still hungover. Debs was waiting for him when they pulled up to set.

"I really like today's scene," Debs told him. "You're a good writer." She wrapped her skinny arms around her clipboard and hugged it to her breasts.

"Thanks," Ricky said. "It just kinda wrote itself." They watched the grips off-load from the truck.

"I have a boyfriend."

"Oh."

"Yeah, so." She looked down at her sandals, then back up at him. "Are you free for lunch?"

"Um." Ricky couldn't recover in time. "Sure."

"I have a present. Last day. And everything." She flashed him a videotape. The tape had a sticker on it, *Life and Death in Little Italy—Rough Cut—Unfinished*. "Not yesterday's stuff, of course, but everything else. I swiped it from Renée's Winnie."

"You did what?"

"I thought you would like to see it." She slipped it back behind her clipboard. "We'll eat in your trailer and watch it together."

"It's a date," Ricky said. Her smile grew, her green eyes sparkled. She walked backwards, then turned and skipped to the AD office.

DISSOLVE TO:

Mikey took a long time to die. As Charles had pointed out, there were a lot of loose ends. For the big scene, Video Village had been moved closer to set. Ricky watched the monitor and sipped his soup. They were out of headphones, but he could hear it whispered through Renée's set.

Ainsley was holding Kevin's head on her lap. "Hold on, Mikey," she said, wiping saline drop tears from her cheeks. "We've called the ambulance." Kevin shook his head, and worked more stage blood out of his mouth.

Renée leaned in close. "They worked on it all day," she whispered. It showed, Ricky felt. Not even Edward's direction could water it down—although he tried.

"Too late." Kevin rasped and wheezed with every shallow breath. "Too late for me, but not too late for you and your father."

"He tried to have me killed!" Ainsley curled her fist, careful not to break a nail.

"He didn't know it was you." The words were coming with more difficulty, and Kevin fluttered his eyelids. "Forgive him. He still has love to give, if you let him. He wants to be your father again."

"What do you want me to do?" Ainsley begged for an answer. "Tell me what to do!"

And Kevin smiled, the first and only time Mikey the bad cop smiles in the entire movie. "Take him for a picnic." His hand slipped from hers. His eyes closed. Ainsley let him go. The camera whirred.

"Cut," Edward whispered beside Ricky.

"Cut!" Walt yelled. The floor erupted into cheers and applause. People pounded Ricky on the back. Some wiped at the corners of their eyes. "You got me," Steven, the thin Wardrobe guy said, shaking his finger at Ricky. "Oh my God, you got me." Charles met Ricky's gaze and nodded. Thanks for leaving me out of it, his look said.

"Wonderful, Richard honey." Renée rested her cigarette on his shoulder and left his cheek heavy with her lipstick.

"Going again," Walt called. Everyone turned back to the monitor. Ricky slipped out.

DISSOLVE TO:

Ricky was sitting on his suitcase, trying to get it to latch, when Debs knocked at his door. He unlocked it and she climbed in. She hugged him.

"That was a really great speech." Her mouth tickled his ear. "Better than yesterday's."

"It was terrible," Ricky said. "It was clumsy, full of exposition, and worst of all, clichéd."

"Then why…"

"It was honest." Ricky smiled at her. "Heartfelt. Something the rest of the script is lacking." He shrugged. "And it tied up the plot, got us to the picnic scene."

Debs held up the tape. "Let's watch your movie," she sang and popped the tape into the VCR. He sat down on the couch. She sat down beside him, kicked off her sandals, curled her way-too-thin legs under her, and leaned back onto him. Her hair smelt of apples and springtime.

"What kind of shampoo do you use?"

"Life Brand." She tugged his arm and put it around her. "I get it at Shoppers."

The rough cut was just that—rough. It had no music, no sound effects. The first shots of the prison were uncomfortably silent.

"See if you can guess which scenes were Edward's, and which were mine," Ricky said.

On the TV, Frankie was watching as the two crooked cops busted a witness out of jail. Debs started to laugh at the first dialogue and didn't stop until it cut to the sister working at the brothel. "Definitely Edward's."

"Nope," Ricky said pleasantly. "That was mine."

If the first scene was laughable, the second scene was simply embarrassing. The scene after that was Edward's, but by that time Ricky had stopped caring. As the next scene led into the next scene, Ricky lost track of whether it was his writing or Edward's. He tried to be angry about what they had done to his story, his movie, but he couldn't.

DISSOLVE TO:

The rewinding VCR whirred loudly. Debs stood in front of it, waiting for the tape.

"It was well shot," Debs said.

Ricky sighed and lay flat on the couch. "Yeah, well. Franz Woceski."

"Did you see *The Ways of Man*?" She stood with her back to him.

"It gave me a lot to think about," Ricky said. He looked her up and down. Her toes nervously pulling at the carpet. Her long skinny legs. Her bony ass. Her slender back. Her sharp neck. And the back of her big fat head. Ricky couldn't see her eyes.

"I have to go." She stabbed at the eject button until the tape slid out. "I arranged things with Walter, but I've been gone too long." She stepped into her sandals, and paused at the door. "He probably thinks I fucked you." She let herself out.

Ricky arced his ass off the couch and dug in his back pocket for his wallet. He dumped the maxed-out credit cards and video store memberships on his chest until he found his American Dental Association card. It was expired.

CUT TO:

"Richard honey?" And now he was angry. Renée yanked open his door, spilling her champagne and almost falling over. "Come to my trailer with me. I've got some paperwork, but god knows, we should talk before you go." Ricky automatically followed her through the quiet rows of trailers. She waved her bottle of champagne at him. "Wrap night! I love it! You have no idea. No matter what goes wrong, everyone's your best friend."

CUT TO:

Hillary and Debs drank beers in the light of the AD office. Renée gave each of them a kiss and told them how much they saved the show from disaster. She was careful to avoid getting into a position where she would have to say their names. Ricky stood back, said nothing, and waited for Renée to finish. "Come on, Richard honey. Let's go get some more champagne."

CUT TO:

Renée cleared a pile of flowers from her table, but found that every other surface was already covered with flowers. She dumped them on the couch. "From Cathy," Renée told him. "The champagne is from David." She pointed to a few more flowers by the sink. "From the cast, I love them all." She poured herself more champagne. "Except for that fucker Myles Day." She left a glass for Ricky to fill. He didn't feel like celebrating. Renée spread out her folders.

"You did some good work on this one," she told him as she signed. "You saved us, and that is no lie. This picture is going to be huge. Edward is talking about week four, that's how excited he is."

"Edward is an idiot."

"Yes, but he has his charm. I would show you the film, except the office lost the rough cut I had the editors Fed-Ex from LA." She sucked deeply on her cigarette. "But it's the last day, so I love those office girls to death."

"When will I get my fee?"

"Well, Richard, to be honest with you, with the overages and unexpected expenses, like flying you up here, you know, and all this champagne, it might be some time before I can clear the money through Cathy and Michael. You know how tight they are with money." And she went back to her paperwork.

He checked his watch. It was almost time to leave for the airport. He felt drained. Emotionally exhausted. He just wished she hadn't wasted the last five years of his life. Kept alive with an irregular drip of cheques and broken promises. He wished Renée had never come to hear the pitches from that stupid workshop. He used to enjoy writing at night, after work. Maybe someday he would enjoy writing again, but he doubted it. Only a virgin really believes that love and sex are the same thing.

"So, Richard." Renée startled him. "What are you working on next?"

Richard got up from the couch and slid onto the bench opposite Renée. He pushed her paperwork aside to make sure he had her full attention.

"It's about an old, ugly bitch of a producer." He gave it feeling, like he was back in the workshop. Played it out for her. "She goes around destroying people's lives, working her crew all night, and pocketing the budget. She's everybody's best friend, until she steals their parachute and shoves them out the door. She promises glamour and leaves grit." Ricky leaned over the table and did it the way Myles Day would do it. He lowered his voice, drawing her in. "She's not a real person, you see, but a walking, talking, stinking metaphor for the whole fucking movie industry. But there's one guy who for years has believed in her, and she played him like an old game of Pac Man. Because he wanted to believe. He wanted so badly to believe everything she told him. He wanted to see his name on the posters, and go to parties with the people on his TV. And she wrung him dry. So one day he wakes up. Realizes what's going on. And if she pushes him any further, one more nudge, he'll go over the edge and take her with him."

It was the closest Ricky had ever come to making an out-and-out threat against another human being.

In the silence, Renée leaned back, the cigarette trembling in her lips, forgotten. Her eyes were narrow slits behind her shaded lenses. "Does she push him?"

Ricky was breathing hard. "That's up to you."

Their eyes locked. She looked away first. She held her cigarette and watched the smoke swirl up towards the window and slip through the window screen.

Ricky sneered at her, and stood up.

"Let's do it!" Renée smacked the table, cigarette flying as she lunged to her feet. Ricky pulled back, ready to defend himself. Renée dove for her briefcase. Gun, Ricky thought. Jesus, she's going for a gun!

Renée whirled on him and thrust a contract at him. "I think I can get Harvey Keitel for the guy. It'll be *Swimming with Sharks* meets *The Player*."

She stood there, contract outstretched and trembling at the end of her flabby arm. She had that look in her eye. Old prospectors called it gold fever.

If this were a movie, Ricky thought, I'd turn her down.

"Mr. Spellman?" It was Vicki at the door. "We should leave now. You don't want to miss your plane."

"Take the contract, Richard honey."

"I'm a really good dentist," he said. He picked up his briefcase. "My agent will call you as soon as I sign with one."

"There's a lot of money to be made here," Renée said. "We don't need to get agents involved…" But Ricky was already out the door and into the night.

CUT TO:

"I'm glad you're the one driving me to the airport, Vicki," Ricky said as his driver shot out onto Queen East.

"Who else would it be, Mr. Spellman?"

"It's like a bookend. You end the movie the same way you started it. And now the protagonist has learned something about life."

"Did you get a chance to see any sights?" The car rose into the air on the on-ramp, and she picked up speed in the fast lane of Gardiner Expressway.

"No," he said. "But I have learned something about life."

Vicki turned on the radio and hummed along with REM.

"Aren't you going to ask me what I learned?"

"About life?"

"What I learned was that the answer was with me all along. Like *The Wizard of Oz*: classic movie structure. You told me what I needed to know on my first day here."

"I did?" Vicki thought about it. "Huh. Not much of a bookend."

"It's a perfect bookend. Like Glenda the Good Witch." Ricky slapped the dashboard. "It's perfect because the first time around I failed to recognize the wisdom put before me. Only through trials and tests do I recognize what was there all along." They sped by the downtown core of the city. Ricky was overtaken by the beauty of it.

"And what's the wisdom?" Vicki asked him, flicking on the wipers.

"You told me."

"I'm sorry, Mr. Spellman, I must have forgotten." She was humouring him, of course. Ricky was in a mood to be humoured.

"You told me the witness was a prostitute. And now I know that you were right."

"Oh that," she said. The downtown lights retreated into the mist. "I thought that was odd. I asked around and everyone on set thought the witness was the prostitute."

"Perfect movie structure," Ricky insisted. "Syd Field would be proud."

"Oh, I almost forgot." Vicki reached between the seats and handed Ricky his old copy of Syd Field. He wasn't sure if he was going to take it. But then he did.

"You left it behind."

"Thanks for grabbing it."

"Oh, no. Not me. Debs found it. She wanted to make sure I got it to you."

There was something tucked between the pages.

Ricky flipped open the book. Inside was an old call sheet with "WRITER" scribbled on it. From his trailer. And in different ink, "Love always."

Vicki smiled and tapped her fingers on the steering wheel. She sang softly, "Stand in the place where you work…"

Scene One Rewrite

EXT — INDUSTRIAL AREA — NIGHT

A few cars are in the parking lot of an industrial strip mall. The store fronts are all dark, save for the end unit.

A MINIVAN pulls up in front of the end unit.

FX of a camera shutter opening and closing as two women get out of the minivan. They both look like suburban housewives in their late twenties or early thirties.

               EDDIE
               (OS)
    That's them, let's go.

As the first woman pulls the door handle we see a small handwritten sign, "AAAAAA Massage."

INT. PARKED CAR — NIGHT (CONTINUOUS)

In the passenger seat, EDDIE, a cop in his early thirties puts away the camera and pulls his GUN from his shoulder holster.

Beside him, in the driver's seat, MIKEY, a little older, a little more tired, and a lot less interested, drinks coffee.

               MIKEY
    They're just coming on shift.
    Why don't we give them a
    chance to get started, see
    what happens?

Eddie opens the car door and gets out. Reluctantly, Mikey does the same.

EXT. INDUSTRIAL AREA — NIGHT

The two cops walk quickly towards the massage parlour.

                    EDDIE
        Come on. We don't just sit
        around and watch. We make
        things happen.

ACKNOWLEDGEMENTS

For their unwavering support over the years, I would like to thank the following people: Randy McIlwaine and Christine LaFleur, Michel Basilieres and Barbara Gilbert, Allan Levine, Andrew Honor, Campbell Whyte, Maurice Smith, Patrick Aull, Richard Garbutt and that other guy, Scott what's-his-name. And also a big thank you to Karen Haughian and Shelley Breslaw.

—John McFetridge

Thank you to my mom and dad, Henry and Bernice, for their support, encouragement, and love. Thank you to John for making me a better writer through his example and insight. And for figuring out that there were stories to be told on a film set. Thank you to Laurie for her patience and her friendship and her basement. Thank you to Karen for taking a chance on a couple of newbies; the book is so much better for her efforts. Thank you to Julie for her love and boundless creative energy. Our time together made me a better person. Thank you to Michel for his friendship and street-corner guidance. Thank you to Alan, Neil, and Adam for their writing and laughter. And thank you to Stephanie for talking to me at a party.

—Scott Albert

ABOUT THE AUTHORS

John McFetridge and Scott Albert have worked as location managers, transport drivers, production assistants, and assistant directors on both Canadian and American feature films in Toronto.

John McFetridge is the co-author of the CBC radio drama, *Champions*, the story of how Jackie Robinson broke baseball's colour line with the Montreal Royals and the screenplay *The Shrew in the Park*. He and his wife live in Toronto with their two young sons.

Scott Albert recently graduated from the Canadian Film Centre's Prime Time TV Writing Program. He is currently writing for the All-Nude comedy troupe and is developing feature film screenplays. He lives in Toronto.